CONTENTS

THE SKELETONS OF BIRKBURY

Peter Hatherall Mystery Novel #1

COVER DESIGN: DIANA J FEBRY
Cover Image: Bigstock.com

DIANA J FEBRY

Dedication

To Albert, Stein, Paddy & Jaeica.

We spray the fields and scatter
The poison on the ground
So that no wicked, wild flowers
Upon our farm, be found.
We like whatever helps us
To line our purse with pence;
The twenty-four-hour broiler-house
And neat electric fence.

All concrete sheds around us,
And Jaguars in the yard,
The telly lounge and deep-freeze
Are ours from working hard.
(A letter in Farmers Weekly)

ONE

Frank Codrington was running late, pushing his bicycle with a punctured tyre along the lane. He glared at the hedgerow as if it were their fault they had been butchered yesterday by Graham's hedge cutter, leaving debris scattered all over the lane to sabotage his tyre. Frank remembered the pride his father took trimming and plaiting hedges by hand. How he would thoughtfully make sure any offcuts were carefully disposed of rather than abandoned in the road. In those days, ditches were also properly maintained, so the lanes didn't flood every time it rained.

Frank was a slight man. People often assumed he was an ex-jockey although he had never sat on a horse. He had worked at Rooksbridge Farm since leaving school at sixteen. Initially for Mark and Kim Farley. He now worked for their son, Graham, and his wife, Gillian.

He had retained his boyish good looks, enhanced by his wide grin, which was never far away. His dark hair was kept short and neat although usually hidden under a hat.

He leaned his ancient bike against the fence while he fumbled in his pocket for the keys. The pockets of the battered jacket handed down to him by Mark were full of baler twine, nails, screws, bits of straw and sawdust, his cigarettes and at last, the keys. At his age, Frank no longer did wheelies down the road, but he could shift if there was any risk of him missing last orders at the bar. His head hurt from last nights' drinking, and he had hoped the short bike ride would clear his head.

As it was summer, it was light by six o'clock, unlike the dark, cold mornings of the now - forgotten winter months. Once the main gates were unlocked, it was a short ride along the manicured driveway that Graham took such great pride in mowing each week, to the main stable block. There Frank unlocked the tack room and switched off the alarms. Once the stabled horses were checked, he jumped on the quad bike to check the horses in the fields and the fencing.

Frank knew the farm as well as his own cottage, in which he lived rent-free as part of his arrangement with the Farley family. Last night's storm had been severe, but now everything was still. The quad bike skidded as he pushed it to full speed across the homefield. While the rain had left a fresher feel to the air, it had turned the dust to a thin layer of slippery mud. The weather patterns seemed to have gone crazy of late. The seasons all mixed up with extremes of temperature and torrential rain likely at any time. He worried that the strong winds might have upset the horses and possibly brought down parts of the electric fencing used extensively for summer grazing.

Mostly the horses spent the nights in the gully field. They enjoyed the breeze that came across the top of the ridge when temperatures soared. On colder nights they huddled in a tight bunch at the bottom, using the steep banks as a shield from the wind and rain.

Approaching the top of the gully, he noticed the huge oak tree had come down overnight and taken half of the ancient hawthorn hedge with it. The horses were nowhere to be seen. As he approached the base of the fallen tree, a shadow ran across the landscape. The temperature dropped as the passing cloud blocked out the morning sun. Among the upturned roots of the tree and hedge and dislodged earth were the decomposing remains of what appeared to have once been a person.

He steeled himself to move closer and double-check before raising the alarm.

Frank muttered, "Bloody 'ell. This ain't my problem," before setting off to the farmhouse at speed. The quad bike skidded to a halt underneath the bedroom window. Frank tossed up a handful of gravel from the garden path as gently as he could. As the second handful scattered across the window pane, Graham's head appeared. Frank tried to concentrate on the collar of his paisley pyjamas rather than the annoyed face with ruffled bed hair glaring down at him.

"What is it, Frank?"

Frank checked himself. He knew Gillian must not be upset under any circumstances. News of a skeleton was likely to do just that. He tried to convey the urgency with his eyes and arms.

"The big old oak tree in the gully field has come down."

"So, what's the emergency?" Graham asked.

Frank put his finger to his lips and waved frantically for Graham to meet him downstairs.

"Hang on. I'm coming."

Graham quickly checked that Gillian was still sleeping as he hopped about on one leg, pulling on his jeans. He nearly fell, knocking into the chest of drawers. He stood silently, one leg through the jeans, trying to control his breathing while willing Gillian not to stir. A sigh of relief involuntarily left his body as Gillian carried on snoring. He continued dressing, carefully. Before leaving the room, he looked back at her motionless body and wondered why he had worried. She was always in a deep sleep whenever he was in the bedroom.

Frank could think of nothing useful to say and felt uncomfortable alone with Graham in the confined space of the old Land Rover. The vehicle's suspension thudded their spines as they sped back across the fields towards his discovery. Graham was clearly not best pleased with having been disturbed and made no attempt to hide his irritation.

Frank fidgeted in the passenger seat while Graham became increasingly annoyed by the vehicle struggling to gain friction on the greasy layer of mud on the steep incline. Graham broke the heavy silence and said, "I will telephone the police after I have seen this body myself. I'm not making a fool of myself on the basis of what you think you might have seen, Frank." He added irritably, "Just how many did you have last night?"

Frank shrugged and looked out the window. He had known Graham since he was a child. There was no point even trying to discuss anything with him when he was in one of his moods. When things weren't going his way, Graham oscillated between shouting unreasonable accusations and feigning partial deafness to show his complete contempt for anything anybody else may have to say. Instead of responding, Frank counted silently to ten.

Skidding to a halt, Graham demanded, "Get the gate, Frank."

Frank waited at the gate and let Graham go on ahead to the base of the tree. He had seen enough already. This was nothing to do with him. There was nothing he could do or say to improve things, so it was best to stay out of the way. He tried to avoid eye contact when Graham returned looking shaken and pale from what he'd seen.

"Frank, this spot can't be seen from the road. I want you to go back to the main gates so you can show the police where to come when they arrive," Graham said, pulling his phone from his pocket. "I'll ring them now. And Frank, no wandering off anywhere; just wait at the gate until they arrive." He added, "If you see Gillian, don't tell her anything. Leave that to me."

Frank watched Graham return to his battered Land Rover, slump his long body over the steering wheel and shut his eyes. Part of Frank felt sorry for his employer, but Graham shouldn't take his frustrations out on everyone else, especially him. He hesitated, unsure if he should offer to do anything else, but Graham gave him a withering look and pulled out his phone, so he turned to leave.

Graham took a deep breath, before speaking into the phone. "Hi, Gillian, it's me. A tree has come down. The horses are okay. Umm... there's something caught up in the roots. It's probably something to do with Robin Bailey. Nothing to worry about, but the police will be coming to take a look. I'll be back as soon as I can. No need for you to worry or to come up."

TWO

Detective Inspector Fiona Williams was singing in the shower at the top of her voice. She was washing away the weeks of sleepless nights Callum had given her. Another one to chalk up to experience. She was striking rather than beautiful, with huge green eyes and red hair. She drew the attention of men wherever she went and yet always dated the wrong ones.

No longer would she lie awake torturing herself, reliving their last few weeks together, playing the impossible game of "if only" over and over in her mind. She wasn't over him yet...but she was getting there.

She wrapped herself in her dressing gown and sat staring at her reflection. She managed a smile, enjoying the luxury of feeling comfy rather than on show. Callum had been wrong to mock her. The things he criticized her for were so unfair and unreasonable. His chief complaints were her dedication to the job and her willingness to do the extra background work. It was these attributes that had gotten her noticed after all. He'd been happy to share the financial rewards of her dedication. He should have been able to accept the occasional rearrangement of their social life as well. She'd not considered herself ambitious before, but now she was hungry for attention and respect at work.

Callum's accusations about her new senior partner, Peter, were equally ridiculous. They said more about his own insecurities. Along with her many failings at creating his idea of domestic bliss, he claimed all she ever said was, "Peter this and Peter that." This of course was absolute rubbish. How many times had she said, it's just work? Peter is happily married with kids and about ten years too old for me to be interested.

She was pleased Callum had never met Peter, who she'd described to him as bland and unattractive, as he was handsome in a clean-cut type of older person way. Well-proportioned with a smart dress sense, he often drew the looks of older women although he seemed oblivious to the effect he had on them.

She was learning new things every day from Peter. Not just systems and procedures, but how things really worked. How different people behaved and thought. She was also learning things about herself.

"Why don't you ask for a transfer or a promotion?" Callum moaned.

"Yes. Just like that. That'll work then," she'd replied sarcastically. "And what will your objection be to my next partner? Maybe she'd be female, and then I'd be a lesbian."

Fiona had already seen a few too many cases of domestic violence to submit to that type of jealousy. If he was like that when they were dating, what would it have been like a few years into marriage? She knew she'd made the right decision, so why did she miss his toothbrush so much? Why couldn't she stop going over and over those last bitter conversations? Wishing somehow the outcome could have been different.

She tried to concentrate on the day ahead. Today was Peter's first day back after a two-week break with his family. Before leaving yesterday, she had diligently made notes on the few case developments in his absence and left the reports neatly stacked on his desk.

There were no grounds for Callum's stupid jealousy. Apart from being older and married, Peter wasn't the most communicative of people to work for. At first, she'd taken his aloofness as dislike of her but over time had accepted this was just the way he was. Mostly he was laid back to the point of laziness, but on a few occasions, she had witnessed a sudden change of mood. She had been surprised the first time she saw the sudden fury of previously hidden frustration when a case wasn't going his way. But then, surely it was good that after all the years in the job he still cared? That he was still prepared to allow himself to get involved and show some real emotion. Nothing like the succession of men she dated.

During Peter's absence, she'd worked a little with Detective Chief Inspector Jenkins. He was completely different. He was placid and straightforward. His genuine interest in some of her ideas contrasted with Peter's often cool indifference. But she still preferred to work with Peter.

As she got dressed, she tried to convince herself that Callum was just not worth it. As she grabbed some toast for breakfast, she concluded he was a self-absorbed and immature pig.

THREE

Detective Chief Inspector Peter Hatherall walked into the coffee shop on his way to work. Tanned from his holiday with Sally and the twins, on the outside he appeared calm and relaxed. Despite the early time, the temperature was swiftly rising, so he took his cardboard cup outside. He scooped the surface foam from the top of his cappuccino with his index finger as he watched life pass him by. While he'd been keen to leave the house this morning before anyone else awoke, he was in no rush to get into the station. As soon as he arrived, he would become immersed in his cases, the benefits of the two-week break promptly lost.

He watched the people of different shapes and sizes hurrying by to their places of work. Linked only by their choice of dark business clothes and their desire to avoid contact yet moving together in a choreographed dance. He smiled at the sharp contrast with the groups he'd watched only yesterday meandering their way down to the beach carrying towels and beach balls. He took out his phone and called Amelia. "Amelia please, can you ring me? We all got back yesterday. Where are you? I miss you."

Once in the station, Peter briefly scanned the note concerning a body turning up at Rooksbridge Farm in the village of Birkbury. He was sure it was the same farm involved in the old Robin Bailey case. It was way before his time, but for a short while, the story had made the area infamous. It had recently been in the news again as Robin Bailey had died shortly before being considered for release from prison. The media had tried to suggest foul play and conspiracy theories to keep the story alive long enough to sell a few more copies of their papers.

He looked up as soon as Fiona walked in. While she looked good, he wasn't sure her smart dark suit and a perfectly pressed white shirt was the best attire for wandering about a farm. "Don't settle yourself down just yet," he said as Fiona began to slip her handbag from her shoulder. "We're going straight out." As Fiona hoisted the bag back over her shoulder, he added, "Don't suppose you have any flat shoes with you? We're heading off to a village farm." He was pleasantly surprised when she pulled out a pair of neat pumps from somewhere under her desk. "Brilliant. Let's get going." If he noticed Fiona's slight annoyance, he didn't show it as he headed down to the car park, automatically assuming Fiona would be following behind.

The first half of the journey was in silence, but as they were about to leave the motorway, Fiona asked, "How was the holiday?"

"It was good... This farm we're going to, it has an interesting history. I don't expect you've ever heard of Robin Bailey?" He looked across at Fiona who shook her head with a blank expression.

"It was a big story at the time. A bitter boundary dispute between two farmers got terribly out of control. All sorts of tit-for-tat nonsense went on. Leaving animal carcasses on doorsteps, sheep heads on fence posts, blood smeared on walls. But an affair between Bailey's wife and the other farmer was a step too far. Bailey attempted to murder his wife by placing a bomb under her car."

"Wow!" said Fiona. "What on earth was the wife thinking? Anyway, what happened?"

"The bomb didn't kill her, but she lost both legs in the explosion. Bailey tried to frame the other farmer, Oscar Conley, for the explosion."

"Christ, you can't be serious?" She looked across at Peter who was grinning away. "Then what happened?"

"That was about it, really. Robin Bailey was arrested and charged. His family moved away, as far as I know. He was due to be released about a year or so ago, but he died just before his release hearing. The press tried to make much more of it at the time. I checked this morning, and Oscar Conley's son still lives on a nearby farm. It could even be that this unearthed body relates back to that time."

"Weird. They say all sorts of things go on in small villages." Fiona gave a mock shudder. "I wouldn't want to live where something like that happened."

Peter laughed. "I expect the present owner got it cheap because of the farm's history and the family's need to escape the area. Tight as they come, a lot of these farmer types. I think I read somewhere there's an old black plague cottage on the farm somewhere as well." Switching the car indicator on, he said, "Well this is where we get off."

As soon as they pulled off the motorway, they were plunged onto small country lanes as they descended a steep incline towards the village of Birkbury. A small sign announced they had entered the village. Fiona said, "It looks too quaint and peaceful to have such a horrid history."

"It has a decent pub as well," Peter replied. He brought the car to a standstill by the sign for Rooksbridge Holiday Cottages and Livery yard. They were met at the gate by a small man in a cloth cap who seemed to belong in a much earlier era. Peter flashed his card to the man as he asked where they should go.

Frank touched the rim of his cap. "So, you'll be the boss man. Follow me up on the bike. I've been ferrying your guys up there all morning. Looks like something from TV up there." They waited while he closed the gate behind them and jumped onto a mud-splattered quad bike parked alongside the entrance.

"Probably the most exciting day he's ever had," Peter remarked.

FOUR

They followed the quad bike through a concrete yard area lined on both sides with stables and on towards another gate which led out to open farmland. Waiting for Frank to open it, they came to a standstill beside a large muck heap with biting insects hovering above. Fiona closed her window, wrinkling her nose at the smell.

Peter said, "Not a country girl then?"

Fiona replied flippantly, "More of a shopping mall girl, I'm afraid."

Once they were through the gate, the ground rose sharply. At the top of this field, they came to yet another gate. The farmhand jumped nimbly from his bike opening it and directing them through. Pulling forwards, they found themselves looking back down a steep incline. A third of the way down, a scene very familiar to Peter was spread out before them.

From what he could see from their elevated position, the specialist scene of crime teams was in place, and he could just make out the small white tent at the base of a fallen tree. Peter decided to park his car near the gate where the ground was level and walk down the slope to where he'd spotted Ross Phillips, the coroner. They hadn't walked far when they saw a tall, solidly built man in faded work jeans and sweatshirt striding purposefully up the hill towards them. Peter noticed he manoeuvred himself to higher ground before reaching his hand out to greet them.

"Hello. I'm Graham Farley. I own this farm."

The man appeared drawn and tired, but there was an unmistakable arrogance about him. The way he planted himself with legs braced at a hips-width apart and his instant claim to ownership grated on Peter. He felt a little protective towards Fiona, as he noted her good looks were not wasted on the guy doing his lord-of-the-manor stance. He shook hands, introducing him and Fiona stiffly and added, "It probably would be best if you returned home now. We will take a statement from you later. We need to keep the area secure. We also will want to see the person who found the body this morning."

"That will be my employee, Frank."

"Can you make sure he's available? Now if you'll excuse us, we have a lot of work to do."

A flicker of annoyance crossed Graham's face at his abrupt dismissal. It was quickly covered by a false smile, more of a pulling back of the lips with no attempt to disturb his stony facial muscles, which remained set in a frown.

Peter shook his head in amusement as he watched Graham march over to Frank, who was sat astride the quad bike watching developments as he smoked a cigarette. Graham shouted, loud enough for everyone to hear, "Can you get on with what I've asked you to do, Frank, back at the yard? And don't disappear up The Bull Inn until the police have seen you."

"Of course, boss," Frank replied, showing no signs of moving.

"Frank! I need you back at the yard now!" Graham shouted, as he stomped to his waiting vehicle.

Peter watched with amusement as Frank casually finished his cigarette before starting the bike. Graham stomped to his Land Rover and over revved it, skidding slightly as the wheels threw up a spray of mud behind the vehicle. Peter said to Fiona, "Someone forgot to take his meds this morning," before turning his attention back to the crime scene. He was glad to see his old friend, Ross Phillips, in attendance. He was equally sad to think Phillips was shortly to retire and knew he would miss him. Walking down the steep slope, Peter said, "Fiona. See that gate just over there?"

Fiona followed the direction of his arm and nodded.

"I'm pretty sure we passed by there on our way into the village. Can you go over to check that it does open straight onto the lane?"

Phillips turned and waved as Peter approached. "Good to see you. It's been a while."

"I agree. We haven't met up for ages. Not long now and I won't even bump into you at times like this. Any plans for the future?"

"We've nothing definite. All sorts of vague ideas, but nothing agreed. But tell me, how are Sally and the twins? They must be...three now."

"Yes, they're all doing well. We've just got back from a short holiday, in fact."

"That explains the tan. And how's Amelia?"

"I haven't seen her since we've been back. I've been trying all morning to get hold of her. But...Well, you know how it is some-times."

Phillips placed a friendly arm on Peter's shoulder. "I know. Make sure you do give me a call to arrange a night out. Okay? Let's make it soon?" He removed his arm as Fiona joined them.

"Yes. You were right," Fiona said. "The gate opens onto the lane we drove down."

"Great. Thanks." Peter half turned back to Phillips. "Can you tell me anything about the body, yet?

"Initial thoughts only, mind. What we have here is a young fe-male, possibly a teenager. My guess would be early twenties at most. I'd say she's been here around fifteen years. Twenty years tops."

"Too recent to be related to the Bailey and Conley dispute?"

"I'm afraid so."

"And is there any chance of an early identification?"

"You might just get lucky. The victim was wearing what seems to be high quality and quite distinctive jewellery. A matching bracelet and necklace set, along with a couple of rings. We think there's an inscription on the bracelet. It might be a name. I'll get it sent off for cleaning."

"If there's any way you could provide me with a name, that would be fantastic," Peter said.

"I take it if I can come back to you with a name I'll be in your good books forever more?"

"You sure will. The drinks will be on me," Peter joked. His face turned suddenly serious "Is it likely?"

"It's possible. We'll be moving her soon. And yes. I will get my report to you as quickly as I can. There are a couple of other things, including a set of keys. We'll get everything bagged and sent over to you once we've finished with them."

"Brilliant. Thanks, Ross." Peter turned to leave.

Ross called after him, "I'll be waiting to hear from you about that drink."

Peter raised his hand in acknowledgement as he started walking up the steep incline to their car. As Fiona caught up with him, he said. "I don't think there's anything more here we need to see. If they find anything of interest, they'll let us know. With the close proximity of that gate to the motorway exit, it's possible this case will be passed back to wherever the girl disappeared."

As they reached the car, Fiona asked, "So what are we doing now?"

"We'll interview the landowners, along with the employee who found her and then the previous owner and write it up," said Peter as he pushed the key into the ignition. "I don't like dealing with such old cases. Lines of enquiry are usually long cold. The welly, flat hat and wax jacket brigade can be difficult to deal with at the best of times. While they're very observant, they often fail to pass on relevant information. Maybe it's because they're all so deeply suspicious of what they consider to be outsiders. They close rank and hold on to useful information. Factor in that we'll be asking about things that happened fifteen years ago, and we've no hope."

FIVE

Arriving back on the yard, they were directed by a cheery plump woman leading an even plumper horse, towards the farmhouse, set back from the yard. Approaching the front door, they heard a chorus of dogs barking. They were greeted by Graham, who assured them the dogs were quite friendly as he kicked one of them across the small porch to prove his superiority.

"Take your shoes off, please," Graham demanded and indicated the neat row of various types of footwear.

The assortment of dogs eyed them suspiciously from their baskets in the corner of the porch as they removed their shoes and carefully placed them in the line. Slipping through the front door, Graham said. "Please close the door behind you. We don't allow the dogs in the house."

They were led into a traditional style farmhouse kitchen with massive, solid wood furnishing and an oversized table probably capable of sitting twelve comfortably in the middle of the room. What was unusual was how spotlessly clean and tidy the room was. Not a speck of dust or anything left out, the floor a perfectly polished surface. A neat pile of trade magazines, booking diary and paperwork sat in the centre of the table. A small notepad and pencil were lined up in perfect symmetry next to the ordered pile.

Graham made them coffee and invited them to take a seat at the table. It was only when they reached the table that either of them noticed a dark-haired woman they assumed to be Graham's wife sat in the corner on an armchair. She was watching a television mounted on the opposite wall with complete concentration. Even though she sat curled in the easy chair with hunched shoulders, it couldn't disguise how tall she must be. When Peter introduced them, her lifeless eyes briefly left the screen, giving him a critical glance before she returned her attention abruptly back to the television. The disdain in her eyes left him cold.

There was a vast array of surveillance monitors lining the rest of the wall. They covered not only the entrances but most areas on the yard, the stables, the various car parks and the holiday cottages. While the woman continued to sit stony-faced, it was obvious from her red eyes and blotchy skin she had recently been crying. The uncomfortable silence that fell was only broken by Graham carrying the matching coffee cups and biscuit barrel to the table.

"Well, how can we help you?"

"Just some routine questions about how long you've been here, access to the farm, that sort of thing," Peter replied.

"Well, I've lived here most of my life. My parents moved here when I was eight. So that would be getting on for nearly twenty years. And Gillian came here as a groom when she was sixteen."

Fiona noticed Gillian flinch and stiffen slightly at the reference to her as a groom, but her eyes remained resolutely fixed on the screen.

"Could we take contact details for your parents? We will want to see them as well."

"Of course, that's not a problem," Graham said. He pulled his phone from his jeans and copied down the number from the screen. As he passed over the slip of paper, he said, "I could contact them now, if you like."

"That won't be necessary," Peter said. After taking a sip, he added, "I noticed when we were there, that the field has another gate that opens directly onto the lane. Is there any reason why you didn't bring us in that way?"

"I hadn't really thought about it. The farmhouse was easier for you to find. If you would prefer access that way, it could be arranged. It's padlocked, but I could give you a key," Graham said.

"No, that's okay. Hopefully, we won't be here for too long."

"That's quite all right. I understand you have a job to do. We will help you in any way we can."

While Graham's words were aimed to convey a willingness to help, Peter sensed a note of irritation at their presence and reluctance to have them hanging around his property. Peter was also finding the sullen silence of his wife unnerving.

After a short pause, Graham added, "I don't suppose you are able to tell much about the body or how long it's been there?"

"I'm afraid not."

"I'm guessing you know all about Robin Bailey?" Graham asked.

"Yes. I do know something of the case."

"The media can't leave it alone. There was talk recently of a film being made about it all. The media try to convey the impression the area is filled with mad Heathcliffe-type characters and milkmaids running around the village."

"Yes, I'm sure," Peter sympathised. "It's too soon to confirm, but it's unlikely the body found today was connected with that time." This drew a sharp intake of breath from Gillian, causing Graham to look over with concern at his wife still huddled in the chair.

"I don't suppose you can remember any particular disturbance at the farm or in the area when you were younger?" Peter asked.

Graham shook his head thoughtfully. "No. Nothing comes to mind...but if I think of anything, I will let you know."

"Thank you. Before we go, Mrs Farley is there anything you could add?" Peter felt uneasy again as her cold, disinterested eyes held his for a few seconds before she looked away again.

"No."

"Well, thank you for your time. We'll be in touch should we need anything further from you. Could you tell us where to find the gentleman who found the body?" Peter asked.

Graham had been watching Frank on the surveillance cameras while talking to them, so was able to tell them exactly where he was. As they were leaving, Graham added. "You might want to catch up with him quite quickly. He'll be finishing up shortly and heading directly to the pub."

Retrieving their shoes, they heard raised voices from inside.

"You told me they were very old bones," Gillian said.

"I thought..."

"Well, you thought wrong," Gillian shouted. Sounding increasingly frantic, she continued, "There could be other bodies. Disruption all summer. The police will be traipsing around and looking into our business. The cottage guests will leave. Or not come at all. Or we'll have unsuitable people here. Coming to gawp and speculate. The media! They'll all be back. They'll say it was me. It'll all come up again; I won't be able to cope."

"No, they won't. This is completely different."

"I'll just have to cope. That or kill myself."

"Please Gillian..."

This was followed by the sound of a door slamming and then silence.

Once clear of the house, Fiona said, "What do you think that was about?"

"Search me, but definitely worth looking her up to see if she has any record of assault. She must have some reason to think we might blame her."

The yard was densely populated, mostly by middle-aged women pushing wheelbarrows and leading or riding various sized horses about, as they returned to the car. While a few of them chatted, the overall atmosphere seemed hushed and muted. "Do you think they know their every move is being captured on film?" said Peter.

Fiona put her lips to her mouth, "Shh. It really wouldn't surprise me if they have hidden tape recorders as well."

Peter smiled. "Feeling a little paranoid? What did you think of them generally?"

"Odd! I can't believe they didn't turn off the TV when we were there, or at least the sound. And she's so pale."

"Yes. They were somewhat weird. Can you think of anything else?"

Fiona thought for a while. "Well, they called themselves farmers. Looking at Gillian, especially her hands, I'm not convinced she ever leaves the house, let alone does anything manual. And did you notice how scrupulously clean the kitchen was?"

"And your point is?" Peter prompted.

"It just seemed a bit too clean and the husband... I could smell his aftershave and shampoo in his hair from where I sat. Something didn't seem right about them. Farmers certainly seemed the wrong label."

"Maybe that's modern farming for you," laughed Peter. "Farmers nowadays don't talk with a piece of straw in their mouth and use baler twine to hold their trousers up. They employ others to do that."

"It looked too clean. Everything about them appeared too clinical."

"Just remember these are not the farmers you find in children's books. He has not toiled the land, scratching out a living. He inherited the land from his father and has worked out the easiest way to make more money from it. And what did you think of his age? By my maths, he's only in his late twenties."

"He looked older." Fiona thought about it a little more before adding, "A lot older."

"Not sure how relevant it is to us. But I agree there is something desperately wrong in that house."

Walking across the yard, Peter overheard an impossibly thin girl say, "Maybe someone has strangled Gillian at last." This was closely followed by peals of laughter.

SIX

They found Frank where Graham told them they would, outside a small workshop mending the puncture to his bicycle.

"Hi," Peter stretched out his hand. "Frank Codrington? We met earlier at the gate?"

"Yup. I take it you're here about that, there body," Frank replied, without looking up.

Peter nodded.

"Gave me one hell of a shock, I can tell you."

"I'm sure it did. What were you doing up there anyway?" Peter asked.

"I was doing my normal rounds. Do them every morning. Check the fencing and horses all round. Course I saw the fallen tree...and well... there it was." Frank moved across to an air feed attached to the side of the workshop to pump up the repaired tyre.

"What did you do then? Did you touch anything?" asked Peter.

"Did I heck. I got myself back down here as quick as I could. Let Graham deal with it. He then rang you. It's nothing to do with me, really."

Peter left a pause. "Why would we think it was?"

Frank stood up and faced them for the first time. "Well, that's my tyre mended. I got that puncture this morning. Damn twigs and thorns all over the road. Graham really ought to clear up the mess he makes when he cuts the hedges. No thought for anybody else at all."

"Maybe he should. How long have you worked here, Frank?"

"A long time," Frank mumbled as he prepared to leave.

"How long's that? Ten years? Fifteen years?"

"I said a long time."

"Can you give some idea of the number of years you've worked here, Frank?"

"Let me think," Frank said as he scratched his head under his cap. "I guess it could be maybe twenty years or so."

"So, you worked here before Graham took over the farm from his father?"

Frank nodded, avoiding eye contact, hands gripping the handlebars. He started to push his bicycle backwards and forwards.

"Does Graham always speak to you like he did earlier?"

Frank grinned and shrugged his shoulders in reply.

"You can go now. But we will want to see you again."

As they watched Frank peddle his bicycle up the drive, Peter said, "Well, did he fit your ideas of what a farmer should be a bit better?"

"Yes, I get your point," Fiona smiled.

"Do you think he's hiding something relevant, or just worried generally about talking to us?"

"Not sure."

"We'll sit on the fence concerning him for now," Peter said. "It could be nothing. His type often becomes nervous and evasive when talking to us. Could be he's just feeling guilty about a bit of poaching or cash in hand work. Let's go and see what the parents are like."

As they reached the gate that led out from the yard and onto the lane, a vision straight from a 1950s fashion magazine appeared. A gleaming white convertible vintage car glided towards them. The silver of the grille and headlamps reflecting the sun blinded them. As they passed, Peter saw the driver wore a cap and gloves, his passenger a headscarf.

"That's what I call motoring! What was it? Looked like a classic Rolls Royce. Didn't think they came as convertibles!" said

Peter.

"Actually, I think it was an MG sports convertible from around nineteen fifty."

Peter looked at Fiona in amused surprise.

"Sorry. My dad and brother are into classic cars in a big way. I've spent a lot of weekends being dragged around the country looking at them. Guess some of the knowledge has stuck."

"And I assume it's worth a small mortgage," Peter said.

"Surprisingly, it's probably not. It would cost about the same as a top of the range four-by-four."

The address for Graham's parents was in a neighbouring village a short distance away. The house was on the outskirts of the village and resembled a scaled down version of a stately home. It was set behind a high wall with security gates. A long driveway took them past a small lake, the perfect shape and symmetry a clear giveaway it was man-made.

A smartly dressed man with neat, white hair greeted them at the heavy oak door. Despite the heat, he wore a shirt and jacket. He was very quietly spoken, sounding almost effeminate. He took them through a grand hallway with a sweeping staircase and into his study. Peter couldn't resist checking to see if the books lining the room were fake dummies.

"What a dreadful, dreadful business. My son has told me all about it. Do you know yet who the poor person was? Or how long they have been there?" Mark Farley asked.

"No, we're still waiting for reports," Peter replied.

"How can I help your investigation?"

"We just want some background information. When you bought the farm? Whether you noticed anything unusual happening around that time? Gates being forced or ground disturbed? Can you remember anything like that happening?"

"That's such a long time ago," Mark said, as he pulled a pile of neat documents from the drawer of the oversized desk. Putting his glasses on with a flourish, he read: "I bought the place in two thousand and gave it to my son as a wedding gift in two thousand and ten. I thought it would make a nice little project to start them on their way." He smiled over his spectacles. "I can also give you details of the Stokes, from whom I bought the farm."

"Someone else owned the farm after the Baileys?"

"Yes. I don't think they were there long. I dealt with the agent. I don't think I ever met them or spoke to them directly. Not that I can remember anyway. I've written down the agent's details for you as well," Mark said, passing the paperwork over to Peter.

"Thank you for this. But you can't think of a time when there might have been any disturbance at the farm. Signs that maybe someone had been in the field?"

"No. I'm sorry. Nothing springs to mind. It was all such a long time ago, you see." Mark took off his glasses and carefully re-turned them to their case. "If there is anything at all we can do to help, please let us know. Now can I get you both something to drink?"

"No. We're fine, thank you," Peter replied.

"Did you speak to Pauline when you were at the farm?"

"Pauline?"

"She works at the holiday cottages. Well, runs them really. They couldn't cope without her. She's another ex-employee of mine." After a pause, he added. "They all are."

His claim of ownership made Peter shudder.

SEVEN

Back in the station, Peter felt hot and claustrophobic. The old building was not built to deal with the heat. Despite the windows being open and fans everywhere, the stale air remained warm and oppressive. It only seemed to affect the paperwork which was now pinned down by any heavy object that could be found to stop it swirling around the office. The fact Amelia still hadn't returned any of his calls was playing heavily on his mind. He could stand it no longer and announced he was going home for the day.

"I'll stay on a bit longer. See you in the morning," Fiona said. She watched him close the door before she pulled out the Robin Bailey file. She hadn't wanted to admit it in front of Peter, but she was intrigued with the case. She convinced herself it would be of some relevance. If the two farmers had been disturbed enough to leave animal blood and sheep heads on gate posts over rights to a field, what else were they capable of? She found it disturbing to wonder why the wife of one would decide to have an affair with the other one when such a bitter dispute was raging. She could see in the circumstances why Robin may have wanted to kill her. That sort of tension in a small community wouldn't quietly go away. Everyone would have their own opinions and loyalties. And of course, Peter had said Oscar Conley's son still lived in a nearby farm.

Once she'd read the file, she couldn't help but think of the type of person the son must be. The antics of his parents must have left him confused and in despair. Continuing to live in the same community would have taken either great strength of character or insanity. Such a betrayal of trust must have affected all his adult relationships in some way. She tried to make connections between the damaged person he must be, and the body discovered out of thin air. She was quite convinced there was a connection somewhere and the matter warranted further investigation. But with nothing to go on except her imagination, she had to concede after a while that maybe she was just avoiding going home to an empty house.

At home, she did what all lonely singles do. Threw a meal for one in the microwave and realised she'd become a cliché. She didn't feel remotely hungry. The empty spaces in her cupboards said it all. She leant her forehead against the coolness of the fridge, willing herself not to cry.

After the bright-sounding ping of the microwave echoed through the empty spaces, she carried her meal to the living room only to be confronted by the same empty spaces. The gaps in the DVD collection, the picture missing from the wall and the empty coat peg. She bit on her lip hard.

With the plate balanced on her knee, she flicked through a magazine and then the TV guide, but nothing interested her. She could read a book. The pine bookcase had been bought because it was the right size and complemented the rest of the furniture, rather than for any literary need. She hoped there would be something capable of holding her attention for a few hours at least. A cursory look told her all she needed to know. There was nothing that would hold her interest for longer than the first page.

Maybe she could take up knitting. But first, she would have to learn how. While she was visualising the grotesque, stripy sweaters she could knit for orphans all over the world, the phone rang.

"Hello, darling. How are you?"

"I'm fine, Mum."

"Are you sure? I'm worried about you now that you've let Callum go. Are you lonely by yourself?"

"No. I'm fine."

"Not getting down? You sound a bit down."

"Mum! I am absolutely, totally fine. Honest." Fiona felt like screaming but knew it would only make things worse.

"Well. I just wanted to check you were all right by yourself. Just so long as you are. Your father wanted me to check."

"Really, Mum. It was all for the best. I am quite content by myself."

"Well, if you're sure."

"Yes, Mum. I am sure. I promise I'll ring you if I need anything."

"You can ring anytime, even if you just want to talk."

"Yes. I know. Thank you, Mum, but I really am fine."

By the time the call was ended, the microwave meal was cold, and the little appeal it had when heated was gone.

The phone rang again half an hour later.

"Hi there, little sis, how are you? Mum asked me to give you a ring. She said you sounded a little down earlier."

"For goodness sake, what's wrong with you all? Do you think I can't cope by myself? I'm fine. I'm enjoying the peace. Well, I was."

"Okay, okay. I'm just checking."

"No. I'm sorry. I shouldn't have had a go. It's just Mum. You know, worrying. Her worrying then makes me worry, and so it goes on. You know how it is."

"Yes sure. Look, if you're free why don't you come over this weekend? Emma and the kids would love to see you. We haven't seen you in ages. Give us a ring later in the week."

"Yeah sure, I'll let you know."

After putting the phone down a second time, Fiona realised she still had two hours to kill before it would be a reasonable time to go to bed. The boredom was killing her. Maybe there was a point to all the dating agencies. She turned the television on, determined to find something to occupy her for the next two hours. Something that would stop her thinking about Callum or reminding her she was alone with nothing to do.

Failing dismally, she spent another sleepless night tossing and turning. Going over and over in her mind whether she'd made the right decision. If only she'd done this or that, maybe the outcome would have been different. Maybe Mum was right... a career does not keep you warm at night, and her expectations where men were concerned were just too high.

She got up early the next morning without any conclusions and decided to go straight into work. She was surprised to meet Peter in the car park equally early. She wondered to herself what was going on there and why he wouldn't talk about the holiday, but she knew there was no point prying.

Walking across the car park, Peter asked, "Good evening?"

Fiona tried to sound bright. "Yes. Good...and you?"

"Yes. Good," Peter replied.

Despite the early hour, there was already a close muggy feel to the air. The sky was an intense azure blue, promising another beautiful day for sun lovers everywhere. When they arrived upstairs, they found the windows to the office shut and the air unbearably heavy and stuffy.

Fiona poured herself a coffee and sat down to write a rough to-do list. The first thing on her list was to continue going through the missing person database. Until the parameters could be narrowed down, the computer's list was still far too long, and the thought of trawling through all the names of missing girls seemed daunting and depressing. But still, she hoped a name would leap out at her, one that would have some link to the area and Oscar Conley.

She was distracted by Peter's sighs and walks from his desk to stand by the now open window looking down on the slowly filling car park. The claustrophobic atmosphere lifted slightly following a call from Ross Phillips.

"Hi, Peter. I was right. The jewellery worn was expensive and as I thought, once cleaned up there was a name inscribed on the bracelet. Jennifer Turner."

PC Rachel Mann, a petite blond who regularly loitered near Peter's desk, beat Fiona to quickly entering the name into the missing person register and got a match almost immediately. "Jennifer Turner was a sixteen-year-old girl who disappeared without trace from Cheltenham on 25th May 2001."

"Excellent work," Peter said, taking the details from her. "Remind me to ring Ross later to thank him." Peter wandered over to the window to check the brief details. He noticed the tension between the two women but chose to ignore it. After Jordan, his request he not work with women officers had been humoured for a short while. By the time of the arrival of Detective Chief Superintendent Rogers, it was all deemed to be past history, and his request was forgotten.

"It's likely the matter will be transferred back to Cheltenham. Let's head out now to the farm and complete our report so it can be passed on," Peter said.

"Yes. Sure. What are we going to do out there?"

"Get out of this stuffy office for starters. We'll check up on the crime scene guys. See if anything new has been found and then interview this Pauline woman."

"I'll just grab my bag," Fiona said.

"And I thought if we time it right, a spot of lunch at The Bull wouldn't go amiss. Come on, let's make the most of our brief respite from a far too heavy workload. It'll catch up with us soon enough."

Out of courtesy, they caught up with Graham on the yard, told him of their intentions and asked whether the day 25th May 2001 rang any bells with him. Graham thought for a while before replying, "The year means nothing. I would have been nine or ten. But that's my parents' wedding anniversary. I could ring Father to check."

"No, that's quite okay. Could you tell us where we could find Pauline?"

A pleasant wooded walk separated the holiday cottages from the main yard and farmhouse. Shielded on one side by the wood and overlooking a lake, the location was incredibly beautiful with a strong sense of seclusion and tranquillity. There were three terraced and two detached cottages set around an old stone courtyard. The outside of each was decorated with over-flowing tubs of flowers and hanging baskets. In the middle of the courtyard stood an authentic old stone water trough, no doubt found discarded somewhere on the farm. A path to the rear of the exclusive village of cottages led to a low wood cabin which served as a reception area and booking office.

Pauline was dusting the reception desk in the log cabin when Peter and Fiona arrived. She was small in stature but gave the immediate sense of being a rock of stability and efficiency. An attractive woman smartly dressed in a dark knee-length skirt and short-sleeved blouse with a dash of colour from a multi-coloured scarf neatly knotted at her throat. She greeted them with an open smile. "Hello. Can I help you?"

Peter formally introduced them as Detective Chief Inspector Peter Hatherall and Detective Inspector Fiona Williams.

"Oh, yes. I was told you might be calling," Pauline said, as she came out from behind the desk. "Let me just put the closed sign up, so we're not interrupted," she said, walking towards the door. "Shall we sit here?" she said, indicating the comfortable-looking floral armchairs by a low coffee table.

"It's a beautiful place here," said Fiona. "It's so peaceful and quiet."

"It has its moments," Pauline replied.

"Who told you we would be calling to see you?"

"Mark. I mean Mr Farley rang me yesterday to say you may be around."

"We're here just to ask a few simple questions. We understand you have been with the Farley family a long time?" Peter asked.

Pauline straightened the tourist leaflets on the table, showing her perfectly manicured nails. "Yes. Believe it or not, I used to be their housekeeper and childminder for young Graham." She added, "Seen a lot of changes here in my time."

"What were they like to work for?"

"Not too bad. A few up and downs over the years, but we survived."

"We know it's a long time ago, but can you remember any

particular disturbances or events around the farm or the village shortly after the Farleys moved here? May 2001 is the time we're really interested in."

"Well. Let me think. Would you like a drink at all?"

Peter waved the offer away.

"Graham would have been a boy then," Pauline said, shaking her head. "Is that when that body was buried?"

"We believe so."

"I'm trying to think what else was going on then. It was the year of the Twin Towers, wasn't it? I remember being really shocked at the time."

"Yes, we're talking about the same year," Peter replied.

"Sorry, irrelevant I know to your investigations, but it was so shocking at the time. It would also have been around the time poor Frank lost his young bride to cancer. Poor man. He's never been the same since."

"Well, thanks for your time," Peter said as he rose to leave.

"Have you been to the house this morning? Do you know how they're coping up there with this entire thing going on?" asked Pauline.

"They're coping just fine, so far as we're aware," Peter replied.

Fiona couldn't resist saying, "Why do you ask? Is there a problem with them?"

"No. No. I just haven't had a chance to see Gillian, that's all."

Peter was edging towards the door, but Fiona continued. "Mrs Farley does seem a little withdrawn?"

"Well, that's families for you. You know. Things can become very complicated at times," Pauline replied.

As they walked back through the wood, Peter said, "We're not investigating the family, you know. Chances are the girl was killed in Cheltenham. They just chose to bury the body here as the first suitable place they came across when they pulled off the motorway."

"Sorry," Fiona said, blushing slightly. "I'm just a bit intrigued. They seem so odd. You said so yourself."

"So, I did. Well, never mind. Let's enjoy the last of our freedom and get some lunch. We're not going to escape our responsibilities for long. Chances are there's already something else waiting for us when we get back."

◆ ◆ ◆

James Turner couldn't explain the collision of emotions he felt when he heard Jenny had been found. The overall effect of everything he felt at once paralysed him physically and mentally for a while.

He thought it odd that one thing he felt was relief. Relief that Jenny was no longer lost. She had at last been found. He would now have to accept she was finally gone. No longer be convinced he had caught glimpses of her in the street. Go off on mad searches for her. Stop believing she had been spirited away temporarily and would one day walk back into his life and explain where she had been. Explain why any of it had happened.

He used to dream sometimes when he was younger that she had gone through her wardrobe and was having the most wonderful time in Narnia. Aslam was caring for her, keeping her safe and warm. She was having the most amazing adventures while he was left behind. He hated and resented her then. He was so angered by her betrayal. He locked her wardrobe door, so when she just felt like breezing back, she wouldn't be able to. She would be trapped on the other side of the door. Was that wrong?

Anger was the hardest thing to deal with. It was a reaction he could not explain to anyone. It made him sound so callous and self-absorbed. How could he be so angry with Jenny for leaving him? Angry at all he had to contend with. Such uncontrollable anger when he thought of the betrayal and his lost childhood. He also felt anger towards his parents. Angry he couldn't heal their wounds. Angry how he felt, because every time they looked at him, they wished it were Jenny they were seeing. Beautiful Jenny, a girl with boundless energy and life, an exciting future ahead of her she was never going to live.

Angry how they all pretended on the surface everything was

normal. They were coming to terms with their loss. They were all being terribly brave on the outside while on the inside, within the privacy of their home, they were all silently screaming, alone. Angry he was told, "Mummy has become a little overwrought and has taken too many pills and is now resting in hospital." How bloody naive did they think he was? He was still living the hell every day. How many times had he thought of taking "a few too many pills?"

EIGHT

The Bull Inn was far busier than they expected for mid-day in the week. Peter squeezed his car into the last parking space in the front.

"I hope the driver of that car is as small as I am," Fiona joked, as she was forced to sidle sideways to exit the car.

"I'm sure they'll complain if there's a problem." Peter started to walk away but then turned back. "You've probably got a point. You wait here. I'll move the car and park it up in the rear car park."

The pub looked the idyll country retreat. From the car park, stone steps worn concave by many past travellers led up to the heavy oak door. They walked up the steep steps passing between terraced gardens on either side overflowing with flowers. At the top of the steps across the entire front of the building was a narrow stone terraced bar, bathing in the bright midday sunlight. It was just wide enough for small narrow tables, all of which were taken. The huge oak doors were held open by chains, inviting a soft breeze into the building. A sign on the wall told them on their left was the lounge and to the right the bar and to leave their muddy boots outside.

Peter and Fiona turned right into the bar. It was quieter than the lounge area they'd seen through the large bay windows. One man sat at the bar. A couple of the mismatched tables in the corner were occupied by a group of women. The sound of chattering stopped for a second, holding its breath as they entered.

Eyes looked towards them, the moment passed, and the chattering noise restarted.

The girl behind the bar did not fit the 'olde worlde' image at all. She had jet black dyed hair, cropped short and spiked. Peter guessed her to be in her late teens, and while her black gothic clothes were unappealing, she had an amazing welcoming smile and the most piercing blue eyes he thought he had ever seen, reminding him of Amelia.

Serving their drinks, she told them there was a lounge bar next door. The hint was obvious but not barbed.

It was difficult to estimate the age of the man who sat at the end of the bar. His heavily lined face and weather-beaten skin gave him a reptilian look. The only active things about him were his quick, small, pale blue eyes. Otherwise, he seemed to be totally motionless. In front of him was a full pint of beer, an empty pipe and a folded newspaper. Attached to the bar, hanging directly above his head was a sign saying, "Noggin the Nogs' chair." Noggin, assuming that was his name, nodded a greeting of sorts and said in a wonderful deep voice, "You the police, then?"

Fiona smiled and nodded back, before turning bright red when Noggin added, "You 'aving a thing, then? The two of you?"

The barmaid, whose name was Rose, found this very amusing. "Leave them alone, Noggin." She turned to Peter. "Sorry about him. We can't get rid of him. He's become part of the furniture." She laughed and touched Noggin's arm. "I'm only joking. I couldn't survive a shift without you." She leaned forwards across the bar. "So, can you tell us anything about this body? Are there others?"

Peter shook his head.

"We've all been racking our brains thinking of who has gone missing round here in the past few years. We've been trying to work out who the body might be and of course who the murderer could be." She continued, "I think most of the village has been in since yesterday lunchtime and we're expecting the rest of them to be in tonight. Quiet now, but I'm to call the landlord down if it gets busy later."

Peter left Fiona to chat with Rose while he pulled up a bar stool next to Noggin.

Noggin sucked on his empty pipe and looked Peter up and down, and then took his time taking the first sip from his pint. He gave the impression he took his time with everything. That all about him moved at a slower pace than normal. Eventually, he said, "Ah, a lot of you lot 'ere before, bowt the Oscar Conley and Robin Bailey thing. Take it you knows all bowt that?"

Peter replied, "Only what we have read in the old reports," hoping Noggin would continue and give his version of those events. Instead, there followed a long period of silence broken only by Noggin taking occasional puffs on his empty pipe. Peter looked over to Fiona who was in animated, lively conversation with the barmaid and oblivious to his predicament.

Peter was reading the labels on the spirit bottles hung at the back of the bar for the second time when without preamble Noggin said, "David Conley. He ain't what people think he is, mind. You mark my words."

An elderly couple came up to the bar, making a point of ignoring Noggin's audible sigh. Rose served them real ale in their personal matching pewter mugs, without asking them what they wanted. She quickly returned to her conversation with Fiona. The elderly man introduced himself as Derek Alley and his wife Laura, tenants of David Conley, before asking, "Are you investigating the corpse Frank found?" His wife Laura smiled and nodded encouragingly.

"Yes, we are," Peter replied.

Derek frowned at the group of women of mixed ages who sat in the far corner table. "That's where we normally sit. They're not even locals. They are from that horse place you visited today. The farm where that body was found." He leaned forwards, invading Peter's space. "Do you know they drive past my house at five-thirty every morning? What sort of time is that?"

Peter merely shrugged, hoping the irritating busybody would select another table quickly and disappear with his drinks.

Unfortunately, Derek had more vitriol to share. "I expect you will be visiting David Conley as part of your investigations? I'll warn you he is the rudest, most arrogant man I've ever met. He is obviously as insane as his father and sister. You really should look very closely into his activities."

Laura, his wife, continued to smile and nod in the background.

"Well. Thank you very much for your insight," Peter replied, stiffly.

Once Derek was satisfied he had done his duty in pointing out his landlords' failings, he passed a card with his contact details to Peter. "We are both retired and have lived in the village twenty-five years. We will be keeping our eyes and ears open. We'll help you with your enquiries as much as we can. Well, good day to you."

Rose had been listening in as she pretended to wipe glasses. She'd only just managed to resist the urge to laugh. "I'll be keeping my eyes open," she mimicked. Throughout the exchange, Peter had noticed Noggin from the corner of his eye, raising his eyebrows as he occasionally puffed on the empty pipe.

Peter was about to join Fiona when he was tapped on the shoulder by Noggin. "That body. It must 'ave been put there by a huntsman, a local landowner or a farm worker."

Peter asked, "Why do you say that?"

"Ah, well. The Earl, you see. 'E owns most of land 'e hunts on. Rents the farms out, see, so the hunt can go where it likes. On the edge of 'is huntin' land is some privately-owned farms, like these 'ere. Earl don't like to 'ave places he can't cross whenever he feels like, in case he loses a fox. So he makes the private farms use his padlocks. He likes to make sure they all 'ave to use the same number. They all have the same code like. So, if a fox crosses land, they all knows the code to unlock the gate. Always been that way. The same number is on all the padlocks on all the gates. Dead bodies are heavy. And would need a spade so would 'ave to drive through the gate, so would need to know the code."

"Would that have been the case fifteen years ago?" Peter said, suddenly interested.

After an infuriating pause, while Noggin sucked on his pipe, he replied, "Aye."

"Can you tell me who would know the code?"

Noggin took another long pull on his pipe. "Huntsmen, estate workers, local landowners, farm workers and anyone else they told." He added a short while later, "A rule of friendship with Mark Farley, is he sets all the rules. And that son of his, Graham, he's the same. Best person to ask 'bout things up there is Frank. He may not say much, but it's all going on upstairs, if you know what I mean."

Peter called Rose over and asked if their food could be delivered to the rear garden. As soon as they had some privacy, he updated Fiona and rang the station to ask them to delay agreeing to pass the file to Cheltenham as there may be a strong local connection after all.

"Once we finish our meal, we'll pop back down to Rooksbridge," Peter said.

They found Graham and Frank together, mending some broken fencing when they arrived to ask about the padlocks.

"We use the hunt padlocks now on all our boundary gates. Fifteen, twenty years ago, I'm guessing we did as well. Can you remember, Frank?" Graham asked.

Frank reluctantly shuffled forwards. "I would have thought so. Back then as I remember, that gate was covered in barbed wire and blocked with fallen trees. We had some problems with travellers. They used that gateway to get in. Problem was once they got in and settled it was a hell of a job to get rid of them again. The answer was to stop them getting onto the farm in the first place. Local people kicked up a stink about access. Check with Mark if I was you."

"I don't suppose you have any idea where the travellers came from, do you?"

"I can tell you it was a little bit to the west of Wales. They used to turn up with their caravans and all their junk every summer."

As soon as Peter and Fiona were out of earshot, Frank said, "Graham, do you remember when you used to sleepwalk? When you were a lad?"

"Vaguely, why do you ask?"

"I just wondered if you remembered once, when you were quite young. You would have been about ten, I think. There was one evening, quite late, when I found you by the old caravans?"

Graham seemed uninterested, but Frank continued, "You gave me quite a fright at the time, I can tell you. Do you remember?"

Graham snapped, "Again, vaguely. Why?"

"No reason. I just wondered if you remembered, was all."

"Not really, Frank, and why are you asking daft questions? And what exactly do you think you were doing wandering around the farm in the dead of night?"

Frank shrugged. "Are we done here for today?"

On the way back to the station, Fiona asked, "What did he mean by a little to the west of Wales?"

Peter gave a broad grin. "Think about it. He meant they were Irish."

When Peter and Fiona returned to the station, they were greeted by PC Rachel Mann. "I've checked, sir, and I can tell you Mrs Farley doesn't have a record. She's had no previous contact with the police at all, as far as I can tell."

"Thank you," Peter replied, as he picked up the files left on his desk. "Has any further information come in on the girl?"

"Not yet. PC Bains has requested a copy of the missing person report. Shall I chase it up?"

"Yes, please," Peter replied. "And could you also run checks on Frank Codrington and David Conley? While I'm thinking about it, could you also run one on Derek Alley as well?"

"Should I assume they all live in Birkbury?"

"Yes, they're all resident in the village.

Detective Chief Inspector Jim Harris poked his head around the door. "We've had a bit of a result today. Some of us are heading over for a drink. You interested?"

"I need to get home tonight, Jim. I'll have to pass on it this time," Peter replied. "And well done on your result."

"Fiona?" DCI Harris said.

"Well. Is that all right with you?"

"Yes, of course," Peter said. "Off you go. I'll see you in the morning."

Detective Inspector Steve Jackson appeared shortly after. "Hi. I heard you were joining us in the pub. I thought I'd do the gentlemanly thing and walk you over."

Peter noticed Fiona blush and turn away as she began to tidy her desk and collect her personal belongings. He was sure he hadn't sensed anything before he went away. But then, he thought with regret, recently he'd been so wrapped up with his own problems he had missed a lot of things. He wouldn't have noticed anything if something was going on under his own nose.

He felt a little ashamed at how little interest he'd taken in Fiona as a person since she'd joined him. He had no idea whether she was in a relationship or not, or anything else about her. He'd come a long way since refusing to have a female DI, but it suddenly became clear to him he had a long way to go.

Peter stood at the window as he watched his colleagues cross the car park to the pub opposite. He didn't know why he'd refused the offer. He was in no hurry to get home. He just didn't feel in the mood for all the backslapping and high spirits. Plus, it would end up being another call from a pub, explaining to Sally he would be late home. He tried Amelia's number again. Getting no reply, he headed out of the station.

When he parked in his driveway way, he felt the sheer weight of his worries pinning him to the seat. His whole body felt leaden. It was all he could do to unlatch the seat belt and let it slide across his body. He tried to find some motivation to leave the car. Sally must be getting sick to death of me by now. The holiday was hardly a resounding success.

NINE

By nine a.m. the heat in the office was oppressive, as they waited to hear whether the case was going to be transferred back to Cheltenham or stay with them. Peter felt irritable. He wasn't too troubled about the outcome. He was annoyed someone else would make the decision, based on area politics rather than the facts of the case. He frowned when his phone rang.

"You did it again, Peter," Sally said.

"Did what?"

"You left early. Before the boys were up. They like to see you in the morning."

"Sorry. I'll make it up to them tonight."

"Like last night?"

"No. Not like last night. I'll be back by bath time. I promise." There was a tense moment of silence. The sense they both felt unsatisfied but were equally unsure why. Peter asked, "Has Amelia rung?"

"No. You've got three children, Peter. Not just Amelia," Sally said.

"I know. But the boys have got you."

"I give up. We'll see you tonight." And the phone went dead.

Peter leaned back in his chair. The holiday had turned out to be a turning point in their relationship. Unfortunately, a negative one. He flipped open his wallet and glanced down at the most recent picture he had of Amelia.

Would the holiday have been much better if Amelia hadn't

cried off at the last minute following that stupid argument with Sally? For Peter, it would have been a better time. But he couldn't say the same for Sally with any confidence anymore. He could understand Amelia not backing down, but Sally should have made more of an effort. She could have offered an olive branch of sorts. Not let it fester. If it was on purpose, she'd gained very little.

Amelia is so much like her mother. She needs someone to keep an eye on her. She needs to know I'll be there for her. And I can't be if I haven't a clue where she is.

It's something about the way she moves, the lopsided grin that hides her fears, the way she always sidles as if she doesn't want her slightest movement to be noticed. Sometimes it feels like living with a cat that doesn't want to take up too much space. So much like Jordan. Not wanting to be a burden to anyone, locking everything up inside.

With Jordan, everything was so real. It was so natural. Was it because we were so much younger all the emotion felt so raw and immediate? With Sally, it's closed and tight. But wasn't that what I wanted, less complication and drama? Recently everything seems to be an effort, a performance. The intensity, the inevitability is just not there anymore. I'm not convinced it ever was.

Peter was knocked from his thoughts by the reappearance of Fiona, carrying two coffees along with a couple of pastries and the simultaneous ringing of the telephone. There was a short delay between experiencing these events and recognising they required a reaction.

"I'll get the phone," Fiona called breezily, as she juggled the snacks and her handbag and picked up the ringing phone with a mysterious third hand.

"Well?" asked Peter, once the receiver was replaced.

"The case is being passed to us. There's an officer on his way over with the evidence boxes, but we should receive a faxed copy of the main reports shortly."

They both looked to the fax machine. With perfect timing, it whirred into life.

Fiona started to gather the pages as they spilt out. "And check this out." Fiona held a dramatic pause.

"There's a statement here from the missing girl's brother saying she was hit on at the Cheltenham Race Festival a month prior to her disappearance... By an older man with a West Country accent offering her a career with horses."

"That's interesting, and it puts the focus back on the farm. I'm going to have to go and deal with the media shortly. If you could start going through the faxed report and drawing up a list of the people we might want to see, that would be helpful."

"There's one more thing," Fiona said, gathering up the faxed sheets. "A cousin is coming over to identify the jewellery. He was contacted yesterday and went straight to the local station. He suspects it was a sixteenth birthday gift from her parents and apparently her twin was given a matching set."

"She had a twin! The disappearance must have been hard on her."

"Him, she had a twin brother. Anyway, the cousin is coming over with the..."

They were interrupted by Peter's phone ringing. "Amelia! Where have you been? I've... we've been worried sick."

"Chill out, Dad. It's cool. I was just hanging with friends."

Peter made a fist with his free hand, fighting the urge to scream and shout. Demand his baby come home immediately. And it definitely was not cool, as he felt a bead of perspiration run down his cheek. He wiped it away and said, "Could we meet this evening after I've finished work?"

"Sure."

Fiona found an excuse to leave the office rather than listen to a call which was obviously personal. When she returned, the office was empty. She settled down to read the original missing person case notes. She was pleased the body had a name. Jenny Turner had been a very pretty girl with a promising future ahead. It was no longer an abstract find in a village which had an intriguing and colourful past. It was a real person with hopes and dreams, with family and friends left behind to wonder what had happened. Fiona was so totally immersed in the report she jumped when PC Rachel Mann appeared from nowhere in front of her desk.

"Sorry to disturb you, but there's a young man downstairs." She looked down at her notebook. "It's a Richard Turner. The cousin of the body found at Rooksbridge."

"Thanks," Fiona said, rising from her desk.

"Is DCI Hatherall about somewhere?" Rachel asked, her facial expression screaming, 'You can't interview him without supervision.'

Fiona bristled at the slight. "He's with the media." She added more confidently than she felt, "I'll come down and see him."

She left a note for Peter on his computer and took a deep breath. "I'm coming now," she said, as she followed Rachel's blond ponytail, which jauntily whipped side to side, out the door.

She collected Richard from the front desk and ushered him into one of the side rooms, trying to ignore the thumping of her heart against her chest wall. She felt unnerved by how closely he resembled the girl in the photographs she'd been looking at upstairs. A few years older and the features were a little more defined, but overall the similarities were startling.

He had the look of a lost boy about his face. With his dark curly hair and bright blue eyes, he was very attractive. His athletic figure showed off his expensive chinos and denim shirt to perfection. Almost too perfect looking. The look of deep sadness in his eyes added further to his appeal. When Fiona showed him the evidence photographs showing close-ups of the jewellery taken from the body, she saw a look of raw grief on his face.

"Were you very close to your cousin?"

"We all played together as children. It was a tough time for all of us. My mother was distraught when she lost her sister-in-law as well, due to all this," Richard said, waving his hand dismissively over the evidence folder. "They had developed a very close friendship over the years. We used to go on holiday together every year. Naturally, everyone felt for James, but our family was very deeply affected as well."

He held the photographs for a long time. He turned them over several times in his hands, squinting to read the blown-up inscription before nodding. "Yes, I'm sure they are hers."

He pulled from his holdall what appeared to be a matching set of jewellery. It was more masculine but had the same distinctive style. He turned over the bracelet to show the inscription, "James Turner." He handed them towards Fiona reluctantly, as if he couldn't bear to be parted from them. "I'm quite sure they were a sixteenth birthday present from their parents."

Fiona thought she saw tears well in his eyes when she gently took them from him.

His voice sounded educated and calm when he softly asked, "Will we be able to have them back at some stage?" He added quickly, "Can I have some sort of receipt? I'd like to have something to give James when I get hold of him?"

"Of course, that won't be a problem. We will take good care of them until they can be returned," Fiona reassured him.

Richard asked for the name of the village where the remains had been found and said he intended to stay in the area for a few days. Fiona gave him the name of the holiday centre and suggested some other local places for accommodation. Then, she took him back to the entrance of the station, gave him her card and asked that he let her know where he was staying. She hastily added, "We will probably need to speak to you again as part of the investigation."

When Fiona returned, Peter was back in the office and stood gazing out of the window overlooking the car park, her scribbled note in his hand. When she joined him, he asked without turning towards her, "Was that Richard Turner in the denim shirt? I think I just saw him leaving?"

"Very possibly, he was wearing denim and has just left." She too peered out of the window, but he was long gone.

"What did you think of him?" Peter asked.

"Upset. Quite moved by the sight of the jewellery, but nothing

I wouldn't expect, considering. He is planning on staying in the area for a bit. I've asked him to let us know where."

"We need to keep an eye on what he's up to while he is here. I don't want him carrying out his own investigations and making a nuisance of himself. Could you find out a bit more about him? I've heard he runs a private investigation business."

TEN

Rose had finished her lunchtime shift at the Bull and was heading up to Hillend Farm where she kept her horse. She'd briefly tried stabling her at Rooksbridge but had fallen out with Graham Farley very quickly. She was too much of a live wire for his controlling ways.

Cathy and Tim Potter, who owned Hillend Farm, were far more laid back and easy going. Recently she'd been doing a bit of work for them, helping with their horses. She sensed she would be losing her pub job shortly and was angling for more horse work.

Part-time casual jobs suited her best. She had tried a "proper" job once and hated every second of it and the restrictions it made on her time. She enjoyed it at the pub, but the landlords had three daughters, and they were all keen to become more involved. Rose was sure she was being squeezed out. As it was, she was only allowed to serve behind the local's bar and even there, she seemed to be getting fewer and fewer shifts. John and Pat, the landlords, had insisted to Rose they had no intention of excluding her and once the summer season was in full swing, her shifts would increase again but Rose was unconvinced. Family always comes first, thought Rose, and she would rather leave by choice than suffer the indignity of being pushed out by those girls.

The key is to keep moving on. The only other place to work in the village is Rooksbridge Farm. Not a chance in hell that's ever going to happen.

She'd read somewhere, 'We are all masters at talking ourselves out of a change that will take us into the unknown.' She thought this was probably very true, but it was so easy to live at home and to do the bare minimum of work locally to get by.

Her parents were cool. Mum could be a little embarrassing after a few glasses of red wine. Sometimes she got what she called the "blues," but these usually lasted only a couple of days. During that time, whatever Rose did was wrong. Dad would often slip her extra money on the quiet when she was short. She guessed her parents were happy and liked having her around still. And she felt she had plenty of time in the future to take on the mundane responsibilities of taking control of her life and trying to finance her lifestyle in the wide world.

As she passed the farmhouse, heading off to catch her horse, she passed one of Tim's vintage cars parked in the driveway. She waved to Cathy, who was filling her wheelbarrow with cut flowers from her garden.

Rose exclaimed, "Aren't they lovely!"

Cathy looked around her garden with pride. She tended to it mostly by herself, even the heavier work, despite fast approaching sixty. "I was planning on taking these up to the church. But if you would like some, you are quite welcome."

Rose couldn't care less about flowers but thought her mum might like them, so she replied, "That would be lovely, and they really are quite stunning. If you don't mind, that is?"

So, for the first time, she was led up to the house while Cathy sorted the flowers and wrapped a bunch for her. Tim was at the kitchen table poring over maps. He looked up briefly and smiled when they entered. Rose thought he was quite striking for an old man. Tall, slim and with a full head of blond hair. The son, Grant, wasn't bad either, but he was engaged, and Rose was fully aware the whole family was well out of her league. The old class system was still firmly in place in the British countryside, and she knew her place.

"Don't worry about Tim," called Cathy, who had disappeared into their pantry. "He's planning a road trip for us down to the

Rhine, so he can fill the cellar with even more wine. I've refused to go into an airport with him again after the scene he made at the check-in desk last time, so we're driving down."

She came back into the kitchen with a large bunch of assorted flowers bound together at the stems, and a sheet of brown wrapping paper. "If you pop them in a bucket of water when you ride, they'll stay fresh. Then you can wrap them yourself when you leave."

Rose faked a gushed thank you and asked if there was anything she could do for them. Cathy considered for a moment before saying, "Well, we will shortly be bringing the hunters in. If you could help with getting them fit for next season that would be wonderful."

Rose positively beamed in reply.

"And how's Frank been since his gruesome discovery? I expect he's been holding court in the pub, telling everyone about it," Cathy asked.

"I've no idea. He's barely been in since."

Tim looked up from his maps and said, "Unusual for him. I expect he's going up to The Star instead."

"I really don't know. Well, I'd best be off. Thank you very much for the flowers," Rose said, as she backed out of the room.

After Rose left, Tim said, "What a strange little thing," before returning his attention to the maps.

"Well, I think she's delightful, like a gust of fresh air. And she could be very useful with the horses," Cathy said. She made them both a cup of tea and feigned interest in Tim's maps for a while before exclaiming, "It is quite disturbing about that body being found." Getting no response, she added, "Well, I still think we should go down there and offer our support as neighbours."

Tim sighed and petulantly said, "I really don't enjoy that man's company. He bores me," before he turned his attention back to the maps spread over the table.

"And I don't really have time for playing childish charades with Gillian, but I feel it's our duty as neighbours," Cathy replied.

Tim continued planning their route through Germany. Cathy finished her cup of tea and said, "Well, I'm going to take some of these flowers down to Gillian. She must be distressed by such a terrible thing. I'll see if Grant wants to come with me if you won't."

"Up to you, dear, but I doubt if they'll thank you for interfering," Tim replied.

◆ ◆ ◆

Peter waited outside the station until seven-thirty for Amelia to arrive, constantly checking his phone. His call to Sally explaining he was going to be home late after all had not gone well.

Waiting for Amelia had left him with far too much time to brood and he fell into his worn-out way of thinking. As hard as he'd tried over the years, he could never forget the look on Jordan's face, that terrible day. It was etched forever into his brain cells: the raw hurt in her accusing eyes at his betrayal. His guilt would never go away. He knew he deserved to be haunted by that face forever more. Just when she'd needed him, he had failed her. Unable to cope with his own childish fears, he'd turned away from her. He tried over and over to justify what he'd done. It wasn't his fault. He was just too young at the time to understand. They both were. He'd no comprehension of what she was going through. It was only later when he'd had to face the same dark demon, he'd really understood. But by then, it was far too late. Amelia was a constant reminder. And a second chance for him. He was determined he would not fail again.

ELEVEN

Early the following morning, Fiona and Peter read the computer screen with disbelief. Surely it couldn't be that simple? Mr Frank Codrington had been arrested in Cheltenham on April 2nd, 2001 for assault on a prostitute.

"We've no choice. We have to bring him in," Peter said, his voice filled with regret. "I've got to be honest, I'm finding it hard to take in. Killing and burying a girl and then continuing to work on the farm? He was jumpy when we spoke to him, but I wouldn't have thought he was capable of that. My gut instinct says it wasn't him, but then possibly I'm trying to make things too complicated."

Fiona quickly did the arithmetic. "The statements refer to Jenny meeting an older man in Cheltenham. Surely that would make him too young?"

With a heavy sigh, Peter replied. "When you're sixteen, anybody over twenty could be called an older man. At forty we're ancient."

"Yes, but offering her a job with horses? He just works for the Farleys. He wouldn't be in a position to offer her a job surely?"

"Don't be naive. You've never been spun a line by a bloke in a pub?" Peter said.

"That's a fair point. It must have been awful for him. Losing his wife so young."

"Exactly, we have to take that into account. That sort of grief can make people do odd things." Peter watched Fiona's face carefully for any reaction, wondering whether his past was such old news nobody mentioned it anymore. Seeing no obvious sign, he wondered whether that was a good or a bad thing. "We'll arrange a search of the house as well."

They were leaving when they were told a Mr and Mrs Alley had come in to see them. Peter was annoyed at the delay this would cause. He wanted to get things with Frank over and done with as quickly as possible, acutely aware of the line of questioning he would have to take. The memories and old wounds he knew he would be opening filled him with a sense of dread and also distaste for himself. It all felt a little too close to home. "Where have you put them?"

"They're in interview room one. I've taken them some tea. Aren't they a sweet old couple?"

Peter's blood pressure was raised a notch when he recognised the sweet old couple as the two busybodies from The Bull Inn, so anxious to point out their neighbours' shortcomings. The fact they looked so relaxed and at home with their cups of tea wound him up further. Derek had a notepad and pen laid out neatly in front of him as though about to start an exam.

"Please turn over your papers now," Peter remembered his old school teacher saying with a shudder. He sank into the chair opposite them, smiled weakly and asked them how he could help.

Derek leaned forward, his face eager, tapping his notepad. "It's how we can help you."

Laura smiled and nodded her head encouragingly at his side.

Peter tried to hide the irritation he felt. "What do you want to tell us?"

"Well, we watched the news the other day. And we talked about what we should do. Didn't we, Laura?"

Laura nodded and smiled. She reminded Peter of a nodding dog on the rear shelf of a car.

"The girl came from Cheltenham. We decided we should let you know. Normally we wouldn't have a bad word to say about him. But around that time, he was very affected by his grief. And well, I'm sure you know, sometimes when people are under a lot of stress, they do things they wouldn't normally do. We're not accusing him of anything, of course. We just wanted to bring things to your attention. As our duty..."

Peter held up his hands. "Whoa! Slow down. Who are you talking about?"

Derek didn't like being interrupted; he was building up to the name. This was all part of his drama training.

Laura leapt in to fill the silence. "Frank Codrington, of course."

Derek gave Laura a sideward glare before he looked down at his notepad and continued as if his wife had not spoken. "Frank Codrington..." He paused to give Laura a second black look, "lost his wife in the summer of 2000. It completely devastated him, and everyone says he's never been quite the same since. Don't they, Laura?"

Laura, presumably forgiven, returned to her role of supportive, nodding and smiling.

Peter stood up. "Thank you for your time. We are already aware of this."

Derek looked crestfallen. "But we need to tell you..."

"We know about Mr Codrington and the death of his wife. Thank you."

"And did you know about his flat in Cheltenham?"

"Yes. Thank you again for coming in."

Peter stood up and marched out of the room, leaving Fiona to gather her things and show Derek and Laura out.

"Well, I must say! Is your boss always so rude? We've taken a lot of trouble to come in here today and do our duty."

"We really are very busy at the moment, but we do appreciate you both coming in," Fiona said.

"It's no wonder the public doesn't want to become involved with the police if this is how they are treated."

"I'm sorry you feel that way. You have been very helpful, but I'm afraid I really must go now," Fiona said, as she held the door open for them to leave.

She caught up with Peter who was waiting for her in his car. As she climbed in, he couldn't contain his frustration and anger any longer. He hit the car ceiling with his fist and said, "God, I can't stand people like that. Just the look on his face was so condescending. Sheer malice. That's what it was, malice and the opportunity to stick the knife in someone's back. Let's get this over and done with."

Fiona quietly put her seat belt on, confused by Peter's reaction to the news about Frank.

Pulling away, Peter said, "Do you know what he reminded me of?"

Fiona shook her head in reply.

"He reminded me of a toddler presenting his mother with his artwork from nursery school. He sat there as if anticipating approval and maybe a biscuit for his clumsy splodges of paint, regardless of whether it deserved any merit."

"Funny you should say that, sir. Something about him reminded me of my school days."

"Well. When we get back, arrange a good look into his background. Find out if he's not trying to distract our attention away from him with his schoolyard tales. He would have been around at the time Jenny disappeared." Before they'd gone far, Peter's phone rang.

"Amelia. What happened to you yesterday?"

"Sorry, Dad. Something came up. How about we meet up tonight instead?"

With the phone on loudspeaker, Fiona couldn't avoid hearing the conversation. She watched Peter's knuckles turn white as he gripped the steering wheel before she decided to stare resolutely out of the window.

"Tonight? Come over to the house."

"Umm, is...?"

"Sally and the boys are spending a few days with her mother. She hasn't been too well recently."

"See you later. I'll bring round a bottle of wine."

Peter gave Fiona a sideways look that said, "Not now." And they continued the rest of the journey in silence.

As they pulled into the yard, they noticed Graham and Frank

were travelling behind them in a green tractor.

Peter inhaled deeply as he pulled himself from the car. He walked the short distance back to the tractor and called, "Frank. Frank Codrington." He watched him climb down the steep steps from the cab, dreading the words he would have to say. Graham joined them from the other side. Peter walked up to Frank and said, "We would like you to come back to the station with us to answer some questions about the disappearance of Miss Jennifer Turner."

Frank looked bewildered while Graham stood staring open-mouthed. Peter noticed the colour drain from Frank's face and thought for one moment he was going to bolt. Instead, he stood completely still as if paralysed with shock. Fiona was as gentle as possible, firmly insisting a very nervous and immobile Frank get into the rear of the car. Frank was looking furtively around the yard at the group of women who had stopped to stare. He looked as though he was going to be sick. Driving out of the yard, Peter noticed Graham striding purposefully towards the farmhouse talking into his phone.

TWELVE

Gillian looked up in surprise when Graham rushed into the kitchen as she was laying the table for lunch.

"You are not going to believe this. The police have been here. And they've taken Frank in for questioning! It's got to be a mistake, but that's no help to me. I'm going to be stuck the next couple of days without him. I can't do it all by myself."

Gillian looked at Graham with complete shock and amazement. "Frank? What? They're suggesting he had something to do with that poor girl. No."

"They met us in the yard just now and said they wanted to have a word with him back at the station. Didn't you see it on the cameras?"

Gillian gave him a withering look. "So, they haven't arrested him then? He'll probably be released by this evening. Sounds like you're overreacting."

Graham did a double take. Gillian accusing me of overreacting, now that's a good one. He persisted, "They must think he knows something to take him in. Either way, he's not here to help me this afternoon."

"Well, maybe I could help you?"

"No, that's fine. I'll manage. I'd prefer you stayed here to manage things."

Gillian sighed and returned to preparing lunch.

"Maybe I could give Keith a ring, see if he could help out a bit. Or I'm sure Helen said recently her husband had lost his job.

Maybe he could help for a few days. I'll ask her when she gets here later."

The last thing he wanted was Gillian back out on the yard getting increasingly stressed and upsetting everyone. Gillian on the yard was always a total nightmare and led directly to a loss of clients. Her wild accusations drove some away and led to ridicule from others. He wasn't sure which was worse.

"Well, if you are sure?" Gillian placed the casserole dish in the oven and curled up in the armchair to watch TV.

Graham watched his wife for a while.

"Are you still here?" Gillian asked, without looking from the screen. "Lunch won't be ready for another hour."

Graham opened his mouth to speak, closed it again and turned to leave. He kicked over the neat row of wellington boots in frustration on his way back out.

There were a handful of women in the yard, standing around in shock discussing what they'd just seen.

"Frank? Who would have thought it of Frank?"

"It seems so unbelievable."

"The police must have it wrong."

"I think it's totally bizarre."

"Frank a cold-blooded murderer? No way, I can't believe it of him."

"Frank has the patience of a saint."

"You'd have to be a saint to put up with the Farley family and the goings-on round here."

"If it had been Graham or even that friend of his with the limp, maybe I could believe it, but not Frank."

"Or Graham's father, what was his name? Mike, I think, or Mark, something like that."

"But then you never know... it was years ago. Maybe Frank was different back then?"

"Don't they say murderers hang around the scene of their crime?"

"Well, who would have thought it of Frank?"

Ros and Lisa had been the closest and overheard Frank being

taken away and were revelling in their moment of glory and enjoying being the centre of attention. All thoughts of their horses being ridden that day were wiped clear away. They stopped gossiping briefly when Stephen, a local riding instructor, drove onto the yard before jostling to be the first to pass on the gossip to a fresh pair of ears.

Stephen had been surprised when he first arrived not to see his morning clients already warming up their horses ready for their lesson. It didn't take long for him to be drawn into the huddle. He would be running at least an hour late all day, possibly longer as he retold the story. He disliked the Farleys and knew they barely tolerated him. If he weren't so popular with their mutual clients, they would probably ban him from their farm. He genuinely liked Frank and was as surprised as everyone else at the revelation.

"Wow! All this happening on our doorstep. Nothing so exciting has ever happened like this, before. Normally the highlight of the day is someone falling off, a lost shoe or a lame horse," Ros said.

Pat, the next arrival to be greeted excitedly with the news, was also the first to spot Graham coming across the yard. As he approached, she said, "Graham, it's not true, is it? About Frank? Do you know anything more?"

Graham had a lot planned for the day and didn't like gossiping with the daft women that kept their horses on his yard. But today he would make an exception. Due to the Farleys' temperament, the yard had a high turnover of clients, the average stay being about three years so none of them would have known anything about Frank's past. They were all surprised to hear Frank was a widower and were happy to hang attentively to Graham's every word. Most had assumed Frank was a confirmed bachelor, too much of a free spirit to be tied into a conventional marriage with 2.5 kids in tow.

"The suggestion he murdered the poor girl while suffering a severe breakdown following the death of his wife, still seems a bit farfetched to me," Pat said firmly.

Graham replied, "You never know what goes on behind the scenes. The police must have good reason to suspect him." He had no qualms at all about planting a negative opinion of Frank in people's minds for once. It annoyed him how popular he was on the yard. Everyone liked good old Frank. Not any more, if he had anything to with it. He continued to plant a seed of doubt in everyone's mind for the rest of the day.

No one stopped to think Graham had been a boy at the time. He knew nothing of Frank's state of mind at the time of his wife's death other than what his father had told him. He didn't remember it ever being suggested Frank had suffered any breakdown. Comments had been made about him having a drinking problem back then, but in Graham's opinion, he still did. He could vaguely remember Frank as a young man visiting the yard with his wife. He seemed to recollect she was pretty and had been kind to him. She used to chat with him and bring him sweets.

Once the conversations about Frank were repeating themselves in a perpetual loop, Graham disappeared to his workshop, his inner sanctuary, to telephone his father. Mark seemed equally shocked by the news and berated Graham for not contacting him sooner or finding out more about what was happening. Did Frank need legal representation, for instance? Graham was surprised his father thought they should provide legal assistance at their own cost. Frank had a long-standing relationship with his father. But paying for legal representation? That seemed completely out of character. Not like him at all. But then it dawned on Graham. Father meant he should be paying.

From his pocket, he pulled out the card the police had given him on their visit. He was unable to get through to Peter or Fiona, so left a message. He then worked out how much of the afternoon's planned work could be salvaged. He soon found himself distracted by his thoughts, not just about Frank but also about Gillian's recent behaviour, including her frequent disappearances.

Gillian didn't usually go anywhere by herself. Even before all the medical problems, she preferred to hang on his arm. And now the idea of Gillian making secret trips terrified him, especially with the police hanging around the area. Previously, the only visits she had ever made alone were to the doctor or the supermarket. And then he always tried to make sure he was at home when she returned. He would find himself getting increasingly anxious if her return was delayed for any length of time.

Her lack of independence was one thing that had attracted him to her. He would never have to worry about her straying too far or questioning his judgement. The business ran so much better with one person clearly in charge. But still there were times her total dependence on him was a drain, and a third incident would not be so easily explained.

He was padlocking the workshop when he was interrupted by Joyce, a life-long friend of Frank.

"Please God tell me it's not true. They haven't really taken Frank in for questioning, have they?"

Graham was saved by his phone ringing. He raised a finger to her, asking her to wait while he took the call. It was his father, wanting to know if he had spoken to the police.

"Look, Graham," Mark said. "We have to accept that twenty years ago Frank was a mess. He was under a lot of stress and drinking very heavily. Whatever he has done, I think we should stand by him. I'm going to speak to the police myself to explain what he was going through at the time. And I realise you are going to need some help with Frank gone. I've got a bloke I can send over to you tomorrow. Not the brightest, I admit. Heroin would probably make him sharper, but he could help you out for a few days."

Still shocked by the sudden concern, Graham thanked his father and turned back to Joyce. "Yes, I'm afraid it is true. Father is doing all he can to help. When I find out more, I will let you know. Now, I've got work to do," Graham said, before heading back to the house.

Joyce was shocked by Mark being prepared to help Frank. It was most peculiar. Could it be, he felt some gratitude for the way Frank had worked for his family all these years?

Over the years, James had dreamt many times of what he would do if he ever came face to face with the person who had destroyed his life. But now he didn't have a clue how to react. What was he capable of doing? He didn't even know what he was feeling. He stomped around the cottage, banging off the walls, flicking channels on the TV. He picked things up to give him an excuse to slam them back down again. His heartbeat was racing. He was losing it.

He thought about how everything he ever cared about had been taken away from him and how unfair it was. It didn't seem to matter how much he cared or how hard he tried to hang on. His feelings always seemed to be tossed aside, leaving him to grieve a further loss. And each time it seemed to bring it all back.

His entire family wiped out. He always knew Jenny was dead, not missing. Something inside of him had died that day, too. He was left to spend the rest of his life in search of his missing half. Waiting and watching and feeling inadequate.

THIRTEEN

When Peter and Fiona returned to the station, they escorted Frank to the booked interview room and left him there to wait. The room was hot and stuffy. Peter had noticed the small window was shut but made no effort to open it.

Peter did not want to hold Frank for longer than necessary. Despite what they'd found out, something told him Frank was not responsible. But he was equally convinced he knew something, something that was the key to finding out what really happened. If making him feel a little uncomfortable would speed the process, he could live with that. He wished he could think of a way he could spare Frank the anguish of dredging up the loss of his wife. But he couldn't, and he had a job to do.

In the back of his mind, he feared he may be allowing his own personal experience to cloud his judgement. But even when he made full allowances for that worry, he still came to the same conclusion. Unfortunately, it was a conclusion based on a feeling, with no evidence whatsoever to support it. While he felt Frank was not their man and the questioning was going to be cruel, he had no option other than to put him through the ordeal. He was not going to feel good about himself by the end of the day, but it had to be done. There was no way he could explain his reluctance to interview Frank. His only hope was that Frank would tell them quickly what he did know about the girl and how she ended up on the farm.

They were delayed going down to the interview room by a

telephone call from Mark Farley. "I'm just ringing to see how things are with Frank. And to ask you let him know if he needs a solicitor or any other help we're happy to help him."

"That's very thoughtful of you," Peter replied.

"Well, Frank's been with us a long time. He's a good employee. And we know what he went through."

"How was he around the time of his wife's death?"

"As I'm sure you would expect he was absolutely devastated. We all were. Maggie's death hit us all hard. At that age, you think you are invincible. Death happens to old people and strangers. She was a lovely girl. Frank was besotted. It took him a while to get back on track," Mark said.

"Do you think he would have been capable of murdering a young girl?" Peter waited while Mark fully considered the question.

The reply was very calculated. "Frank was in a terrible way. Sometimes people do things they wouldn't normally do when under a great deal of stress."

"Thank you for that."

"But I want you to know Frank is one of the good guys. We will be standing by him. I want him to know that."

"Thank you for the call, Mr Farley. I will pass on your comments when I speak to him."

Frank sat in the interview room shaking and sweating. His condition wasn't helped by the fact he hadn't been eating or sleeping properly since his discovery and had doubled his smoking and drinking at home.

He looked up at the window several times. He daren't move or ask the uniformed officer to open it. He tried to sit as still as possible, looking down at the cassette recorder placed on the side of the table, then at the two empty chairs on the opposite side. He was full of dread. What had they found out? What were they going to say? Would it be best if he said nothing? If he closed his eyes, would this all go away?

They had told him he was not under arrest. Could he just get up and leave? What would happen then? He didn't understand what was happening. They hadn't grabbed him or anything. He hadn't been manhandled into the car or been handcuffed to anything. But he didn't think he could just get up and walk out. He had also not missed the policeman standing between him and the door. He had not been left alone at any point since his collection from the yard. Would Connie be okay?

He had refused legal representation. He didn't know why they thought he needed a lawyer. It must be a mistake. Hopefully, one he could correct. He couldn't afford a lawyer. Having one might make them think he had something to hide.

His thoughts were making his head hurt. The questions were coming so fast he couldn't make sense of them. They were chasing round and round in his head too quickly. He sat glumly waiting for the interrogation to begin.

He nearly fell from his chair when Peter and Fiona did come in. Under the artificial light in the room Frank's skin had taken on a grey hue, and the smell of sweat hung in the room.

"Are you feeling all right, Frank? Would you like a drink before we start?" Fiona asked.

Frank shuffled in his seat but replied he felt fine. Peter noisily scraped his chair along the floor before shuffling it into position, which made Frank flinch and move his hand to his chest.

"Are you sure you're okay?" Fiona asked again.

Frank gave a quick nod of his head, avoiding eye contact and lowered his arm. Fiona sat down quietly with her hands in her lap.

Peter went over the statement Frank had previously given. Peter constantly had to repeat simple sentences before Frank could confirm them as correct. Fiona spoke only to encourage him to relax. She reminded him they just wanted him to tell the truth and that he was not under arrest.

Frank went through again how he had found the body and what he had done after. He confirmed his employment record with the Farleys and that he would have been working at the farm twenty years. They moved on to talking about his marriage, his wife's illness, the treatment and his state of mind in the months following her death. The questioning appeared kind and considerate of his feelings, but it was hard to talk about the things that happened so long ago.

Frank froze when they started to ask questions about his flat in Cheltenham.

"Why were you staying in Cheltenham? Why did you rent a bedsit for your visits rather than seek hotel or bed and breakfast accommodation? Surely that would have been a cheaper option? Your visits, while regular, were often weeks apart and your stays were always only a couple of days, three at the most. What was the interest in Cheltenham? What were you doing that required the privacy of a flat? Did you lend the keys to anyone? Did anyone else ever stay there? Did you attend the races at Cheltenham in 2001?"

Frank's replies went from monosyllabic to shrugs and looks of despair. He rubbed his temple furiously. "Please, could you slow down, I need time to think."

"What do you need to think about, Frank? Just answer the questions," Peter fired back.

"My mind is all mixed up now. I can't think straight," Frank pleaded, as a bead of sweat ran down the side of his face.

"Frank. Please, could you answer our questions?" Peter said.

"I have been. I've answered all your questions the best I can. You're just confusing me now. I don't know what to say anymore."

"I think we will take a break, Frank. When we return, we do expect you to answer our questions. Do you understand?"

Frank nodded.

FOURTEEN

Joyce had been upset all day hearing the way people were gossiping about Frank. Friends she had once thought of as loyal to Frank were far too easily influenced by all the excitement. People were far too easily swayed by others. They all seemed to be swept away with the drama of the whole thing.

That was possibly what bothered her the most. People viewed the whole thing as something thrilling to spice up their own boring day. Didn't they realise it was Frank's life they were greedily dissecting while behaving as if they were part of some long, drawn-out soap opera?

If they just stopped and thought, they would realise how stupid it was to suggest Frank capable of hurting anyone. Clearly, pathetic, stupid people with no personal integrity. Frank would be devastated if he could hear how ready people were to turn against him. Does nobody have a mind of their own, capable of thinking independently anymore? Have they no compassion or awareness of the feelings of others?

Joyce didn't know who she despised the most. Those who had known Frank for years or those who had only known Frank's kindness in recent years, pretending they knew more about him than she did. She felt disgusted and disappointed. They were pulling Frank's private life apart like vultures, taking pleasure in every new twist that came to light in their desperate need to feel part of the drama.

The only person who appeared to be doing anything for Frank

was Mark, and she had an uneasy feeling as to what his motives might be. Part of her wanted to see some good in him, to trust that Frank's friendship and loyalty over the years meant something to him. But bitter experience told her Mark only cared for Mark. But just maybe he did want to help, even if it was for selfish reasons. At least he was a strong man. He at least stood by his principles and was a leader rather than a follower.

She thought of going away for a few days. Maybe going to see her sister, Jill. But what if Frank needed her? The police said she couldn't see Frank but what about when he was released? They would release him, she felt sure of that. Then he would need a friend. Maybe they could go somewhere together then?

If she went away, who would look after Connie? Could she take Connie with her? Although the car journey was only about forty-five minutes, Connie was old and often confused. Jill was very house-proud. Would she want an old and somewhat smelly dog in the house, especially one that couldn't be guaranteed to do her business outside?

What if Frank were charged? Found guilty? Could she reconcile the Frank she knew with a killer? He was in a state back then, didn't know what he was doing. But any harm he'd done had always been to himself. If he had done something like murdering a young innocent girl, how had he kept it hidden from her all these years? What if her most important friendship was a sham?

She tried to push these thoughts from her mind. Even thinking them made her feel guilty.

She would go to Frank's to feed Connie and check the house was locked up and secure. Then she would have a good long think. Decide what to do.

While she normally wasn't one to pry, the situation was exceptional, and maybe there was something in a drawer somewhere in the house which would explain Frank's behaviour. She didn't quite know what she had in mind...an old photograph or letter, a clue left lying around which she could retrieve and save the day. Well, that sort of thing always happens in television dramas. Look at Miss Marple and all she unearths.

There would be no one to disturb her at the house, and Connie gave her a valid reason for being there. And while she was having a look about she could telephone Jill and ask her what she thought she should do.

When she pulled up outside Frank' cottage, she sat in her car and wept. Frank's house was being searched by the police. It had been surrounded by tape, and there were no less than three police cars parked outside with their lights flashing. After she dried her eyes, she took a deep breath and stepped out from her car.

She explained to the officer who stood outside, who she was and insisted he allow her to see to the dog. She was horrified to learn arrangements had been made for Connie to be taken to a local shelter. After a lengthy discussion, she was allowed under close supervision to see to the dog. She could see someone in the living room through the half-open door and heard movement upstairs. She let Connie into the garden while she spooned out her feed. Once Connie was settled back in her basket, Joyce walked out to the back garden with as much dignity as she could muster. She quietly chanted, "I must not cry. I must not cry," and it seemed to work. She marched back in, slipped on Connie's lead and said, "Connie is staying with me. Don't you dare try to stop me."

The officers inside were struggling to find anything of relevance in the house. They had all complained about the smell, despite the windows being flung wide open. One of the officers found an old shoebox full of photographs under the bed along with a great deal of dust, discarded shoes and socks. They were an odd assortment going back at least twenty to thirty years. They were worth taking if only to show a likeness of Frank at the relevant time.

The officer had almost given up on the bedroom when he found an envelope taped to the bottom of a drawer. The envelope was new, but the three photographs he found inside were old. They looked like they had been moved very recently from the shoe box.

The first photograph showed a group of six men in a bar setting. The men were aged between twenty and forty years old, he guessed. On the back, it was written "Cheltenham Gold Cup 2001." The relevance of the other two pictures wasn't obvious. One was of a teenager washing a couple of old caravans which seemed to have been recently gutted. The other was of the same boy holding a shotgun posing with an older man. He guessed it was probably the father as he stood with his hand on the boy's shoulder. The look of pride and happiness on the boy's face made it stand out. He decided he should take them to the station straight away.

After Frank's interview, the tension in Peter was palpable. Fiona thought it best not to say anything when he threw himself into his chair. "Well, that was a total waste of time."

Fiona wanted to say, well maybe you should slow down a bit, but she chose to bite her lip instead.

She watched, unsure how to react when he headed towards the door. He said over his shoulder, "I'm out for a bit. Can you chase up the results of the house search and finalise a list of others in the area we should see? I also want full background checks on Derek Alley and Mark Farley."

Peter felt much better after his walk. The tension which had built all day within him seemed to have subsided a little. It felt as though a light had come on when he'd decided to meet up with Ross Phillips to talk things through later. He knew things looked bad for Frank, but the pit of his stomach told him that, although Frank knew something, it wasn't him they should have in custody. But with everything going on with Sally and Amelia, he wasn't sure he could trust his own judgement in the matter and be certain how objective he was being.

When he walked back into the stuffy incident room, he couldn't miss the look of concern on Fiona's face as she looked up from her desk. He asked, "Do you have that list of people we should be seeing? I think we'll leave re-interviewing Frank until tomorrow morning."

Fiona handed him the sheet of paper with a worried look on

her face. "I think you should see these," she said, as she handed him the photographs.

Peter felt the knot in his stomach tighten when he turned over the picture of the group of men and saw the inscription. He ran his hand through his hair as he felt the knock to his confidence. Frank had denied being at the races that year.

Peter walked backwards and forwards as he read the list of names Fiona had prepared. Sounding as decisive as possible, he said, "Make sure Frank knows we will be interviewing him later today. I'll see if I can get hold of David Conley."

FIFTEEN

David Conley picked up his phone on the third ring. He told Peter he was delivering haylage but would be back at the farm within an hour. Peter saw the uncertainty in Fiona's eyes when he said, "I've spoken to David Conley. We're seeing him in an hour."

"Okay," she replied as she started searching through the untidy stack of paperwork on her desk.

"I thought you'd be pleased. You're the one interested in the family's skeletons," Peter said.

Fiona looked up. "Yes. I thought you might be interested in this." She looked down at the sheet of paper she'd retrieved. "David Conley was arrested in 1999 for driving his muck spreader past a camp of travellers on his farm."

It brought a smile to his face. That and the fact Derek Alley so obviously disliked him made him warm to the guy he'd never met. "By the way, do you know if the check on Derek Alley has been done like I asked?"

"Not sure sir. I will check as soon as we get back."

When they got in the car, Fiona asked the question he'd been dreading. He'd hoped naively by the time the question was asked he'd have more than a feeling to substantiate a meaningful reply.

"Why don't you think Frank killed the girl? It all seems to fit."

"Maybe that's the problem. I don't know he didn't do it. I just think there are other things we should be looking at before jumping to conclusions."

Peter waited for Fiona to say more. He sensed she wasn't sat-isfied by his answer, but she settled back in her seat and didn't push the subject further. Before turning into the stone court-yard at the front of Grange farm, Peter said, "I know you've been looking forward to meeting David Conley. Feel free to ask some questions of your own if you think of something."

They couldn't fail to notice along the right-hand side of the small yard in front of the impressive stone farmhouse it was neat and tidy whereas the left side was a jumbled mess. Parked in the middle of the yard was a white Land Rover with a flatbed trailer attached, presumably just returned from the delivery Conley had made. Next to it was a modern, expensive-look-ing tractor. The farmhouse itself was far more substantial than Rooksbridge. Peter had the impression the farmhouse would have looked the same if he'd arrived in a horse-drawn carriage a century earlier.

As they were getting out of the car, David came out of the house to greet them with three dogs at his heels. He was not what Peter had expected. He was a large man with a round face, clean-shaven and wearing round glasses. His jeans and sweat-shirt, while casual, were neat and clean. His wide smile made his small eyes disappear behind his glasses, and he gave them both a firm, warm handshake.

"Please do come in," David said, as he led them to the front door. "The kettle is on ready, but perhaps you would prefer a cold drink?"

"Coffee is fine," Peter replied.

It took a while for Peter's eyes to adjust from the bright glare of sunshine outside to the dark, cool interior of the kitchen. Again, one side of the room was spotlessly clean and neat, the other untidy and grubby. A line of insulating tape not only ran across the floor but along all the surfaces, separating the orderly from the cluttered side. The solid kitchen table was split in the same way.

David invited them to sit down, but as they went to sit, he said,

"No. Sorry. On the other side of the table, please."

Peter shot Fiona a quizzical look as they shifted along to the other side, noticing the sticky remains of food on the table. Peter moved a stack of old newspapers from the chair, so he could sit back down.

David returned with their drinks and joined them on the left-hand side of the table. He enquired earnestly, "How can I help you?"

Peter noticed even the dogs seemed to keep to the left side of the room. "It's about the body found at Rooksbridge Farm."

"Yes, of course. I've heard all about that. And naturally, I was expecting you to contact me. I am quite sure everyone is suggesting it has something to do with my family. It's okay, I'm resigned to all the fanciful things people say about me and my family. I've gotten used to it over the years. Not a lot of choice, really. In fact, I find it all quite amusing at times."

"It must have been difficult for you," Fiona said tentatively.

David's face showed a mixture of surprise and possibly hurt pride. "Honestly, my dear you don't have to worry about my feelings." He held out his hands with his wrists pressed together, and said with a smile, "Well? Am I under arrest?"

Fiona played with her mug of coffee. "No, of course, you're not. We're talking to everyone."

"One thing we are interested in, is this system of using padlocks provided by the hunt on farm gates. Can you tell us a little more about it?" Peter asked.

"Well, it's an informal arrangement. But yes. The hunt was losing foxes when they couldn't get access to some fields. The old Earl came up with the idea. As far as I know, there's never been a problem."

"And you use them? You would know the codes used?"

"Yes, of course. The Hunt used to meet here regularly in the old days."

"How do you get on with the Farleys? Have you had reason in the past to be on their land?" asked Peter.

"I used to get on well enough with Mark and Kim. Saw them a

bit socially when we were all a bit younger. And yes, I've visited them on the farm in the past. I know the farm well enough."

"So, you would know the farm's general layout?"

"I would, along with most people in the village. In fact, they would have more reason than me to cross their land. A lot of people walk their dogs over Farley's fields. Why would I want to wander around their land? In case you haven't noticed, I do have my own." After a brief pause, he leaned forward conspiratorially and whispered to Fiona, "Perhaps I've buried so many people on my own land I have no more room left." He then added, winking at Fiona, "Having run out of space, I had to start branching out, so to speak."

"I take your point," Peter conceded. "We are talking to everyone who would have lived around here fifteen or so years ago and asking whether they knew about the codes."

"I take it you've seen Toad of Toad Hall, then?"

"Sorry, who is that?"

David banged his hand on the table twice "Beep. Beep. Tim Potter and his silly cars!" he laughed.

"I think we may have passed them in the lane the other day," Fiona smiled.

"Have you spoken to Simon Edgar and Susan Fisher?"

"We've heard of Simon, the local historian. But who is Susan Fisher? I don't think we've heard that name," Peter said.

"She lives up near Frank. She has a small cottage at the end of the lane with a couple of stables behind. She worked on and off for Mark Farley for years. Stepping into the breach when he'd upset his staff. Taking out rides and looking after the ponies."

"Did he often upset his staff?" Peter asked.

"He probably wasn't the nicest of people to work for. The girls were expected to show total deference. If they stepped out of line, they were out. Sent packing with their tails between their legs. And of course, they were too young and homesick to do anything other than obey."

"Was there any particular incident at the farm that makes you say that?" Peter asked.

"No, nothing in particular. It's just a general observation."

Peter pulled out the photographs they'd found in Frank's house. "Could you have a look at these, please?"

David looked first at the group photograph. "Goodness! Don't we all look young? But then I guess we were."

"Who are the people in the picture?"

David pointed in turn. "Well that's me, and these are Frank, Mark, Tim and Taffy. I can't remember this gentleman's name. I'm pretty sure he was a friend of Mark's who came along for the day. I think he was involved for a time with Mark in some sort of property deal."

"Did you often go out in a group like this?"

"Mark was always arranging trips when he was at Rooksbridge. He was always quite sociable. Not like his miserable son."

"And could you tell me anything about this guy?" Peter asked, pointing to the sixth man in the picture David had called Taffy. "Do you know where we could find him?"

"That's Taffy. He was a real nice straightforward guy. But you won't be able to find him. He was killed in a farm accident about ten years ago."

Peter drew out the photographs of the boy. David was at a loss to explain any connection between the two photographs other than they were obviously taken at around the same time and were of Graham and Mark Farley.

"Do you have a clearer picture of yourself taken around 2001?"

"No, I'm sorry I can't help you there. I don't have any," David replied.

"Surely you must have at least one?"

"No, I don't. I do not like being in them, looking at them or keeping them."

Fiona asked if she could use the bathroom and excused herself briefly once given directions. Peter watched her go, hoping she would be observant. He returned his attention to David. "We understand you've had problems in the past with travellers?"

David replied, "I'm sure it's all in your records. But yes. You lot were useless when we asked for help moving them on. I dealt with the problem my way. And it worked. Do you know we've never had a problem since?"

They looked up as Fiona returned to the kitchen and asked, "Where's your wife today, Mr Conley?"

"No idea."

She pulled a pen and notepad from her bag and asked, "Do you have a contact number for her?"

"No."

Fiona looked up sharply. "You must have? We'd really like to contact her. Or perhaps you could contact her now for us?"

David thought for a while. He eventually said, "No. But you could leave a note for her."

Fiona quickly scribbled a note, asking her to contact them, ensuring she placed it on the other side of the table, under David's watchful eye. "What time will she be home?"

David shrugged.

Peter wasn't quite sure what Fiona was getting at but guessed she'd seen something upstairs. He asked, "You have an interest in horses, don't you?"

"I have a passing interest, yes."

Peter pulled out a photograph of Jennifer Turner. "Have you seen this girl?"

David shook his head.

"At the Cheltenham Race Festival perhaps?"

David shrugged. "I wasn't really part of the gang. I didn't spend all day with them."

"You're quite sure you do not recognise this girl?" Peter asked.

"I recognise her from the news report last night. But no, I had not seen her previously."

Peter asked a final time, closely scrutinising David for any slight reaction which may give him away. "You are absolutely sure you did not see this girl when you were in Cheltenham in 2001?"

David casually picked the photograph up from the table, and said, "No."

Peter was convinced he was lying as he stood up to leave.

"Thank you for your time. We may need to contact you again."

David followed Peter and Fiona back out to their car, his round face positively beaming, claiming how much he had enjoyed their company. His three dogs trotted faithfully at his heels. He shook their hands and wished them well with their further enquiries.

Driving back to the station, Peter asked, "Do you think he was lying about seeing the girl?"

Fiona replied, "His whole attitude changed as soon as he was asked about his wife. He became much more defensive. He reacted in the same way when you asked whether he'd seen the girl. Yes, I think he was lying."

"What was that about the wife?" Peter asked.

"When he said he had no photographs, I just thought I'd take a look around. There was not a single photograph or even a picture anywhere in any of the hallways or rooms upstairs. The walls were totally bare, as were all the table tops and window sills. Unless you include the thick layer of dust and grime on one side of each room. Upstairs, it felt as though it had been abandoned. As if nobody actually lived there. It occurred to me, there was nothing at all to suggest the presence of any woman, although our records say he's married."

"What was the rest of the house like, generally?"

"Dingy and dark and separated with insulation tape, the same as downstairs. Long uneven corridors leading off everywhere, it was like a maze. It was very run-down, and the floors were covered mostly with threadbare rugs. It seemed...sad."

"And what did you think of David?"

"He's not what I expected. He's certainly not stupid," Fiona replied.

"I agree. Let's pay a quick visit to this Susan Fisher before we go back and see Frank again."

After a long pause, Fiona said, "You're convinced Frank didn't do it you, aren't you?"

Peter sighed. He didn't know how to explain what he felt and so had hoped the subject had been permanently dropped. "I think he knows something. I want to see all the men in that photograph, but I really want to see Mark Farley again. I'd like to find out a bit more about him."

"You think...?"

"I don't know. It's just... I don't know...a feeling."

"But the evidence..."

"I know," Peter said sharply, leaving it in no doubt he wanted the subject dropped. "Do you have any other thoughts about David generally?"

"Odd. The way the house is split up. His amusement at his own peculiar traits, the way he stiffened as soon as I mentioned his wife. Something's not quite right there."

"That seems to be a bit of a trend around here." Peter decisively added, "We're going to quickly see this Mrs Fisher. It won't take long."

SIXTEEN

They found Miss Fisher's home around the corner from Frank's house. It was a solid looking three storey stone cottage, set in its own small plot of land. Some tired-looking ivy had taken over the front wall of the house and was threatening to block the front door. After knocking on the door, they waited a short while before they heard shuffling steps from the other side. The door was opened by a squat lady with a heavy bust straining to be released from the tight tweed jacket she wore. She leaned heavily on a stick as Peter introduced himself and Fiona. She viewed them suspiciously before saying, "You'd best come in, then."

As they followed her down the hallway, the smell of boiled cabbages and cat urine became stronger. The living room contained an odd assortment of chairs and sleeping cats. Peter was pleased he chose the hard-back chair when he saw Fiona sink deep into the seat of one of the armchairs, having to use the armrests to pull herself forwards out of the broken seat.

"We understand you used to work for Mark Farley?" Peter asked.

"Yes. But that was a long time ago, before I did this stupid leg," Miss Fisher replied, slapping her thigh like a pantomime dame.

"Could we call you Susan?" Peter asked.

"Miss Fisher is better."

"You helped out when there was a problem with his usual staff? Is that right?"

"That's pretty much the size of it."

"How did you get on with Mark Farley?"

"I did the job when I got the call. He paid the money," Miss Fisher replied.

"Did he often have cause to ring you?"

"Yes, it became quite regular. It ended up being every year. Those young girls he took on were always disappearing off without good reason."

"He had quite a problem with girls leaving?"

Peter watched as Miss Fisher considered his question, running her tongue over her pale, thick lips. The image of a lizard on the lookout for a juicy fly came into his mind.

"You are obviously here about that body Frank found. Why are you asking me these questions? I don't know anything about why one of them might have ended up buried on the farm."

"Why do you think the body found was one of the girls employed by Mark?"

"I'm just assuming. Well, was she?"

"As far as we know, she was not," Peter replied. "Could you answer my earlier question about the girls leaving?"

"Well, I don't see that's relevant if you say the girl wasn't an employee. Are you quite sure about that? None of them stayed very long. Except Gillian of course, that silly misguided girl thought the son was a real catch." Miss Fisher started to cackle madly which resulted in a long coughing fit."

"Are you all right, Miss Fisher?" Fiona asked. "Would you like a glass of water?"

"No, I'm fine, thank you. I'm sure that's one decision she's lived to regret."

"What makes you say that?" Peter asked.

"No reason at all," she replied and began her cackling noise again.

Keen to avoid a further episode of her coughing and spluttering, Peter quickly interrupted, "Do you have any idea why the other girls didn't stay very long?"

"I expect it was a mixture of things. Dislike of hard work, dislike of Mark." She paused to lick her lips before adding, "He's not a nice man. They found that out the hard way. Then, of course, there were the rumours."

"What rumours would they be?" Peter asked.

"Just rumours. Some of them were very silly little girls."

"Just rumours?" Not receiving any further comment, Peter asked, "Did you ever see him acting in a way that might suggest inappropriate behaviour towards any of the girls?"

Miss Fisher leaned forwards on her stick. "He had a violent temper, that one. He was real nasty if you got on the wrong side of him. He'd become as vindictive as anything. He had them all under his control." Her eyes darted around the room before she heaved up her heavy body onto her stick. "That's all I can tell you, you can leave now."

Mrs Fisher pulled in her cheeks and it seemed quite apparent they would receive no further information from her. Peter stood up from his chair and offered her his card. "Would you contact me if you think of anything else that might be relevant to the young girl?"

"I'd like you to leave now."

"Okay. We're leaving now, but we may want to speak with you again."

"And if I don't want to speak to you again?"

Peter shrugged in reply. "We'll see ourselves out. But can I just ask if you know Frank Codrington."

"Of course, everybody knows Frank."

"Could you tell me what he was like?"

"He has the patience of a saint, unlike me. Goodbye."

Once outside, Peter said, "I want to see Mark Farley before we go back to the station. But I don't want any mention of the photograph when we're there, not yet anyway. I want to ask him again about access to the farm and whether he attended Cheltenham Races in the past. Get an idea of how he reacts."

Fiona said, "What did you think of Mrs Fisher? She seemed quite confident the girl would have been an ex-employee."

"I know. But she's also as mad as a box of frogs."

"Shouldn't we be getting back to interview Frank?" Fiona asked.

"We won't be long. I'd like to speak to Mark Farley first."

SEVENTEEN

Since they arrived unannounced this time, the security gates did not swing open as they approached Mark Farley's house. Pressing the buzzer on the side of the wall, Peter looked around and said, "I wonder if they have surveillance cameras on the gate, same as at the farm?"

A female voice crackled on the intercom agreeing to open the gates. As they swung silently open, Peter said, "Well, there goes any element of surprise."

They were met at the house by a slim, very well-dressed, severe-looking lady. The perfectly applied makeup could not hide her sharp facial features and the pinched nostrils. They could hear an engine running as the woman led them towards the rear of the house. They passed under a wooden trellis heavily burdened with roses running the length of the side of the house. Mark Farley waved to them from astride a sit-on lawnmower. He raised the cutting blades and drove towards them as the woman returned to her garden chair and magazines under the shade of the large awning hanging from the rear wall of the house.

Parking the lawn mower at the edge of the decorated stone patio, Mark said, "Shall we go through to my study?" It felt like an order rather than a suggestion. "Has all this nonsense been sorted out with Frank?"

"I'm afraid we have a few more questions for Mr Codrington," Peter replied.

The woman removed her sunglasses and putting down her magazine said, "I will join you in a moment with some drinks. Fresh orange juice I think would be most suitable."

Mark had shed the jacket, but he still wore a smartly pressed shirt and tie albeit short-sleeved. "What brings you back so soon?"

"New information has come to light concerning access to the field, the gully, I think your son calls it?"

"Yes. Yes. What new information would that be?"

"We had wrongly assumed as the gate opened directly out onto the lane, access would be fairly easy. We now understand not only was the gate padlocked, but also covered in barbed wire and often further blocked with old machinery. Can you confirm that was the case in 2001?"

Mark, who had positioned himself in the padded chair at his desk, leaned back slightly. "Who can tell when it was so long ago? To be honest, I was always very lax about security back then. It was a different world."

"But we understand you had problems up there with travellers moving in and camping in the fields. That's why you blocked them."

"Some years we did. Some we didn't. We often got a few days' warning if a convoy was on its way. I'm afraid I really couldn't say whether access was blocked or not on any one particular day years ago."

"But if it was blocked, the only other access would be through your yard?" Peter asked.

"I guess so," Mark replied. "But the bottom gate is a long way from the house, and I can't remember when we started locking that gate at night."

They were interrupted by the arrival of the tray containing a large jug of orange juice. Mark swivelled his chair around. "Kim. Just in time. I'm feeling quite parched." As he poured himself a glass, he asked, "Do you remember when we started locking the gate to the main yard at night?"

"No idea," Kim replied, as she poured out three more glasses.

"You really should have offered your guests a glass first." As she handed each of them a glass, Kim added, "Should I stay, or would you prefer I leave you to it?"

"Please stay," replied Peter, walking across the room to pull up a chair for her.

"We now know the young girl found on your farm disappeared from Cheltenham on twenty-fifth May 2001. We wondered if you could tell us if that date means anything to you."

A huge smile spread across Mark's face. "Yes. It most certainly does. I thought Graham told you." He looked fondly across at his wife. "It happens to be our wedding anniversary. We celebrate every year with a meal."

"Does the year mean anything to you? Is there anything at all about that year that could jog your memory?"

Mark said, "As a matter of fact, I could tell exactly where I was that day." He pulled out the bottom drawer of his desk, taking out a slim document. "My favourite mare had a foal that year. I was lucky enough to witness the birth. Sadly, it turned out to be no good, which was such a shame. We had such high hopes for that horse."

Peter took the document from Mark. He'd never seen a Horse Passport, but inside he noticed the birth of a horse registered to Mark had been born on 25th May 2001. The date appeared to have been officially stamped and signed by a vet. "Could we hold on to this?"

Mark looked surprised, but replied, "I see no reason why not. The horse proved to be a sickly thing and was put down a few years later. It was a terrible disappointment to me."

Peter turned his attention to Kim. "Do you remember where you were that day?"

"I remember the day that horse was born. The mare was very special to my husband, so of course, we were present. She foaled around midnight as I recall. It was shortly after we returned from our meal. So yes, on that date I was at Rooksbridge with my husband."

"We understand you employed a number of young girls when

you owned the farm?"

"Yes," Kim replied. "We ran it as a riding school. We employed a lot of girls over the years, including our daughter-in-law."

"And how did you get along with them?"

"Absolutely fine. Our son married one of them."

"It's just that we heard you had quite a high turnover of girls."

"Who told you that?" Kim said indignantly. "Some of the girls were unsuitable. Had over-romantic images of what working with horses would be like. Some became homesick within the first day. Ones who were any good stayed and often returned the following year."

"Would you have records of the girls you employed?"

"It's highly unlikely we would keep records that far back," Kim said, standing up abruptly to collect their empty glasses. She placed them on the tray saying, "If you're finished, I'll take these through to the kitchen."

Peter noticed Mark had a lazy grin on his face. Once Kim was safely out of earshot, he said. "Women can be so oversensitive at times, can't they?"

"Can they?" replied Peter. "You're quite close to Cheltenham here. Do you attend the races?"

"Of course, I do. I don't think I've ever missed a year. Do you enjoy a flutter?"

"Not really my thing. Would you have been at the Festival the year the girl disappeared?"

"I expect I was, along with thousands of others."

"We understand the girl who has turned up buried on your land claimed to have met a man there prior to her disappearance who promised her work with horses."

Mark laughed. "Surely you're not suggesting I had anything to do with the poor girl?"

"We have to ask the questions."

"Well really, that's quite preposterous. You've no evidence at all to support such a suggestion. Is there anything else?"

"That will be all for now."

Mark stood up to show them out. As he followed them to the

car, he said, "In the future, I would prefer you telephone ahead before coming out here. We're often out, and I wouldn't want you to make a wasted journey."

Peter returned his smile and replied, "We'll bear that in mind."

At the car, Mark held Peter's door open for him and said, "I think I'm playing golf with one of your senior officers later this week."

"Well, I hope you have a nice game. Weather should be good," Peter replied brightly.

EIGHTEEN

Before going back into the interview room with Frank, Peter filled a file with a thick wad of paper he took from the photocopier. As they sat, he let the heavy file fall onto the desk with a loud thud.

Frank had resolved to swallow his pride and try to explain why he had gone to Cheltenham. He'd gone there to get pissed, stoned and to contemplate suicide in privacy. He had found it increasingly difficult to hang onto reality and deal with everyday life. Mostly, he'd been incredibly lonely and hurting. Cheltenham was just a good distance away. Not too far to travel but not close enough to know anybody. He went there to be alone to self-destruct. He just didn't know how to say it all.

Fiona checked to be sure the cassette recorder was working.

Peter said, "Can you tell us what you were doing in Cheltenham in 2001?"

"I just went there... I liked it there."

"We understand you were in the habit of using local prostitutes. Do you deny this?"

Frank was totally thrown. How did they know? People generally knew of his drink problem and how he had dabbled in drugs. But this was private. What did they know?

"No response...Can you tell us about the time you were arrested in Cheltenham?"

"It was nothing... It was a misunderstanding." Frank felt the sweat running down his sides.

"What were you arrested for, Frank?"

"It was a misunderstanding," Frank insisted weakly.

"Let me remind you. It was for assaulting a prostitute. We understand she feared for her life." Peter leaned forward, his arms on the table, on either side of the file.

"No. It wasn't like that. What you are suggesting is wrong."

"What was it like, Frank?" Peter asked.

Frank sat slumped back in his chair. He rubbed his hands in circular movements, round and round his face.

"Frank! Could you give an answer for the tape?"

"It wasn't like that. We were both stoned. It got out of hand. I didn't hurt her."

"The bruises tell a different story, Frank."

Frank leapt backwards from his seat and was immediately restrained by the officer by the door.

"Sit down, Frank."

"Is that what happened with Jennifer Turner? It got out of hand?" Peter asked.

"No. I never met the girl. I've told you. Things got out of hand one night. But I didn't kill her, did I?" Frank shouted.

"Frank! Frank. Stay calm. Can you tell us what happened with the prostitute? Something happened?"

Frank couldn't tell them. It was pathetic. He'd failed. He couldn't get it up. He was stoned. Everything was hazy. He was on the point of passing out when he saw the girl empty his wallet. It wasn't the money. She could have taken that. But not Maggie's wedding ring. He just wanted it back.

"Nothing happened. It was all a mistake."

"Is that what happened with Jennifer Turner? It was all a mistake?"

"No. I never met her," Frank said slowly emphasising each word.

"Did you go to the Cheltenham Show on the twenty-fifth of May 2001?"

"No."

"Have you ever been to the Cheltenham race-track?"

"No. Yes, once with Maggie."

"Did you go to the show on the twenty-fifth of May 2001?"

"I've already told you. No."

"Did you attend the Cheltenham Race Festival earlier that year?

"No."

"Really, then how do you explain this photograph?" Peter placed the group photograph on the table.

Frank went white. "Where did you find this?"

"Are you in the photograph?" Peter asked.

"Yes, yes I am. But the date is wrong."

"What date? How do you know the date is wrong?"

"Because it's my bloody photograph. The date is wrong."

"Who are the people in the photograph?"

When Frank picked up the photograph to study it, his hands were shaking. His fingers left smudge marks where he held it. "Myself, Mark Farley, David Conley, Tim Potter, Taffy Williams and a friend of Mark's...but the date is wrong. It was the following year." He tried to wipe away the smudges he'd left.

"And can you look at these two photographs? Who are they?" Peter said, handing them to Frank.

"It's Mark and Graham Farley. I found them when I was going through some stuff. I put them separate because I was going to give them to Mark. I thought he might like to keep them."

"What did you do during the day on the twenty-fifth of May 2001?"

"I don't know."

"What did you usually do in the daytime when you were in Cheltenham?" Peter asked.

"I don't know. I didn't do much at all. I sobered up, slept in, wandered about and looked in shop windows."

"You're quite sure you did not go to the Cheltenham Race festival that year?"

"No. I mean, yes, I'm sure. I didn't go there."

Peter showed Frank a photograph of Jenny Turner. "Do you recognise this girl?"

"I do, but only from recent photographs on TV and in the news-papers."

"Are you quite sure you have never seen this girl?"

"No. I've only seen her in the photographs," Frank insisted.

"You did not meet this girl at the Cheltenham Race Festival and again at the Cheltenham showground and take her back to your bedsit?"

"No. No. No."

"But you did take prostitutes back to your bedsit on a regular basis?"

"No. It was only the once. It was a mistake," Frank pleaded.

"But you did meet this girl and take her back to your flat?"

"No. I've told you, no. I just couldn't. I wouldn't. I've never hurt anyone. I did not go there. I did not meet this girl or any other girl. I went to Cheltenham to be by myself. I went to get away, to think, to try and forget and to try and find the courage to kill myself. I was different then, but I would not have hurt anyone. I wouldn't."

"Frank, calm down. Things aren't looking good for you. You were in Cheltenham when a young girl went missing. Her body has turned up where you work. What are we supposed to think?"

"I know. But I swear to God it's nothing to do with me!"

"Then who is it to do with?"

Fear spread across Frank's face for a split second before he re-plied. "I don't know."

"You do know, Frank. Who are you protecting?" Peter asked.

"Nobody, I'm not protecting anyone. I don't know."

Peter sat back in frustration, drumming his fingers on the desk. He leaned forwards. "You need to tell us what you know, Frank. Do you want to stay here overnight?"

"No. But I don't know anything," Frank pleaded.

"Interview suspended."

Peter stood up abruptly and left the room leaving Fiona to fin-ish off and trail after him.

"Do you still think Frank knows nothing about the girl?" Fiona asked, as she played with the bottle of water back at her desk.

Peter moved to the window. "I really don't know. I'm convinced he knows something. I think he is protecting someone. He doesn't seem to realise the position he is in. The issue with that prostitute really doesn't help."

"She withdrew her complaint later," Fiona said.

"But we don't know why."

"Maybe she just sobered up," Fiona suggested.

"I know he is hiding something," Peter said. "But, if we hold him tonight, is he any more likely to tell us anything new tomorrow? Will an evening sweating in a cell make him say more?"

"It might," Fiona said.

"I'm not convinced he's responsible, but I think he does know who is. Or thinks he does."

"So, you think if we keep him in overnight, he'll tell us?" Fiona asked.

Peter sighed as he flicked through the file on his desk. "I don't think so."

Fiona said, "He has a record of violence against women. He was stressed following the death of his wife, he works with horses and he was in Cheltenham."

"But a night in the cells would be very hard for someone like Frank. He's going to suffer as it is with the stigma of being brought in for questioning. You know what these small rural communities can be like. I think he's just as likely to 'sweat it out' in his own home. I just wish we could have gotten something from him today."

"Should he be released?" Fiona asked, peeling the label from her bottle with her thumb.

"We'll release him. We're just going around in circles here. Maybe it will stir something up, and he's unlikely to flee the area. Where would he go?"

"So where do we go from here?" Fiona asked.

"I've told you. We need to see everyone in that photograph."

Peter sent Fiona to give Frank the good news and arrange transport home for him. She hesitated for a moment before doing as she was asked.

NINETEEN

Frank was relieved to be released without charge but was totally unprepared for the media attention. He was taken out the back entrance and straight into a waiting car. He'd seen the waiting reporters but was still shocked at the camera flashlights blinding him as they pulled away.

He was very anxious about his time with prostitutes leaking out and about the photographs. Could the police make the connection among the three pictures he had pulled out? He tried to stop his mind racing. Think logically. Without the distraction of what he knew, no connection could be made, unless somebody else said something. This new worry made his heart sink even further.

Frank fretted about what everyone must be thinking. His initial joy at being released was replaced by a feeling of dread. Fear of being hounded by the press as a man suspected of killing and burying a young girl. Would he be branded as the type of man who paid for sex? Would he be a prisoner in his own house? Would the media be lying in wait for him? His biggest fear of all was would his friends stand by him?

He knew how impossible it was to just forget about the past and carry on. He knew what it felt like to become plagued with guilt. He knew he couldn't just forget and neither would others.

Staring out the window, he began to ponder the mindset of a hardened criminal. They must be immune to the feelings of others to be able to hurt, maim and kill without regret. Have little respect for the life of another. The level of arrogance and self-importance needed! But then, maybe some people could just forget? Wipe whatever they had done from their mind. Not be weighed down every day with remorse or allow it to ruin their lives.

He had gone full circle and did not want to think about it anymore, but thoughts kept swirling round and round in his head. All he wanted to do was to get home to Connie and the safety of his own home. Bolt the door against the outside world and drink himself into oblivion.

He noticed the Bull looked quite busy when they drove past. How would he ever be able to face everyone again? What about work in the morning? Should he just go to work as usual? Pretend nothing had happened? Shrug it off as a minor misunderstanding? A few little queries the police wanted sorted about how he found the body? Only when the car came to a stop did he realise he was back outside his own home. He thanked his driver and hurried to his front door.

Connie wasn't there to greet him. He found the note from Joyce on the kitchen table confirming she had Connie and that he was to ring her as soon as he got home. Good old Joyce. At least he knew he had one loyal friend. He looked towards the phone. Even talking to Joyce would be too much. He decided he would ring her in the morning.

He sat on the end of his bed trying to sort everything out in his mind. He shuddered at the thought that strangers had been through his personal stuff. He felt dirty and grimy. He quickly showered and changed.

Feeling a little fresher, he forced himself to eat a couple of pieces of cheese on toast although it tasted like cardboard. He reached for a bottle of Jack Daniels. A few glasses were just what he needed to relax and get a good night sleep. Tomorrow was going to be a difficult day. He needed all the help he could get. He decided he was going to get on with things and act normally. If anyone asked, he'd explain the police just wanted a little more information from him about finding the body.

He didn't notice the man sitting on the wall outside watching the house. He dozed off for a short while in the armchair before waking with a jolt. He'd started to dream an old dream he used to have shortly after Maggie died. It reminded him that the first time he'd woken from that dream was the last time he had felt totally happy. In the dream, Maggie was still alive. She had, against all the odds, recovered somehow and her reported death was all just some terrible misunderstanding he had to explain to their friends.

A brief respite from grief before reality crashed back in. She was gone. He was alone and empty, feeling guilty that in the dream he was more concerned about what his friends might think of him than the joy of Maggie still being with him. He felt disgusted by his selfishness. He was disgusting inside. Not good enough for Maggie in the first place. He would never be good enough.

He remembered how shocked it had been to find the emotion he felt most strongly after her death was anger. The anger and hurt multiplying inside until it choked everything else, drowned out all his other feelings. So bitter that daily life continued. Anger at the doctors for failing to save his wife. He hated the aching loneliness he felt, his inability to care for anything again spiralled to further emptiness. Too numb and isolated to keep up with daily life he had nothing left to offer anyone else.

Frank noticed the whiskey bottle was empty as was his crushed packet of cigarettes. There was always another bottle in the kitchen and another packet in a drawer.

Opening a new bottle, he began to think about Jennifer Turner. Somebody's daughter was lying in the ground all this time. Somebody's hopes and fears were crushed and covered in that ground. Somebody had felt the pain he had felt.

The crippling pain when the worst thing you could possibly imagine happening does actually happen. It's not an irrational worry, it is here and now and really happening. It's all slipping away while you stand hopelessly watching. Nothing you can do. No matter how you try, how you pray, how many deals you make with God, no matter if you're prepared to sacrifice your own life. There is nothing you can do except be a silent by-stander. He still remembered how it felt to desperately hold on with your fingertips while forced to watch everything quietly slipping away. And then the light being switched off.

TWENTY

While locked in his own thoughts, Frank was unaware how much he was liked and respected in the village. Or that the treatment of him had sparked anger in his fellow drinkers at The Bull.

Derek and Laura Alley had walked hand in hand down to The Bull for their supper as they did several nights a week. Both in their 70s, they appeared a sweet couple. Most people fell for the impression Derek gave of a forgetful dotty old fool until they crossed him in some way. He could then be as sharp an adversary as a man half his age. Laura was difficult to get to know. She was rarely seen without her husband. When with him, she was happy to stand in his shadow. She smiled a lot and mostly agreed with whatever opinion Derek cared to express. Whether she agreed with him or really couldn't care less was a complete mystery.

They were both very fit and agile for their age and always smartly dressed. Especially Laura, who still had traces of the very attractive woman she must have once been and carried the poise of a professional dancer. At the top of the lane, they waved to Tim and Cathy Potter driving out of the village in their convertible Morris Minor. They were possibly the only locals who were getting some respite from the stifling heat that continued throughout the night.

Walking hand in hand across the car park, Derek spotted a reporter sitting in his car with the window open. He went over to exchange pleasantries, leaving Laura to wait. Derek returned to her, full of his own self-importance.

Unaware they had been watched, they walked towards the bar door with relaxed smiles. The smiles were frozen as their entrance caused an abrupt end to the usual bar chatter. Total silence fell, no one broke ranks. Most turned their backs or looked down. Some stared defiantly and slowly shook their heads.

Colin stood at the far end of the bar and looked sternly at Sue who was standing in for Rose. He held her eyes and quietly said, "Don't you dare serve them."

Sue looked to Noggin and Joe who were sitting at the opposite end of the bar. Noggin slowly nodded.

Sue looked back to Colin and whispered, "What do I do?"

"Do nothing. In fact, why don't you go out in the cellar to change a barrel?" Colin said.

"What are you going to do?" Sue asked.

"It'll be fine. Go on," Colin replied.

Sue didn't want to get involved but was worried about what might happen. She hid around the corner, playing with the phone in her pocket.

Derek and Laura were still standing in the doorway. An invisible barrier was holding them in place. Laura nervously pulled Derek's sleeve. "Come on. Let's go."

Derek shook her off. "No, I'm going to the bar."

Laura followed nervously, one step behind her husband. She tried a smile and then looked down at the floor. As Derek approached the bar, Joe, still covered in dust from his job on a building site, turned around slowly on his stool and said, "You're not welcome here."

"Don't be so ridiculous. Get out of my way," Derek blustered, trying to push his way past.

"Yer won't get a drink in 'ere," Noggin said, puffing slowly on his pipe.

Derek was about to open his mouth when he sensed somebody large stood behind him. He turned around to face him.

"I want Myrtle Cottage back. I'll be posting notice for you to quit tomorrow," David Conley said, before walking out of the pub.

"You can't do..." Derek said, to his disappearing back. He looked around the bar in defiance realising all eyes were on him. A few looked away, most continued to hold him in a hostile stare.

"We know who has been telling tales to the police and media. You were seen at the station this morning, just before the police picked up Frank," Joe said.

"Come on, dear," Laura pleaded, moving backwards toward the doorway.

Derek hesitated. He felt torn between holding his ground and retreating. A furtive glance around the room told him he had no allies. He started to open his mouth to protest before accepting the village opinion was unanimous. Feeling the heat rise in his cheeks, turning them a crimson colour, he turned and walked out of the bar to the sound of a slow hand clap.

Derek pushed Laura's hand away as he marched through the car park. "I've never been so insulted in all my life." Passing the journalist, he'd spoken to earlier, he said loudly, "And why hasn't David Conley been arrested yet? That's what I'd like to know." He stomped up the hill with Laura running behind to keep up.

The cheering in the bar was short lived. It felt like a hollow victory. There was a lot of anger at the police's stupidity, thinking Frank could be a serious suspect. They had no idea who put the body on Farley's place, but they were agreed it certainly wasn't Frank or any one of them.

Sue returned to the bar. "I won't be in trouble, will I?"

"Not at all," reassured Colin.

"I'm sure if landlord bin 'ere, he'd done the same," Noggin said.

"Rose would have done the same," Joe added.

"Who's going to go and see Joyce? Sort out that earlier little misunderstanding?" Colin asked.

Pauline, who had just come up for a refill, said, "I'll pop in and see her tomorrow after work. How she thinks we've all turned against Frank, I don't know. We were only having a bit of a laugh about his tankard holding less than a pint. No need for her to go storming out like that."

"How are things at Rooksbridge?" Colin asked.

"More bizarre than normal," replied Pauline.

"Is that possible?" Joe joked.

Pauline shrugged and said, "Thanks, love," as she took her drinks back to her table.

Matt, the local farrier, came in with his friend Ross.

"Landlord not around tonight?" he asked, seeing Sue behind the bar.

"No, he and Pat have taken Phyllis out to dinner somewhere. Castle, I think," Joe said.

"Have we missed anything?" Matt asked.

"We've had Joyce storming out and Derek being thrown out. All pretty regular stuff," Joe replied.

"Really? How come I miss everything?" Ross asked.

"What was it all about? That body Frank found, I bet," Matt said.

"Police are barking up the wrong tree," Colin said. "It's got nothing to do with any of us. I reckon it was someone just dropping down from the motorway. Be pleased when they get fed up and go back to whatever station they came from."

"Mind you, I've been up at Grange Farm today. David Conley has been acting really strange lately," Matt said.

"Well, he was a bit of a star in here tonight," Colin said. "Told Derek he wanted him out of Myrtle Cottage. David's an odd one. But I reckon harmless enough."

"Just saying." To change the subject, Matt added, "I reckon the daughters will be running this place soon. I heard the oldest wants to convert the old stables around the back into guesthouses. Run them herself. Is that right?"

"Yeah, I'd heard that," said Sue.

"That'll please Farleys then."

Varney, a local builder, came in with his dog, Dino. "Pint, please. Any more bodies turned up today?"

"Don't go there, mate," Matt said.

"Everyone's just a bit upset about Frank," Sue said.

"Yeah, I heard about that insanity. They probably only took him in because he found her. He'll be out soon. Anyway, Noggin, I heard you were in the frame," Varney joked.

"Noggin, ha. He's never gone out of a five-mile radius from here. Have you, Noggin?" Joe said.

"Anyway, who wants another? We all know it's nothing to do with any of us. Police will work it out eventually and leave us all alone," Colin said.

"You're probably right," admitted Joe. "Pint, please, Sue. And where is the delectable Rose tonight?"

"Hot date, I believe," Sue said, filling his glass.

TWENTY-ONE

The support Frank was receiving was the exact opposite of that being given to Graham and Gillian by his parents.

Mark, as was his usual practice, had rung Graham a few hours earlier to say he and Kim were visiting. There was never any thought as to whether it would be convenient. Graham closed his phone and went upstairs to warn Gillian, who had locked herself in their bedroom following their recent argument.

"It will have to be okay," Gillian replied, from the other side of the door, resentment in every word. She hated the way, after so many years of the farmhouse being her home, Kim walked straight in as if it was still hers. It made her feel like she was still sixteen and should be terrified of being summoned to the house by them. She wanted to stay locked in her room with her own bitter thoughts, but now she would have to go downstairs to ensure everything was tidy and prepared for their visit. And to make sure the door to the second sitting room was locked.

She sat on the end of her bed and looked around the ugly, damp room. She wanted to feel mentally prepared for the visit. If only Graham would accept how much she hated the place and wanted to leave. The room, the house, the liveries, the chalet guests, the phone... she hated everything. As her tears started to fall, she realised she hated herself as well.

She'd been lying under the damp and cold earth just as much as the poor girl up in the gully. Her death was slow and painful in comparison. Her death was one of slow suffocation followed by emptiness and then nothingness. All she had left was time, and that was constantly slipping away from her.

Gillian dried her eyes and walked downstairs, stopping only to check that the door at the bottom of the stairs was locked.

"I was worried earlier because I didn't know where you were," Graham said, as soon as she entered the kitchen. "I wanted to check what time you needed a lift to the doctors."

"So, I'm not safe walking about your farm now?" Gillian said, picking up the mop and bucket to clean the floor.

"I'll do that if you like," Graham offered.

"It's fine."

"What time is your doctor's appointment?"

"It's in the diary," Gillian told him gruffly.

"Where were you today, anyway?"

"This would be easier if I had the place to myself," Gillian replied, and started to mop the floor. She felt it a minor victory when Graham eventually gave up and left saying he had some fencing to finish. His recent whining and self-martyrdom was more annoying than his usual bad temper.

Pushing the mop around the floor, she wondered if things would have been different if they hadn't been given the farm. Would things have been easier if they'd built their own place up from scratch together, as a team? Probably not, she thought. It still would have ended up being Graham's. He still would have been the one in control.

Gillian didn't fully understand her feelings, but she had the strong sense she was approaching a major turning point in her life. A decision her whole future depended on. A strange sense that the answer was close, even though she wasn't sure yet what the question was.

Gillian had just sat down when Graham returned. A short while later, Mark and Kim breezed in without knocking, dressed to the nines. Kim's expensive perfume wafting in and scenting the room.

"Can't stop long, we have a table booked at nine-thirty at The Castle," Kim announced, looking critically at the homemade cakes Gillian had set out on the table. Gillian felt the anger rising inside her as Kim turned to Mark and said, "Don't ruin your appetite before we get there."

Mark gave the cakes an insincere look of regret. "What a shame. I hope you didn't go to too much trouble on our account." Not giving Gillian time to reply, he asked Graham, "Have you heard any more from the police?"

Kim airily said, "Two gormless idiots came to see us. No wonder crime is out of control. I don't think they could find their way out of a paper bag."

Mark's silky voice contrasted with his wife's shrill tones. "A most unfortunate thing, but they should be looking for whoever put the poor girl there rather than wasting time with us just because we happen to have owned the land at the time. They're starting to get quite tedious."

Gillian focussed her attention on the TV screen following the slight to her cakes. It was a cheap American drama, but it was preferable to listening to Kim's barbed comments. She ignored Kim's tut at the programme. Everyone knew Kim had a bee in her bonnet about the Americanisation of British culture.

Mark's attention rested briefly on the TV following his wife's tut. He mockingly said, "Here we are looking for a murderer when those scriptwriters are walking the streets as free men."

Gillian stood up. "I'll watch the rest in the other room."

After Gillian left, Mark said, "Sorry, son. I was only trying to lighten the mood a little."

Kim said, in a cold tone, "We do try, Graham, but she is just so oversensitive." To avoid dwelling further on her daughter-in-law, she suggested popping the news on before they left. "See what the media are saying about your body before we go."

From the hallway, Gillian heard Graham obediently switch channels. Still looking for Mummy's approval.

The national news was just finishing. Mark commented on the story, "If I had a million people rioting and holding candlelight vigils calling for my resignation, I might start polishing up my C.V. a bit."

Kim said, "I'm sure they will find another job for her, some-where."

Mark laughed. "With her stubbornness and lack of public con-cern, she would do just as well as a bus driver!"

The news reporter reeled off grisly details about the find on their farm and confirmed the victim had been identified as a school girl from Cheltenham who disappeared mysteriously nearly twenty years ago. A different voice asked for anyone who may have information to telephone the local police. And then they were on to the next story.

"Look at the time! We really must go," Kim said. Air kissing Graham, she added, "Why does Gillian have to be so dull and miserable all the time?"

Gillian watched the same news report in her bedroom. Hearing the roar of Mark's Jaguar, she listened carefully to see if Graham was going to follow her upstairs. She let out a sigh of relief when she heard him change channels on the TV.

Gillian thought about the young girl found on the farm. The photograph they'd showed on the news was of a beautiful girl, looking blissfully happy, full of hope. No trace of fear that her future was about to be snatched away. Whatever ambitions or feelings she had when that photograph was taken were irrele-vant. Gillian tried to remember a time when she'd been a happy young girl.

Building the holiday homes had been her idea. While Graham and Frank had worked hard on renovating the old barns and building the log cabin, she had been excited at the prospect of decorating the cottages. She planned to give each cottage an in-dividual style and a suitable name. She'd studied magazines and sent off for material samples. She'd arranged trips to local an-tique stores and learned to drive a hard bargain. Was that the last time she'd been happy? Before Graham said, it would be too much for her and employed an interior decorator to do the cottages.

Gillian's thoughts wandered down their usual worn track without her noticing. Would things have turned out any better even if they had a family? She tried to imagine her two children running happily around the farm, a boy and a girl. Would Kim have stopped seeing her as staff and bitterly regretting the day she employed her? She felt her stomach knot and her back ache.

She fought back another onslaught of tears and tried to block her murderous thoughts about Kim from her mind. She imagined taking an axe to the insensitive cow. It would be a modern twist on the Lizzie Borden story. Chop. Chop. Chop. But then she thought, knowing her luck, the chopped-up parts would somehow reassemble. Then she would have three mini Kims taunting her.

Another wave of self-pity and despair hit her. She was sad and lonely with a meaningless, dried up life, and she didn't know how it had happened. She wanted to feel something other than numb.

TWENTY-TWO

Peter felt a little better than he had for a long time when he arrived at the station. He was concerned about the dark circles under her eyes and the dramatic weight loss, but at least Amelia was back under his roof. He couldn't deny how pleased he was to have her back under his care and without any mention of the recent boyfriend.

Plus, with Sally away at her Mother's, he had the space to think through their relationship. He didn't want to lose her, but something had to change. He found it a welcome break not to come home to a house full of tension. He wondered if Sally thought the same. Whether she had her own doubts and secretly wished for a happier marriage than the one he gave her, or that he had failed her in some way.

The recent strain between them was over Amelia, but there had been other causes of ill feelings and resentment which lay just below the surface. Their recent disagreement on how to deal with his daughter was proving difficult to resolve. Amelia was his daughter, his responsibility, and so this time his feelings were much stronger and the rift far deeper.

Amelia probably needed Sally just as much as she needed him. Once upon a time, they had been quite close. Sally was the closest thing to a mother Amelia had. Sally was the adult, but she had been obstinate and refused to back down before the holiday. Peter had hoped up to the point they'd boarded the plane that Amelia would turn up, only to be disappointed. For him, the holiday was ruined before it started. Sally hadn't seen it the same way. She blamed him for ruining the holiday. He wondered whether under the stubborn behaviour they were both as scared as he was. Problem was none of them was prepared to make that first step to conciliation.

"Morning, sir," Fiona said, as she walked in with a coffee. "Sorry. I'd have got two if I'd known."

"That's fine. Has there been any reaction to the photograph from Jennifer's old friends?" Peter asked.

"Not yet. Do you want me to chase them? I'm still trying to find out a bit more about Derek and Mark. Think I might be getting somewhere with Derek Alley."

"Leave all that to later. I was thinking we should head out to see Tim Potter this morning."

"That's the neighbouring farmer? The one David Conley called Toad of Toad Hall?"

"Yes. I'm interested to know if he remembers anything more about the day trip to the races that day. But drink your coffee first."

The name Hillend Farm, home to Tim and Cathy Potter, explained the farm's location perfectly. It seemed to hang down from the ridge of the Cotswolds Way, giving the impression nothing further existed after its boundaries. Perched a little higher than the other farms in the area, the countryside was more rugged and dramatic. The slopes of the ridges steeper and the outcrops of rock more frequent. Though it was slight, a gentle breeze gave a welcome relief from the stagnant, still air they'd been experiencing lower in the village. The harshness of the terrain contrasted with the pretty, well-tended kitchen garden, and the winding path leading to the ivy-covered farmhouse.

As they were about to knock, Rose shouted, "Hi, again!" as she got out of her car with a good-looking, dark-haired man. She laughed at their blank expression. "We met the other day. I work in The Bull."

"Of course, do you work here as well?" Peter asked.

"I keep my horse here."

"Why don't you keep it at Rooksbridge? I thought that was where everyone kept their horses," Peter asked.

Rose laughed and with a look of mischief in her eyes replied, "I tried it once. It was an absolute disaster, never to be repeated again."

"Let me guess. Was it all those rules we've seen dotted about the place?"

"Partly, but mostly just trying to deal with the Farleys and their erratic moods. Graham hates me," Rose said.

Peter could guess that Graham would not like a livewire like Rose running about the place. He smiled at the thought of her causing havoc with their enforced order. He innocently asked, "How come he dislikes you?"

"They're just both so miserable, and I like to have a bit of fun," Rose said, mimicking the dour impression of Gillian before adding, "But what really freaked me is the way he talks about Gillian. Tells everyone how fragile she is and no matter what she says how everyone must remain very jolly around her. People are only to say very positive, happy things when she's around. It's just not normal."

"She goes out onto the yard then? I didn't think she left the house that much," Peter asked.

Rose raised her eyebrows and said in a mock serious voice, "Not that often, but when she does appear, never ever point out that what she's just said or done is completely insane."

"Is she really that strange?"

"Umm, she's totally deranged. You end up having bizarre random conversations with her. You're not allowed to query anything she says, no matter how crazy or untrue it is. If you do, Graham throws a complete tantrum and blames you for all her emotional problems. That's why she's so back to front if you ask me."

"Is it quite difficult to get to know her?"

"Duh yeah. Graham doesn't allow anyone to get that close to her. She has no idea what really goes on down there. I think

Graham does it on purpose because he's scared she might leave him if she knew what he was really like."

"Surely she has some friends of her own? Someone she trusts?"

"No idea. Don't think so. Pauline possibly. I wouldn't lose too much sleep over those two, they're just odd."

Rose continued on her way with a cheery wave. Once they were out of earshot, Fiona said, "Guess who the guy with her is?"

"No idea."

"It's Richard Turner. And guess where he's staying?" Peter gave her a blank look in reply.

"Over at Rooksbridge, in one of the holiday cottages."

Peter felt uneasy about Richard's accommodation arrangements but didn't have time to question them before the front door swung open. Cathy greeted them warmly and led them into the house along a narrow passage with uneven floorboards. The walls were lined with a variety of framed family photographs, showing the Potters had a wide range of interests and friends, everything from vintage cars to sailing boats and the obligatory horses.

The kitchen was large and airy, the quality furnishings chosen for their comfort and durability rather than the latest fashion. There were overflowing bunches of freshly cut flowers on the table and on the massive sideboard. The room smelt of flowers and fresh coffee percolating. On the mantle above the substantial open fireplace at the end of the room, Peter noticed an invitation to supper with the Earl.

They were quickly made to feel welcome and sat at ease around the huge oak kitchen table. The Potters appeared to be a close couple, comfortable with each other, sharing looks and gently mimicking each other at times. Cathy came across as a robust woman of spirit, but also well-grounded and sensible. While her short brown hair was peppered with grey, she had a girlish open face. Peter noticed Tim was far more reserved. His quiet confidence and his manner gave a sense of class and inherited wealth. He was tall and incredibly thin. Handsome, he had something of the look of Robert Redford about him. Both had impeccable manners and the discipline of good posture.

First, Peter checked what they knew of the gate padlocks.

"The hunt system of padlocking the perimeter gates was brought in sometime in the late 1980s," Tim said. "It was around then we started to have real problems with travellers. They didn't care where they went. Any gate was an open invitation to them. Their ideas on free love seemed to apply to all aspects of their life. A real pain when they were camped. But it was the mess they'd leave behind that was a real problem. Normal rules of behaviour just didn't seem to matter to them. A lot of things would go missing when they were around as well."

"I don't remember them being that bad, Tim. There was never any proof they were actually stealing things," Cathy said.

"But the system was in place and followed by all the local landowners at the time?" Peter asked.

"Well, we certainly used the padlocks. But then, we both ride to hounds. The hunt often meets on our land anyway. We had no objections. As far as I'm aware, everyone else was quite happy to use the padlocks provided," Tim replied.

"The only person who ever had an issue with the system was when Mark Farley moved in, as I remember," Cathy added.

"Really, so what did he do? Did he refuse to use them?" Peter asked.

"He refused outright for a short while. Until it was explained to him how the countryside works. Kim was desperate to fit in. She really is such a terrible snob, so it didn't need too much explaining," Cathy said.

"Mark didn't fully understand how the hunt worked when he first moved here. He was happy to comply once they had a friendly chat with him," Tim said.

"Hrmm. Mark is a control freak," Cathy said. "Always insisting on getting his own way. He didn't think the traditional customs applied to him. And he thought he could bully the villagers. He had to back down to the hunt, though. He always had a bit of a chip on his shoulder afterwards."

"I think you are exaggerating a bit, dear. Once it was settled, he had no problem at all with the hunt," Tim said.

"He's never allowed us to meet on their farm, though, has he?" Cathy pointed out.

"No. But it's a business. He allows the hunt to cross his fields like everyone else."

Peter interrupted, "But he does and did use the hunt padlocks? That's all we really need to know."

"Yes," Tim replied.

"And the previous owners, we believe their name was Stokes? Do you know if they were happy to use the same system?"

"I'd forgotten about them. Yes. They also hunted. We used to get along with them very well," Cathy replied.

"And how do you get along with Graham Farley and his wife?"

"We don't get along particularly well. At least he does allow the hunt access without any fuss," Tim said.

Cathy added, "We're guessing you know all about the baby-snatching?"

"Sorry? Baby-snatching?" Peter asked.

Cathy looked to her husband before continuing. "It seems they have a problem having children. Gillian has taken two babies in the past. The job of returning them has been left to Graham. It was all hushed up, though. Rumour has it the parents were paid off, and the problem has never been properly addressed. In the long run, I don't think he is helping, though. She clearly needs therapy." After a pause, Cathy added, "I feel quite sorry for her."

"We assume you know all about Oscar Conley and Robin Bailey?" Tim said.

"Yes. We do. But thanks for that information about Gillian Farley. We thought something was amiss. That explains a lot," Peter said.

Tim changed the subject to David Conley. "The hunt used to meet on the Conley farm back in the day. Not since all the trouble, if I remember rightly. But David uses the padlocks. Now he really is an odd guy. Never saw him in the company of a woman until his marriage to Hannah."

"And that's another story," Cathy said. "You wait until you see how they've split the house up."

"He's quite a character. Loves winding people up, especially Derek Alley. But then with his family history..." Tim said.

"Derek Alley deserves it anyway," Cathy said.

Peter had to interrupt them again. "We have already seen David Conley. You don't remember a time when any of the padlocks or gates were tampered with in the past?"

"No. I can't think of anything like that ever happening," Tim said. "But then it was such a long time ago. The news reports say that the girl went missing in May and that would have been around the time the travellers used to appear. Personally, I've always thought they parked their vans up in the winter and returned to their cosy homes during the colder months. I expect they all live on benefits."

"That's a little harsh, dear. By the way, how is Frank? It was him who found the body, wasn't it? It must have been quite a shock for him. And I heard you took him in for questioning, didn't you? I haven't seen him in ages," Cathy said, fishing for gossip.

Before Peter could reply, Tim said, "Then look in The Bull or The Star." He added, "He's a genuine chap, Frank, but he is a bit of a drinker. You know what they say, 'work is the curse of the drinking classes.'"

Cathy added, "We were surprised to hear you'd taken him in. But then, we don't know him well, and you do hear such strange things."

Peter pulled out the photographs.

Tim smiled at the group photograph. "They were happy days."

Peter replied, "For some maybe. Can you tell me who they all are?"

Tim looked again and could identify the same five men but wasn't sure about the name of the sixth. He looked blankly at the photograph of the caravans and shrugged. "I think that might be Graham as a boy."

Cathy was surprised by the third picture. "We always have a handful of shoots here every year. Mark used to come. Still does occasionally. But I can't remember a time he ever brought

Graham with him." She looked closer at the picture. "I can't be totally sure, but I think that is the gun Mark used to use. What do you think, Tim?"

"I'm really not sure," Tim replied. "If we're finished here, I have some work to do on the cars."

Taking the photographs back, Peter asked if it was them he'd seen in the vintage car. Tim was pleased at his interest and offered to show them his collection.

"Another time perhaps, when we've a little more time."

Tim excused himself and headed off to his workshop. Cathy apologised. "He's obsessed with those cars. Not sure how many he's got. His father started the collection. The two of them used to go up to Birmingham all the time to see some strange little man, equally obsessed. They referred to him as a genius. It was this guy in Birmingham who found all the cars for them. A harmless enough hobby, I suppose, and he does love to tinker with them."

Before they left, Fiona asked, "I don't suppose you would have any clearer pictures of the group, taken around the time of 2000?"

"We probably do somewhere. Would you like me to look and pop them into the station some time?"

"If you could, that would be great. If you address them to me, I will make sure you get them back," Fiona replied.

As an afterthought, Cathy said, "Have you been to see Henry Tinney?"

"No. Who's he?" replied Peter.

"He used to run a small riding school back then. But I do remember there was a bit of a scandal involving some girl or other. Can't remember exactly what it was about, but there might be a connection."

"Do you have any idea where we'd find him?"

"Yes. He still lives in the area. Probably easiest if I draw you a quick map." Cathy moved the sideboard to get a pad and pen and added, "It's not the easiest of places to find."

TWENTY-THREE

Despite the map being quite accurate, they drove past Henny Tinney's house the first time. The overgrown hedge hid most of the gateway to the short, rutted, mud track that led to the house. On either side of the track was discarded junk of all descriptions, an old washing machine and cooker, rusted car parts and broken oil barrels. What may have once been a cosy detached cottage showed signs of dilapidation, paint peeling on the window sills surrounding dirty unwashed windows, dirty smears covering the once white door next to which was a broken boot scraper.

Peter knocked twice without response, but when he moved to look through the dirty windows, he heard heavy footsteps approaching the door. This was followed by the sound of a key being turned and the pulling back of a bolt. From a partially opened door, a gruff voice demanded, "What do you want?"

When they explained they were police officers, there was a delay while the unseen occupant seemed to be deciding whether to run for it or slam the door shut again. The stockily built occupant finally decided to squeeze himself through the partly opened door and close it quickly behind him. Henry Tinney was unshaven and of medium height and there was something about his neck that reminded Peter of an ox. He spat on the floor before asking them again what they wanted.

"We understand you used to run a riding school in the past, but it was closed down. Could you tell us what happened?"

"I don't like to talk about it," Tinney said, turning as if to go. He suddenly spun round to face them and said, "I'll tell you what happened. Mark Farley, that's what happened. He's one nasty piece of work. He set up his fancy school and bled me dry." Spittle appeared at the side of his mouth, and he began to jab his finger for emphasis. "I kept a few loyal customers. They were just enough to keep me going like. But he wasn't happy with that. He used every dirty trick he could to run me out of business."

He broke off at this point with a coughing fit. His face, which had been slowly turning pink with anger, was crimson. Both Fiona and Peter had drawn back away from his bitterness, keen to avoid a soaking from his spit.

Tinny struggled to control his ragged breathing.

"Did you employ girls to help with the ponies?" Peter asked, after a pause.

"If you want to know about that murdered girl, you go find Mark Farley and leave me alone. He really was messing about with his girls. Well known at the time. You ask anyone."

"So, did you employ girls to help you out?"

"Yes. A few times I employed a local girl. But not like Mark Farley. He brought in girls from around the country."

"We're not asking about Mr Farley. We're asking you about employing girls. Did you ever have any incidents with the girls you employed?" Peter asked.

"I know exactly what you are trying to say, and absolutely not. You're barking up the wrong tree. Mark Farley tried to set me up. I was cleared of everything, but mud sticks around here. You go and check your records and leave me alone."

"Do you have any records of the girls you employed?"

"You can't expect me to have records from so long ago. I can tell you it was only local girls from time to time and none of them went missing." Henry had to stop at this point, unable to carry on, his breathing was so laboured.

When he was asked about the padlocks, Henry managed to draw in enough air to carry on. "I may have made a few mistakes in the past. But I've never had a reason to go hurting girls or opening gates. I know nothin' about the hunt or what their systems may be or about bodies buried anywhere. You go ask Mark Farley about it. I'm not in good health. Registered disabled I am, because of my nerves, because of him. I live here quietly, bothering no one. I've heard bowt things from my daughter. But I go nowhere. I mostly stay here, in the house. My nerves are bad."

The outburst left Henry gasping for air. Peter decided there was little to be gained standing outside the sad-looking house.

As they drove away, Peter was deep in thought. While Henry Tinney was consumed by his bitterness, he was not the only person to raise doubts about Mark and his relationships with the young girls he employed. There obviously was another side to the gentle, quietly-spoken man he tried to portray.

The relationship between Mark and his son also bothered Peter. Even in the photograph of Graham as a young boy, there was something awkward about the two of them. "What do you think of the relationship Mark has with Graham?"

"I would describe it as close," Fiona replied.

"Close or controlling?" Peter asked. "I'm just thinking out loud, here. Just say Jenny turned up at the farm looking for work. Either at the suggestion of Mark or Frank. Suppose Graham had been fooling about with the girl. In the photograph, he looks older than ten. He was already a big, strong lad, used to manual work on the farm. If something had happened, would Mark have covered up for his son?"

"Possibly. Mrs Farley would want to avoid any scandal involving her family," Fiona said. "But surely, ten is too young for what you're suggesting?"

"You're probably right," Peter conceded. "I think it would be worth having a closer look at Mark Farley."

"I've been thinking about what you said earlier," Fiona said. "For a grown man, Graham does seem very dependent on his father."

"Do you think?" Peter said sarcastically.

"Yes. He constantly says he'll check things with his father. His tone is always very respectful whenever he mentions him, as if he's some sort of god."

"I think the entire family is very odd, but how relevant that is I don't know. It could be a sort of 'kick the cat' syndrome."

From the look on her face, Fiona didn't understand what he meant.

"Mark controls Graham, so Graham controls Gillian. I've had a change of thought. I want to see Graham with the photographs now. And then maybe go and see Mark again." He was quick to see the look of doubt on Fiona's face. "Don't worry. It'll all be on my head, and I will be on my best behaviour." He added, "I'd hate to ruin a round of golf."

James had promised himself he would visit the spot one more time and never return, again. He couldn't torture himself any more. He needed to put his demons to rest. Maybe he could bury them in the ground with Jenny.

Dr Grey had told him not to read so much into things. Find connections and patterns that just weren't there. Not to go over and over things in his head. Dr Grey called it ruminating.

All James could think about was finding somewhere quiet and peaceful. Somewhere he could hide all his anger and evil inside. He could reappear when his mask was back in place.

How dare she try to break down my armour?

TWENTY-FOUR

When Peter and Fiona arrived at the Rooksbridge farmhouse, they could hear the TV was on but received no reply after knocking several times. Peter pushed the door, and it swung open. He walked in with Fiona behind, calling, "Mrs Farley." The kitchen, as usual, looked spotlessly clean, and through an open door to the side, they could see the far end of a living room where an open fire was burning. Peter and Fiona gave each other an incredulous look. They could both feel sweat running down their sides in short-sleeved shirts.

Peter walked along to the end of the hallway to the foot of the stairs. He held the bannisters at the bottom as he called up the stairs, "Mrs Farley?"

Fiona checked behind the doors that lined the hallway. She pushed open the second closed door and gasped. She was momentarily confused by what she saw before she called, "Peter? You'd better have a quick look at this."

Peter looked hopefully once more up the staircase before making his way back to the doorway where Fiona stood. He pushed the door further ajar to get a better look into the room. It was decorated as a second living room. The living room of a house that contained children. There was a mosses basket, high chair and an open packet of disposable nappies to the side of the room. The centre was taken up with a large wooden playpen filled with an assortment of colourful toys and fairy tale books.

Sitting in the middle of all this was a realistic baby doll. Peter stepped backwards and closed the door, edging Fiona out of the room with him. "This has nothing to do with our investigation. Let's go out into the yard and see if we can find them."

Fiona nodded her silent agreement.

As they walked towards the stable block, they saw a group of women huddled around a notice board. They overheard one of them say, "What new insanity is this?"

Unobserved by the women, they peered over the backs of their heads to see what they were referring to. On the notice board was a list of over fifty rules and safety notices. The smudges on the board suggested these rules were amended and added to on a regular basis. The most recent rule concerned the correct way to leave a saddle on a stand and pointed out that some saddles had not been put away correctly so had been confiscated. One of the women turned to Fiona and before realising who she was, said, "Can he do that?"

"No idea. But we are looking for him. Do you know where he is?" Fiona asked.

The woman blushed at her mistake before being rescued by one of the others who said, "Yes. He's banging about over by the holiday cottages."

The small group quickly dispersed, grumbling, "He'd better not have my saddle."

The woman who had spoken to them introduced herself as Ros and asked if they needed help finding the cottages.

"No. We know where they are. Thank you." Peter added, pointing to the note about the saddles. "Does he often do things like that?"

"He does sometimes. They're just a bit odd... If you're sure you know where you're going, I'd best get going." Peter sensed an uneasiness and wariness in her voice.

The shaded walkway through the woods gave a brief respite from the burning sun. As they emerged back out into the glaring sunshine, the heat hit them. They spotted Graham mending the handrails to the log cabin. Gillian was sitting on the steps in a heavy sweatshirt watching him, with a tub of nails between her knees. Graham looked up from his work as they approached, beads of perspiration running down the side of his face. "Damn kids swinging off the rails."

Peter stood at the foot of the steps, his hand raised to shield his eyes from the blinding sun. "Could we have a word please, Mr Farley?" He smiled at Gillian, but she turned away. "I'd prefer it back at the house if possible?"

"Yes. I'm finished here, anyway," Graham said, collecting his tools and putting them into an empty wheelbarrow.

Walking back through the woods, Fiona said, "It really is a lovely spot here, quite beautiful."

"Is it?" Gillian said.

They continued in silence other than the squeaking of the wheelbarrow wheel and the sounds of birds singing.

Once the business of removing shoes was over, Graham offered them coffee which they declined. He took his place at the head of the table while Gillian curled herself in her armchair in the corner of the room. She kept her eyes glued to the TV screen. When Peter asked for the sound to be turned down, Graham obliged without any reaction from Gillian. Peter hadn't noticed before that the remote control was kept on the table by Graham's hand.

With all the windows shut, the atmosphere in the room was stifling. The heat was irritating Peter, who quickly pulled out the photographs. He passed over the group picture first. Graham was able to identify his father, Frank, Tim and David from the photograph. He pulled his phone from his pocket and said, "I could ring father. I'm sure he would know who the other two are."

Peter shook his head in reply before handing Graham the photograph of the caravans.

Graham looked at it a while before looking to the window as if for inspiration. Peter noticed him stiffen and clench his jaw. Graham looked back at the picture with a furrowed brow. "The picture is of me washing the old staff caravans. I cleaned them every summer when the girls left," Graham finally said in a monotone, and then placed the picture back down on the table.

Peter looked closely at the photograph himself and said, "But this year they were completely gutted, by the look of it."

Graham gave a "so what" shrug and allowed his eyes to stray to the TV screen.

Peter drew his attention back by handing him the photograph of him with his father. A brief smile crossed Graham's lips before he asked, "Where did you get this?" Peter chose not to reply. Graham continued staring at the picture and almost in a trance said, "I remember when Father gave me his old shotgun. He said he thought I was old enough to handle it as he handed it over to me." He appeared to struggle to pull his eyes away from the photograph before handing it back.

Peter returned it to the pile on the table before asking, "Any particular reason your father thought you were old enough?"

Graham shook his head and returned to staring at the TV.

"What do you think the connection is between the three pictures?" Peter said, trying to draw Graham's attention.

Graham replied with feigned boredom, "I have no idea. I'd hoped you were going to tell me. Where did they come from, anyway?"

"Can you remember why the caravans were gutted that year? Had anything happened to them? Maybe they were damaged in some way?" Peter suggested.

"Look, I'm really busy today." Graham sighed heavily and picked up the photograph again. "I did what father asked. Maybe they were due a re-fit. I don't know. Why don't you let me ring Father? I'm sure he could tell you."

"We'll be speaking to him later. Do you remember when the girls left the caravan that year?" Peter asked, as he gathered the photographs.

A long sigh preceded, "No idea."

Peter turned to Gillian. "Did you stay in the caravans when you worked for Mark?"

Gillian's body tensed, and her eyes widened in shock. "Yes, but it was much later." She added sulkily, "We had to clean them ourselves," and she returned her full attention to the TV screen.

Peter stood to leave and asked, "Before we go, could you show us where the caravans were parked back then?"

Graham made a point of slowly pushing himself up from the table and led them through the garden. They walked in silence around the side of a large barn filled with bales of straw. Once they reached the far side, Graham pointed to a small area of grass behind a tall hedge. "Over there."

Peter asked, "Why were they positioned so far from the house?" but when he turned around Graham had gone. His back could just be seen disappearing behind the side of the barn.

"He'd probably have just said, 'I'll have to ring Father,' anyway," Fiona said, with a playful grin.

Peter walked to where a small patch of cracked concrete could be seen amongst the overgrown grass and weeds. The house could not be seen from where the caravans had been sited. But they did have a clear view across the yard and to the main gates into the yard.

"Nice to see Mrs Farley out and about wasn't it?" Fiona said.

"Sarcasm doesn't suit you," Peter replied.

Fiona shrugged before asking, "Where do we go from here? Do you still want to see Mark Farley?"

"No. I'd like to leave him until the morning," Peter said, looking at his watch. "Graham has probably already rung to tell him about the photographs, so we've lost the element of surprise. In fact, I was planning on shooting off home. If I drop you back at the station, could you do a bit of digging on Mark's history?"

"No problem," Fiona replied.

Retracing their steps back past the house, they overheard an argument from inside.

"See what you have done!" Graham shouted.

"Me?" replied Gillian. "What on earth do you think I've done?"

"Forget it."

"No. I want to know what you think I've done and how anything could possibly be my fault," Gillian said.

"Just leave it alone," Graham shouted.

This was followed by the sound of the kitchen door banging shut as Graham reappeared, pulling on his boots. Peter raised his hand to wave as they walked on towards their car.

Once in the car, Fiona asked, "What do you think they were arguing about this time? What was her fault?"

"No idea. I'm beginning to think both are so screwed up none of their behaviour makes any sense. I'm not even convinced it has anything to do with the murdered girl."

"What did you think of the baby thing?"

"Mostly just sad, I guess. It's not something I know much about." He added, "I definitely don't think it has any relevance to what may have happened here nearly twenty years ago. While that remains the case, I think it best we don't mention it. Those two have enough problems. I dread to think what would happen if the media got a whiff of their life of make-believe babies."

TWENTY-FIVE

"Do you want me to take your plate, Dad?" Amelia asked.

"Thanks, love. That was the best homemade lasagne I've had since last time you made it," Peter replied.

"You wait until you try my chocolate cheesecake," Amelia called over her shoulder as she disappeared out of the dining room.

The sight of Amelia's stick-thin body wrapped in the dress she'd put on especially for him was something he found hard to deal with. It seemed incongruous that such an excellent cook should starve her own body like she did. He'd cleared his plate, watching Amelia merely push the food around hers. Only the odd morsel ever seemed to reach her mouth. He couldn't fathom what pain she must be in to do that to herself, but it tore at his heart.

The cheesecake was sublime. "This is wonderful, Amelia. You really should try some," Peter said.

"Not for me. It has far too many calories."

Peter forced his eyes to his plate, desperately wanting to hide the fear he felt. He was so pleased to have her home with no mention of the boyfriend. Now was not the time to tackle her about her eating, or lack of it.

"How long is Sally staying with her mother?" Amelia asked.

"Not sure. I expect she'll ring later and let me know how her mother is," Peter replied.

"There's not anything wrong, is there? I mean between you

two?"

"No, there's nothing for you to worry about."

After a brief silence, Amelia looked up warily, a timid look on her face that pained Peter and knotted his stomach. "It's not because of me, is it? ...Dad?"

"No, Amelia. It's definitely not because of you. We've got some problems we need to sort out. But none of it is your fault, okay?"

This was exactly why he felt so cross towards Sally. She couldn't see just how vulnerable Amelia was or how deeply she worried about things. It reminded him so much of her mother and while he felt too paralysed to help, he was convinced it was the cause of the eating disorder.

"It's just sometimes... I just wish sometimes things could be different," Amelia said.

"How do you mean different? What would you like to change?" Peter felt his heart quicken. He so wanted his daughter to break down the barriers and explain what was really bothering her. He desperately wanted to reach a place beyond their fears, where they could communicate openly.

"I don't know." Amelia forced a smile, which partly lit her face but did not reach her eyes. "I'm going to clear the table and sort the mess out in the kitchen."

Peter stood up from his chair. "I'll help."

"No," Amelia replied sharply. She softened her voice and added, "You go through to the living room with the wine. Maybe choose a film we could watch together. I'll join you in a bit."

Peter felt he had no choice but to obediently take the half-full bottle of merlot through to the other room and flick through the TV guide. The invisible barrier between him and Amelia was hovering somewhere around the entrance to the kitchen. For the hundredth time, he wondered if the barrier would be broken down if only he could truly confess what had happened with Jordan. How it was all his fault? Was it that awful secret that held them apart? The dread he felt of losing his daughter by telling the truth was matched only with the dread she would somehow find out the whole truth from somebody else.

Nobody had said it at the time, but he remembered the looks he received at Jordan's funeral from her family and friends. Without moving their lips, they said, "unfaithful scum," and he felt the daggers pierce his back. He remembered the coffin in the small church. How he realised it was the last time they would be so close. How he'd wanted to reach out and touch the wood, run his fingers along the cool metal of the handle.

Every day, Peter wished he could go back in time, press rewind and cut out that part of his life. Occasionally, he had a childish dream. He'd be walking in a street or sitting in a restaurant. Jordan would lean over and kiss him, and he'd know he'd been forgiven. The dream tortured him. Jordan had died hating him.

Amelia's return halted his thoughts. "Dad...Dad. Have you chosen a film?"

"Sorry. I was miles away. Here, you'd better get a glass and not leave me to finish this by myself," Peter said, indicating the bottle of wine at his feet. He watched Amelia smile and move to the side cabinet to collect a glass, feeling a stab of guilt in his side. He had robbed her of a mother. Peter poured a glass for her and said, "Earlier. When you said you wished things were different? What did you mean?"

"I don't know. Just sometimes I wish things were different."

"What things would you like to change?" Peter asked.

"Just everything and nothing."

Peter was sure she was going to say more as she silently sat beside him on the sofa drawing her legs up underneath her. They both turned towards the sound of the telephone ringing. The shrill tone cut through the moment. Peter ignored the insistent rings calling louder and louder and said, "Leave it to ring. Start with the things you want to change?" The phone in his pocket started to vibrate and play a tune.

"Dad, you really do need to answer your phone," Amelia said. As Peter reluctantly pulled it out of his pocket, she added, "That's one lame tune. You need to change that to start with."

Peter looked at his screen and felt his entire body sag. "Sorry, I've got to take this." He walked from the room with the phone, hoping he could delegate whatever the problem was.

He reappeared a few moments later. "I'm so sorry, Amelia. I've got to go out. Can we talk about this later?"

"Yes, Dad. That's fine. How much have you had to drink?"

Peter hesitated as he heard the disappointment in her voice. Was it really that essential he attended the scene? He could read the report in the morning. "Only half a glass with the meal, maybe I should stay here."

"Dad, if it's important, you should go."

Peter hesitated. What if this was the moment he let her down and later would be too late? They were so close. Earlier it felt like she needed to talk to him. "Are you sure you'll be okay?"

Amelia picked up the cushion from the chair next to her and threw it at him. "Dad! Go! I'll be fine."

Peter ducked under the pillow and reluctantly picked up his car keys. "I'll ring you in a bit to let you know how long I'll be."

TWENTY-SIX

By the time Peter reached the area, the lane had been blocked off by parked police cars. The flashing lights of the cars and fire engines lit the scene. The ambulance had already sped off carrying Frank Codrington. Peter saw his friend and colleague Rob, who'd called him, momentarily lit up by the lights and walked over to him. He reached out a hand to him. "Thanks for calling me."

"Hi, Peter, it's good to see you." Rob turned to the scene alongside the bridge. "I thought you'd want to know as soon as we realised who it was. Excuse me a minute. They'll be lifting the vehicle in a moment."

Peter took a while to get his bearings as the area was distorted by the flashing lights. He'd driven the road at least twice every day over the last few days and was aware it bordered the Rooksbridge Centre. He could see from the rubble, the small bridge that covered the river must have been hit at some speed. It was one of the few sections of the lanes around the village that was straight, where you could pick up some speed. While it narrowed slightly between the two stone walls built alongside the river below, it was hard to imagine what may have caused the driver to lose control. He thought maybe an animal, possibly a deer suddenly appearing from a hedge could have caused the accident.

Rob returned and said, "Sorry about that, Peter. I called you because there's something a little odd here. It's not just the straightness of the road that confuses me, but here." He led him over to the side of the road where two officers were taking photographs. "Looks like there was a two-vehicle collision just here before the bridge and someone attempted a quick clean up. It ties up with the statement from the witness who heard the accident. He heard what sounded like a two-vehicle collision followed by the noise of something colliding with the bridge. He was too far away to see anything, but he thinks he heard the sound of a vehicle driving away at speed shortly after."

Peter was looking at the two very short skid marks on the road. Rob followed the direction of his eyes and said, "Yes. It looks like the driver only applied the brakes at this point. As if something appeared suddenly in front of him. What we've found brushed to this side suggests the vehicle hit the rear of another vehicle before careering over the bridge. The question is, why didn't he see the other vehicle, earlier?"

Peter looked along the lane and asked, "How long has he been here?" nodding towards Graham Farley, who was standing a short distance away next to his truck.

"Is he still here? He's been asked to leave once already."

"I'll deal with him," Peter replied.

Peter wandered over to where Graham was standing. "Hello. It's a bit of a mess over there. Any particular reason you're here?"

"Yes," Graham said sharply. "I've asked the officers to check whether there's any damage to my fencing. I'll have to move the horses if there is. I'm sure you don't want them wandering onto the road. I'm waiting for them to come back to me."

"I'll go and check for you. But first, can you explain why you're here at all? We're some distance from your home."

"I thought I heard something. And then we saw all the emergency vehicles arriving. This is my land. I have livestock to think about."

Peter registered the look of cool arrogance in Graham's face and voice. "Fair enough. I'll find out if your fence has been damaged."

"It was Frank, though? Wasn't it?" Graham asked.

"I believe it may have been, but I've only just arrived myself."

"Seems a bit odd...I mean, that he should lose control of his car there."

"I'll go and check about the fencing for you. Are there any horses in the adjacent field?"

"Yes. That's why I'm concerned."

When Peter went back to check about the fencing, he was told there was another friend of Mr Codrington called Joyce James waiting on the other side of the cordoned off area. He sent one of the officers back to tell Graham his fencing was undamaged and to make sure he went home.

He walked towards the small car parked alongside his car. Ducking under the tape, he saw a matronly looking lady wearing a wax jacket and stout shoes. She stood very upright by her vehicle with a worried look on her face. "Mrs James?"

"Joyce," she said, in a no-nonsense manner. "Was it Frank?" she asked, fixing him with a hard stare.

"Yes, I'm afraid we think it was."

Joyce staggered back, the façade of her tough exterior fading.

"Are you feeling all right?" Peter asked, grabbing her arm, afraid she was going to faint.

She recovered quickly and pulled back her arm defiantly. "Yes, I am, young man. Is he...Is he still in the vehicle?"

"No. He was pulled out a short while ago and has been taken to hospital."

Joyce turned and opened her car door, Peter followed her and said, "And where do you think you're going?"

"I'm going to the hospital, of course."

"Wait there. I'll get someone to drive you."

Joyce indignantly replied, "I can manage."

"Wait. I'd hate to arrest you for drunk driving, Mrs James."

"You wouldn't..." began Joyce and then stopped.

"On second thought, get into my car, and I'll drive you," Peter said, knowing he would probably still be back before they pulled the vehicle up from the river.

Joyce obediently climbed into the passenger seat and put her seatbelt on. She sat stiffly with her hands in her lap, staring straight ahead.

"Have you known Frank long?" Peter asked, as they pulled away.

"We were at school together. Here in the village."

"So, did you know his wife as well?"

"Of course, I did," she said crossly. "She moved to the village when she was about fourteen. We were all friends. A gang of us, you might say."

"Would you mind me asking what things were like when she died?"

"Yes, I would." But after a brief silence, Joyce added, "I will tell you just to set the record straight. They were childhood sweethearts. They were inseparable, and it broke his heart." Then her anger rose as she added, "But to suggest he would go murdering some poor innocent girl? No way... And then carry on as if nothing had happened. If you think that of him, you're not a very good judge of character."

Her piece said, she returned to staring out the window in stony silence until they reached the hospital.

Peter's offer to accompany Joyce into the hospital was met with a firm, "No," and a slam of the passenger door. The blame for the accident was evidently his. A little harsh, he felt.

He was worried he wasn't the only person who thought Frank knew something. It was only a gut feeling, but the accident seemed too much of a coincidence. Until foul play could be ruled out, he had to assume the worst. If the nearby householder hadn't been working nights and heard the collision, it was unlikely Frank would have survived. He suddenly felt tired and drained. Checking his watch, he called Rob to see if the vehicle had been lifted from the river.

"No. Sorry, mate. We're having some technical problems."

"Why doesn't that surprise me?" Peter replied. "I'm heading off home now. Can I ring you in the morning?"

"Yes, you get a good kip in, mate. Don't think about us out here," Rob joked. "And don't ring too early in the morning."

James sat with a coffee, gazing out the window. Sometimes he really didn't know what he was doing. The only thing he did know was that time had not healed his wounds. He didn't know why he did anything sometimes.

TWENTY-SEVEN

When Graham was sent home from the scene, he found Gillian pacing the kitchen with a frown on her face. He thought she looked more drawn and tired than normal as she silently handed him a coffee.

"I just don't understand how it could have happened." Graham sat down heavily, his hands hugging the warm mug. "How on earth could he drive his car through the bridge like that? It's narrow but dead straight. He knows that road like the back of his hand."

Gillian replied, "I should probably stay up for a full cycle."

Graham sat with his elbows on the table, running his hands through his hair. He looked at his wife with tired eyes. "Sorry, cycle?"

Gillian got up. "Yes, a full cycle." She disappeared into the hall, leaving Graham confused.

When she returned with a pile of washing, Graham said, "He must have been doing some speed. The wall looked totally demolished."

"Graham. Are you sure this is dirty? It looks clean to me." Gillian handed a sweatshirt to him.

He went through the motions of taking it from her and giving it a sniff for good measure. "Yes. It's dirty." As she took it, he continued, "He must have been travelling towards The Bull. But it still doesn't make sense."

Gillian returned to her chair. "What doesn't make sense?"

Graham leaned back in the chair and looked up at the ceiling for a few seconds before answering. "The accident doesn't make sense. How his car ended up going through the wall."

"Oh, that was Frank, was it? He was probably drunk or something. I don't know."

"It's very possible he was. But Frank is used to having a drink...unless maybe a deer or something ran out, just at the wrong moment? That might explain it."

Gillian looked up from playing with the loose thread coming from her jumper. "You're quite sure none of the horses were involved? You did check, didn't you?"

"Yes. The police checked all our fencing."

Gillian returned to playing with her loose thread.

"Well, I'm off to bed," Graham said.

"I'll wait until the washing is finished," Gillian replied.

Graham sighed as he pulled himself from his chair and walked upstairs. He couldn't remember a time when he didn't feel stressed and worn out. He was tired of dealing with Gillian's nerves. He didn't know anymore what to do for the best. He was tired of it all. Running the centre single-handed left him mentally and physically exhausted. He wanted to leave, make a new start away from the gossip. But still part of him wanted to hang on to his childhood home just in case. In case what? Was it still possible to hope that things could be any different?

He couldn't go on like this much longer. He could deny it no longer. Something somewhere had to change. If only he had more support, someone he could rely on. He felt like he was endlessly running from room to room to keep the fires going, to drive out the chill and damp from the house. His insides were churning over and over with the stress and worry that never seemed to end. Constantly keeping so many balls in the air was beginning to affect his health. His biggest fear was the feeling he had no safety net. Everybody was relying on him.

He always worried when he didn't know where Gillian was. That if he wasn't around to protect her somebody would push her too far, not realising her fragile state. That it would push her over the edge and she would do something stupid again. Her depression and need to be protected wore him out. It left no space for his feelings. They'd been forgotten. He didn't even really know what they were anymore. He'd shared the same disappointments, gone through the same indignities. He wanted a son to follow in his footsteps, a daughter to spoil. But then he didn't have a 'biological clock,' so his feelings didn't count. He didn't feel anything anymore except tired.

The photographs the police had shown him had reminded him of the confusion he felt when he was younger. Nothing much had changed since then—the sense that there were things going on around him that he didn't understand, things he knew even at an early age it was best to forget about and pretend he hadn't seen or heard. Play dumb.

That's what Father thought he was anyway. Too stupid to make a success of anything without his supervision. Well, he had. He had shown him he could make a really good go of it. The farm was certainly in better shape than when he'd taken it over. The sad thing was his dream had always been to one day hand the place over to his child.

There were times he hated the place as much as Gillian did. But it was his childhood home, the only place he really knew, a place he could hold the respect his father had. He could keep close control of the land and all the people who stepped foot on it. It was important he had control over something. Without that he would be nothing.

If he thought hard enough, he could still remember the glow of pride he felt when Father told him the farm was to be a wedding gift. All the ideas he had for the farm, how he would never let Father regret his decision.

At the time, he'd felt overwhelmed with gratitude that his father was finally showing some confidence in him and his abilities and that he would do anything not to betray the confidence shown. He'd believed then, despite appearances, it meant underneath Father did have faith in him.

Even though Kim didn't think Gillian was suitable, his father had indirectly encouraged the wedding and given them a way of supporting themselves independently. At the time, people had been surprised at Mark's decision to hand over the reins completely. But he had risen to the challenge.

Things were beginning to settle down before Frank discovered the body. If only that blasted tree had not come down in the storm.

TWENTY-EIGHT

Peter ate breakfast at home for the first time in weeks, in the hope Amelia would join him, painfully aware how he had purposefully been avoiding Sally. She was right on that. He knew he was being unfair to her, but something had seeped into the relationship, something negative that had grown and developed, pushing them farther and farther apart. But he was damned if he knew what it was or how he could sort his mixed emotions out. They didn't even make any sense to him.

The ridiculous dream that had woken him in the night and then kept him awake tossing and turning hadn't helped. When he thought of it rationally, now he was fully awake, he realised it was preposterous. But somehow in his semi-conscious state, it had some logic. It at least caused him to smile over his muesli when he thought of the vision he had of all the villagers getting together to push the tree over as they all knew the body was there and it was time Mark Farley was held accountable.

Totally nonsensical, but then maybe there was a message in there, somewhere. He had grown up in a small village, similar to Birkbury and he knew how things could be. A school friend had been knocked off his bike and killed in the lanes around their home. Nobody ever came forward, although it was always suspected a local must have been responsible. It was one of the random reasons he'd decided to join the police force.

As he drank his second coffee, hoping Amelia would emerge, he thought ruefully back to the time he tried to write out his feelings to try and make sense of them. It was about six months after Jordan's funeral. He remembered how he'd become so tired of going through every conceivable 'what if' over and over in his mind until it started to drive him crazy. He'd naively thought if it was all written down, everything in black and white once and for all, he would be able to forget. Move on with his life. Put it all behind him in a sealed writing pad of his ramblings.

Wrong. Yet another misconception. The idea that he could somehow write his pain away, and then his feelings of guilt and regret would magically disappear as well, was just another fantasy. In any event, over the years he'd accepted he had no right to wish away any of the guilt or the pain. That was his never-ending punishment.

Sometimes he remembered the moments of pure joy the two of them had shared. But those memories hurt so much he mostly blocked them from his mind.

He swilled his empty coffee cup out under the tap, left a note for Amelia and set off for the station. When he arrived, there was a telephone message stuck to his computer screen. "Call Mike Collin, he'll give you the details. I'm asleep! Rob."

Peter picked up the receiver before sitting down and dialled the number given. "Hi, can I speak to Mike Collin? It's Peter Hatherall..."

"Yes. Rob said you'd ring first thing...Let me grab the report." After a short pause, he continued summarising the main points. "Right, you already know about the location, the witness who heard collision and the initial findings at the scene...There are a couple of other things. There is damage to the vehicle, suggesting it collided with something before going over the bridge...umm yes. Broken headlamp and deep scratches along the left-hand side. There were no signs of damage to the wall that side and no way it was an animal. And there was something else? Yes, that's it. There was glass from a rear light kicked into the grass verge."

"What about Frank's vehicle? Were there any signs of defects, tampering?"

"Early indications say no. We are also checking there wasn't an earlier collision in the Star Inn car park where we understand his vehicle was parked previously."

"Thanks for that. So how are you suggesting the accident happened?" Peter asked.

"We really don't know at this stage, but everything suggests there was a two-vehicle collision just before the driver lost control. There's not a lot more I can say at this stage, other than to tell you Rob will ring you later if anything new comes in."

Once he replaced the receiver, Fiona said, "Anything, sir?"

"Yes. Very odd…It does seem likely Frank collided with the rear of a vehicle before hitting the bridge, but the vehicle sped off afterwards."

"What are they suggesting? Someone was driving in front of him? They braked for some reason, and Frank went into the back of them?"

"But that would mean Frank was driving close at speed… I'm not an expert, but would that have made him swerve over the bridge?"

"Maybe someone reversed their vehicle into Frank's path. That might have made him suddenly swerve," Fiona suggested.

"But who would do that? They would be risking damage to their vehicle and at very least a nasty whiplash. The impact could have even pushed their vehicle over the bridge…They're still looking into what they found. But the accident circumstances are suspicious. The witness is adamant he heard a collision before the car went in the river and that was followed by the sound of a vehicle accelerating away at speed."

"You think it may have been on purpose? That somebody was scared Frank knew something?" Fiona asked.

"It looks that way. Hopefully, we'll have a clearer picture of why he lost control of his vehicle later."

"Do you think whoever murdered the girl is still living in the area and prepared to murder again to protect themselves?" Fiona asked.

"Something isn't quite right here." Peter leaned back in his chair. "To be able to quietly cover up what happened without any thought to the family left behind and carry on as normal would be beyond most people. Why would that sort of person suddenly put themselves at so much personal risk?"

"They panicked?"

"Whoever killed and buried the girl is highly motivated to cover up their actions. If they're prepared to kill again to maintain their reputation or something else that's here, we need to find them, quickly," Peter said.

"How sure are we it wasn't an accident? Is it possible Frank drove into the bridge on purpose? He did say in his interview he wanted to kill himself after his wife's death."

Peter stretched and walked over to the window. "Until we know different, we have to consider the other possibility."

"Do you think it's possible over time whoever killed the girl was able to forget what they'd done?"

"I really don't know." Peter slumped back in his chair and ran his hands through his hair. "Do we know how Frank is this morning?"

"Still unconscious but stable. An officer is stationed outside his room at the hospital," Fiona replied.

"Could you give the hospital a call and find out when we are likely to be able to see him? He may be a bit more forthcoming now. Then we'll go and see Mark Farley."

"Shouldn't we call him first, after our last visit?" Fiona cautioned.

"You can call him if you like," Peter said, dismissively. "Tell him we need to speak to him about Frank's accident. He's bound to already know about it from Graham."

Fiona being busy on the phone gave Peter time to think. He pulled out the bottom drawer to his desk and glanced at the old file he kept hidden in there. It was battered and faded, and he'd stopped believing one day he'd find out who killed Jimmy, his old school friend. Back then, he'd felt invincible. Watching Fiona return to his desk, he closed the drawer and said, "Well?"

"He is prepared to see us...But, he did say if we are going to accuse him of anything again, he wants his solicitor present."

Peter stood up, threw his keys up into the air and caught them again. "That's entirely up to him."

This time, when they approached Mark Farley's property, the surveillance gates swung open for them. Nearing the end of the private driveway, Mark emerged from his house to greet them. Peter hadn't even closed his car door when he felt Mark was already on top of him.

"Come in, come in. Good to see you both again. I may have been a little hasty on your last visit," Mark said, jovially. "I was shocked, I suppose, that you could suggest...Well, let's not worry about that now." Mark led them through to his study. "Please take a seat. Graham has told me about the accident and the photographs you have. Can I take a look?"

While Graham pre-warning his father was inevitable, Peter felt a flicker of annoyance as he pulled out the photographs. He'd wanted to have far more control over the order of events.

Mark studied them quickly. "I thought so. The men Graham couldn't identify are Taffy Williams and Gerry Bowden, both of whom were good friends of mine. Taffy died a while back. He was involved in a very nasty farm accident. It was such a shame. I still miss him at times. I haven't seen Gerry in years. We used to do a bit of business together, but then he moved away. I can have a look to see if I can find the last contact details I had for him. I'll contact you if I find anything."

Distracted by the change of attitude, Peter failed to reply. Fiona stepped in and said, "That would be very helpful, Mr Farley."

"Call me Mark," he replied, with a broad smile.

Peter's concentration returned. "Can you confirm the date on the back of the photograph?"

Mark flipped it over. "I've never missed a Gold Cup day. It could very well have been that year. I wouldn't be able to confirm it one way or the other. Do you go to the races?"

"No. It's not something that interests me."

"Well, that's also a terrible shame. A day at the race track is a must."

"I've never had any interest in horses or gambling, so it would seem a little pointless."

"You shouldn't let that lack of interest deter you. It is the atmosphere you go for, the camaraderie, drama and passion. It's all there. But I can promise you one thing. After a day at the races, you would at least have some respect for the speed and bravery of the horses. Of course, the real kings at any race day are the trainers. Everything revolves around them. Next year you must come along with me."

"I hope that's not a bribe, Mr Farley," Peter replied.

Mark gave the other two photographs a quick glance. "What's the connection between them? I don't see one," Mark said, before carefully removing his reading glasses and returning them to their case.

"The caravans were parked quite a distance from the house, Mr Farley. Not a lot of security for the girls staying in them. Was there any reason for that?" Peter asked.

"Never thought of it like that... It gave them and us some privacy. We always considered it a safe area. And there were normally at least four grooms. They wouldn't be sleeping alone."

"Would the girls be using them in May?"

"Very possibly back then, depending on the weather, as God said to Noah. As time moved on, we changed to mostly employing local girls, so there was no further need for the caravans."

Kim walked in with a tray displaying white bone china. She set the tray on the table, avoiding eye contact. "I'll leave you to pour your own, if you don't mind. There's a choice of tea or coffee in the pots."

"We were just asking about the groom's caravans," Peter said. "They were a long way from the house. Did you ever worry about the safety of the girls?"

"It was a safer world back then plus the yard was securely locked at night," Mark said.

"Some would beg to differ," Peter replied dryly.

"Can I leave you to it?" Kim asked, as she edged towards the door.

"You can stay if you like," Peter replied, before Mark had the chance to interrupt. "How did you feel towards the girls working for you?"

Kim sat down stiffly in the easy chair to the side of Mark. "Motherly, I guess. Mostly they were nice girls. I told you before they varied in their ability and attitude."

Peter couldn't see this uptight woman as motherly by any stretch of the imagination. "Roughly what age were they?"

"It varied. Occasionally they would be as young as sixteen, but not often. There were also girls in their twenties. We tried to keep a balance and create a friendly family atmosphere," Kim replied.

Peter was distracted by Mark looking very closely at the picture of Graham and himself and asked, "Do you do a lot of shooting?"

"I used to. Not a terribly good shot now the eyesight is failing with age...You quickly forget how young they once were."

Kim stretched from her chair to take the photograph from her husband.

"Graham said you gave him the gun because you said he'd come of age," Peter said. "Was there any particular reason to say that?"

"Nothing springs to mind. I guess it just seemed the right thing to do at the time," Mark replied, in his soft melodic voice, dripping with charm.

"Do you remember why the caravans were gutted that summer?"

"Which summer?" Mark asked.

"The summer that photograph was taken."

After a long pause, Mark said, "I guess they were in need of a refit. The girl's expectations started to rise. That's why we gradually changed to employing local girls who went home every night."

"Could you tell us where you were last night?"

"Yes, of course. We went out for a meal at The Trout Inn, over at Sudbury. Have you heard of it? They really do excellent food."

"Did you enjoy your meal, Mrs Farley?"

"Yes. Why do you ask?"

"Mr Codrington was involved in a nasty accident last night. I'm surprised Graham hasn't told you."

"Frank!" exclaimed Kim, her hand melodramatically going to her throat. "Is he all right?"

"Hopefully, he'll be fine," Peter said.

"Sorry dear. Graham did tell me a short while ago. I haven't had the chance to tell you." Returning his attention to Peter, Mark asked, "Do you know which ward he's in? We'd like to send him our regards."

"Not sure, you'll have to check. There's one other thing I'd like to ask."

"Ask away."

"Were any of your relationships with the young grooms inappropriate?"

Mark registered a feigned look of hurt and surprise on his face, before Kim said, "You don't want to listen to nasty village gossip. Nothing of the sort went on...Just idle tittle-tattle from people with nothing better to think about."

"Mr Farley?" Peter prompted.

"That's a totally preposterous allegation. Quite categorically, no is the answer." Mark rose from his chair. "I had decided to give you the benefit of the doubt after your last visit. But this is really too much. I will now be making a formal complaint."

Peter maintained his position in the chair. "I'm sorry you feel the need to take such action, but these questions have to be asked."

"But do I have to answer without a solicitor present?"

"Do you think that is necessary, Mr Farley?"

"From the tone of your voice, I think that very well may be the case," Mark said.

Kim interrupted, "My husband is a wealthy and successful businessman, which inevitably leads to petty jealousy and resentment from those less successful. He has every right to feel offended by your comments. He has given you his answer, and now I think you should leave."

Peter slowly stood. "Mrs Farley, Mr Farley. Please be aware we may have to speak to you again."

"That's fine, but we will have a solicitor present in the future," Kim said haughtily, before seeing them out in silence.

Peter had felt his phone vibrate twice during the interview. Outside when he checked, there was a missed call from Amelia and one from the station. "I just need to make a few calls," he said, throwing the car keys to Fiona.

Amelia had left a voicemail saying she'd gotten a new job. She wasn't answering so he left a message of his own. "Congratulations. I look forward to seeing you tonight."

When he called the station, PC Bains told him they'd just received a call saying Mr Conley was in the gully field at Rooksbridge by the fallen tree.

"We're not far away. We'll head that way now to see if he's still there," Peter said.

TWENTY-NINE

Driving down the lane to the village they saw David Conley's white 4 x 4 parked diagonally across the gateway entrance. Peter parked close against the hedge to avoid blocking the narrow lane, but then had to battle through the brambles to escape the car. Over the padlocked gate, they could see David sitting on the trunk of the fallen tree. "Would you mind waiting here, Fiona?" Peter said.

David did not look up until Peter was a few yards away. He was drinking from a can of beer, with several empties scattered on the ground near him. His three faithful companions, the terrier and two black Labradors, lay in the long grass nearby.

"Hi. You shouldn't be here," Peter called, as he approached.

David held out his arms, wrists together. "Well, arrest me," he said, his voice slightly slurred.

Peter sat down on the tree trunk beside him. "Why are you here?"

David smiled to himself and took a slug from the can. After a short while, he said, "Not that it really matters. Most people think I'm mad anyway."

"Why do you say that?" Peter asked, locking eyes briefly with David, willing him to say more.

David pulled the tab on a fresh can of beer and stared out into the far distance. Peter hoped David knew something about how Jennifer Turner ended up under where they sat. During the silence, he strained inwardly to convey the impression he had all day to listen, pushing away all the annoying thoughts telling him he really didn't. After a while, it seemed to work.

"With the disaster that is...was my family," David started to say, then stopped. He sighed and said, "Sometimes I like to play up to them, you know. Do and say erratic things just to sustain their warped gossip-filled minds."

"We all like to play games at times," Peter said.

"You know what they say. Like father, like son... Who told you I was here, anyway? Was it that spineless Graham by any chance, or that weasel tenant of mine, Derek?"

"Call was taken at the station. I've no idea who it was."

"You know, I'm surprised Graham hasn't already chopped up this tree to sell it as souvenirs. He's sick enough to try and make some money out of the situation."

"Would like-father, like-son, apply to the Farleys?" Peter asked.

David thought for a while, taking another long drink from his can. "Mark was ruthless. He could make a slick buck out of anything, that one. But he was more entertaining company than Graham. When he tries to copy his father, it all goes wrong. Hasn't got the gift his father has."

"Did you know Mark well when he lived here?"

"Saw a bit of him. As neighbouring farmers, it would be odd if I didn't. But he had a wide circle of friends. Male and female. It all seems so much simpler when you're younger, doesn't it?"

"I guess," Peter said. "Do you see much of Graham and his wife socially?"

David laughed and took a long drink from his can. "You can't put those two and the word, social, in the same sentence. Instead of going out, Graham power-hoses and polishes his tractor. God knows what Gillian does of an evening. And people think I'm crazy." David paused to open another can of beer. "My parents were very sociable and active. Always parties at the house, trips out, hunt meets and shoots. There was always something going on to keep us occupied. Me and Christina used to...But that was before."

"Christina?" Peter queried.

David gave a deep and heavy sigh. "My sister. She was sectioned a long time ago...It was all a long time ago."

"I'm sorry."

"We had to grow a pretty thick skin overnight. I guess she just couldn't cope. The house used to be full of laughter. Now it's...I don't know what it's full of," David said.

After a brief silence, Peter said, "Is there anything more you can tell me about the day in 2001, when you all went to Cheltenham?"

David shook his head. "I probably should be getting going now."

"Why did you come here?"

"You know, I really have no idea."

"Was it something you remembered?" Peter asked. "The long-term memory can be funny sometimes. Maybe something has jogged your memory? Something from around the time the girl went missing that wouldn't have seemed relevant before?"

"No, I'm sorry to disappoint you." David stood and collected up the empty cans before heading back across the field. Over his shoulder, he said, "It could just be I was thinking about how events on this farm, have a bad habit of affecting my life."

They walked back to their cars in silence. David shooed his dogs into his vehicle. Before getting in himself, he said, "Are you sure you can't tell me who reported me being here?"

Peter shook his head in response.

"Was it that Gillian?" David asked. "That woman has the ability to be complex and yet totally uninteresting. That's quite an amazing feat, really, when you think about it."

Peter stood holding the driver door. "Are you going home now, David?"

"Why, are you planning on following me? Or maybe you should arrest me for drunk driving."

"To be honest, I probably should. Are you going straight home?"

David gave a broad grin, his small eyes disappearing behind his glasses. "Yes, I promise, officer, straight home."

Peter watched David pull away to drive back to his lonely farmhouse. He thought his comment on Mrs Farley was an interesting insight, as he fought through the brambles to get back into his own car.

"Did you find out anything useful?" Fiona asked, once he was seated.

"No, not really. It does make you think, though, when you meet someone like him. Human nature is a fascinating thing at times.

"Is everything okay?"

"Yes, of course, it is. It's nothing," Peter said, starting the car engine.

"I wonder why he never moved away. He could have started a new life anywhere."

"I guess this area is his home. All he's really known."

"I wouldn't have stayed. Would you, if you were him?" Fiona asked.

"Probably not."

"Well, I think it's weird."

"Maybe it is, but it's not something I want to dwell on. I thought we'd head out to the hospital. See how Frank is doing?"

THIRTY

They were told on arrival at the hospital that Frank remained unconscious and he had a friend in with him. Peter poked his head around the door and, as he'd expected, it was Joyce. "Hello again, how is he?"

Joyce came bustling out of the room and into the corridor, bursting with frustration and anger. She'd firmly closed the door behind her, and said, "My friend is seriously ill in hospital. I personally believe as a direct result of your actions. And you have the nerve to ask me how he is?"

Fiona tried to calm Joyce as Peter watched with his hands in his pockets. He'd never understood women. After a short while, Joyce burst into tears. Fiona sat her down on a chair in the hallway and comforted her. Peter remained standing, looking on helplessly. Joyce looked like a semi-deflated balloon as she took the tissues from Fiona and dried her face.

"We just wanted to know how he was," Fiona said.

"I know."

"We need to find out what happened... I know this is a difficult time, but we do need to speak to Frank."

"He's asleep so you can't. I'm not having you two in there disturbing him. Couldn't you come back later when he's awake and feeling more like himself?"

"We could if you tell us a little about Frank. I mean before..."

"Maggie and Frank, they were a lovely couple," Joyce stated, firmly. "It was so incredibly sad when she died. Frank was a terrible mess, I admit. He's never been quite the same since. His drive and ambition disappeared overnight. But I really don't think he had anything to do with that girl." She sniffed into the tissue before continuing more sternly. "And I tell you, Maggie's death was what knocked him back, but it was that bloody Farley family that kept him down."

Fiona took the opportunity to ask, "What was his relationship with Mark, like?"

Joyce's anger and bitterness came to the fore. "It's not a relationship. A relationship suggests some equality and understanding. Everything was terribly one-sided. Frank gave and gave while Mark just took. That man is a terrible bully. He uses his charm and wealth to manipulate and destroy people. And the temper he has! Well! Always determined to get his own way and he usually does."

"Would Frank lie to protect Mark for some reason?" Fiona asked.

"He's incredibly loyal to him and in some situations yes. But covering up the death of a young girl? That I'm not so sure about."

"How about Graham?" Peter asked.

"What about Graham?" Joyce replied, her fierce eyes turned to Peter.

"What was he like when he was younger?" Fiona asked.

Joyce softened and replied, "I used to think, 'Poor Graham.' I don't anymore. When he was a child, Mark treated him harshly. He worked him hard on the farm like a grown man and sent him off to some private school once they made a bit of money. Waste of time as Graham wasn't a bright child. He still struggles to read and needs to ask Gillian to read things for him. Mark used to push him around all the time. Humiliate him for his stupidity. Behind Graham's back, he told everyone he gave him the farm because he was incapable of doing anything else."

"Didn't Kim stand up for her son?" Fiona asked.

"Her? She's as cold as a fish that one. She didn't care, as long as she had status and money. She detests Gillian. I know she's a difficult woman to get along with at times, but the things Kim has said about her…"

Peter listened quietly to Joyce. He didn't think her analysis excused Graham's behaviour, but it explained a lot. As an adult, he shouldn't still be behaving like a bully and a little boy whose toys had been broken.

"Have you ever met any of Mark's family? I mean his parents or brothers and sisters?" Fiona asked, looking up at Peter for direction.

"Nobody knows anything about Mark's past. He simply arrived one day in the area. To the best of my knowledge, he has never spoken of his parents, or whether he has any brothers or sisters. It was like he had no past or family. Even Frank doesn't know anything more about his past," Joyce said.

"Is anything known about Kim's past?"

"Kim, oh yes. She's from a well-to-do family. She has always had everything easy."

"What was the relationship like between Graham and Gillian before their problems with having children?" Fiona asked.

"What have you heard about all of that?"

"Nothing really, other than there was a problem," Fiona quickly replied.

"Things weren't much different, to tell you the truth. Except Gillian had a little more fight then. He's worn her down. He likes to play the martyr, of course. But a lot of it is his fault. I have a phrase I use to describe that whole family."

"Go on."

"Emotional vampires because they suck everybody dry."

"Is there anything else you can tell us about how things were back then? Maybe something you'd forgotten about or something that didn't seem important at the time? Or something Frank has said recently?" Peter asked.

"No. I wish there was," Joyce replied, shaking her head. "There is one thing I should mention. Rumour has it, there's a young man hanging around outside Frank's house. I've not seen him, but I've been told he's been there the last couple of days."

"What does he look like?" said Peter.

"I've been told he's tall and handsome with dark curly hair. He's not from around here."

"Do you know who has seen him?"

"Sorry. It's just something I heard about."

"Thanks, Joyce. If you do see him could you ring us?"

Joyce nodded.

"We really do hope Frank is on the mend soon."

"Thank you. I do think you genuinely mean that," Joyce said, blowing her nose.

"There is one more thing, before we go," Peter said. "When I arrived, you blamed me for Frank's accident. What did you mean by that?"

"I don't know, really."

"You must have meant something by it," Peter persisted.

"Just that he must have been very upset about you taking him in for questioning like you did. Thinking that he was a murderer. Maybe somebody in the pub said something to him, so he wasn't thinking straight when he drove home."

"And that's all?"

"Yes, that as a result he may have drunk a bit too much and that's why he crashed. But I'm sure you've checked for alcohol and all that."

"Thanks again for your help, Joyce, and give my regards to Frank when he comes around." Peter added, "Tell him we will be returning later to speak to him."

Once they were out of earshot, Fiona said, "The guy she described hanging around outside the house sounds an awful lot like Richard Turner."

"Do you think the accident could have been a revenge thing? You thought he was a bit over-emotional when you met him?"

Fiona thought back to when she'd met Richard at the station. "He said events had affected his family. He said they were all very close, but it's a big step to go from that to trying to kill someone."

They discussed the possibility of Richard Turner having something to do with Frank's accident most of the journey back to the station. Peter conceded it was something to consider, but for now, he wanted to concentrate on the Farley family. They agreed to question Richard at Rooksbridge first thing in the morning before visiting The Trout Inn to check Mark's alibi for the night of the accident.

Peter dropped Fiona back at the station and headed back towards Birkbury. He'd decided to pop into The Star Inn on his way home to see if the landlord could give some indication of how Frank had been received.

The Star was a typical village drinking pub, one that had not received the attention The Bull had. The landlord, Phil Morris, was working behind the bar which was frequented by a select few. He gave the impression of a genuine bloke who probably grafted seven days a week to make a living of sorts from the pub. Once Peter introduced himself, Phil called his wife to take over behind the bar.

Settled in a quiet corner of the bar, Phil said, "Your officers were here earlier checking the car park. How can I help you?"

"I'm trying to establish Frank's state of mind when he left here last night. I wondered if you could tell me how he seemed," Peter asked.

"When he left here, he was fine. Has there been any news from the hospital?"

"No change, as far as we're aware. Did everything seem okay when Frank came in last night?"

"Frank is very well liked around here, and no one thinks he could be responsible for murdering that poor girl."

"So, the night passed without incident?"

"It was a little uncomfortable when Frank first came in. You know, the hushed silence with nobody knowing what to say. The awkward moment passed when John Edgar bought Frank a drink and that seemed to break the tension. Following that, as far as I'm aware, there was no problem."

"And Frank seemed happy?" Peter asked.

"Yes. Everyone was very supportive. He seemed relaxed and

happy."

"Could I ask how much he had to drink?"

Phil laughed and replied in a mock official voice, "I can't do that. I've signed the landlords' pledge."

"I'm not interested in whether he was technically over the limit to drive. I just need to know his state of mind and ability to drive when he left."

"I couldn't sign a statement saying he was on orange and lemonade, but he was not inebriated when he left. I would say his state of mind was good and he'd not drunk enough to impair his driving abilities. Is that good enough for you?"

Peter knew that was the best he could ask for. "Yes, thank you. And there was no hostility towards him at all?"

"There was none from what I saw. I understand he'd spoken to Mark Farley earlier in the evening and there was total support there as well."

"Do you have any idea what was said?"

"No, sorry. I don't know any details."

"Thanks for your time."

❖ ❖ ❖

His blood was boiling, bubbling through his veins. He had taken his medication and tried the relaxation techniques he had been taught. None of it was helping.

He could hear and feel his blood racing through his body and pumping his heartbeat. His skin tingled with irritations and his hands clenched and unclenched involuntarily. Thoughts rushed in and out of his brain too quickly for him to hold onto them. He was incapable of staying still. He sat down, stood up, laid down, sat up, stood up and walked around. Every sense felt like it was on fire. He needed something to calm him, but he was out in the middle of nowhere. He picked up a fresh whisky bottle but discarded it again. He couldn't stay here alone, thinking about Jenny. He would go crazy, start bouncing off the walls.

THIRTY-ONE

"Weather's gone crazy," Peter said, as he came through the door. Water from his hair was running down his face and dripping from his nose. His short-sleeved shirt stuck to him from the drenching he'd just received. "It was like someone just threw a bucket of water over me halfway across the car park."

"You don't say," Fiona said. "Five minutes ago, the rain was so heavy it was coming in halfway across the room. We had to shut the windows. Temperature's not dropped at all though."

"I don't think I've ever seen such heavy rain."

"The car park is flooded," Fiona said, as she pushed the window open. "But it's stopped raining."

Pulling his wet shirt from his body, Peter looked at the note on his desk. "They still haven't traced the girl who was with Jennifer at the Race Festival. She'd be the one person who could possibly identify the men who chatted them up."

"Nearly twenty years later?"

"You never know. By the way, any idea who rang in about David Conley yesterday?"

"Yes. I was going to tell you. Derek Alley. And I've done a bit of digging about his past. His last paid employment was as a drama teacher in a private school in Cornwall. He left mid-term due to personality clashes. I'm trying to speak to the headmaster at the time."

"Good work. Keep me updated on that," Peter said.

"Thank you. You seem in a good mood today."

"Credit where credit's due."

PC Baines popped her head around the door, catching the end of their conversation. "Sorry, sir. Just to warn you Superintendent Rogers is looking for you. And I don't think he's best pleased."

"Thanks." He turned to Fiona. "I'm guessing Mark Farley kept his promise. Let's get over to Rooksbridge before Rogers knows I'm here."

Fiona was preparing to leave when the smartly suited Rogers arrived. He was a charismatic man who took on the role of authority with ease, commanding everyone's attention as soon as he entered the room. The type bound to rise rapidly ever upwards unless any skeletons fell out of his closet. His voice was calm and measured, but it was a voice that demanded to be obeyed. "Peter, could we have a word in my office, now?"

Peter asked Fiona to carry on pressing the headmaster while she waited for his return. But as he passed her, he quietly said, "Try and get something on Mark Farley for me."

The conversation with Rogers was exactly what Peter had expected. He could have pre-written the script and saved them both half an hour. The message was simple—leave Mark Farley alone unless you have strong evidence he knew anything about the murdered girl. And even then, all further approaches were to be cleared by Rogers. The one-way conversation left Peter sour and more determined to take a closer look at Mark Farley. He'd had to bite hard down on his lip to stop himself from asking how the golf had gone.

When he returned, Fiona was finishing her call. She replaced the receiver and asked, "How did it go?"

Peter shrugged.

"This will cheer you up," Fiona said. "We may have something on Derek Alley. I've spoken briefly to the retired headmaster. The dismissal was connected to a student complaint. He wants to speak with the present governing body of the school before providing any details."

Peter groaned. "That means we'll get diddly-squat. If they

covered it up at the time, they're not going to want to tell us anything now. Never mind, let's get out to..."

They were prevented again from leaving by PC Rachel Mann. "Sorry to interrupt again, sir, but there's a woman downstairs causing a scene. She looked down at her pad before adding, "She's called Mrs Elizabeth Tinney."

Peter repeated "Elizabeth Tinney?" before remembering the name.

Rachel looked uncomfortable as she rocked from foot to foot. "You saw her father, Henry Tinney a few days ago?"

"Yes, I remember now."

Rachel continued awkwardly. "She wanted to speak to Rogers to make a complaint about you. I've persuaded her to talk to you first."

"Thank you, Rachel. Put her in an interview room. I'll be down in a minute." Peter turned to Fiona and said, "Could you chase up whether Cathy Potter did find those photographs for us and find..."

Fiona finished for him. "Find something on Mark Farley."

When Peter returned, Fiona asked, "How did it go?"

"Luckily she hates Mark Farley. If we can find a reason to charge him, she'll be happy to forget about her complaint. Found anything yet?"

"Not yet," Fiona replied.

"Come on, let's get out of here."

As they walked down to the car, Peter said, "We'll probably give a visit to Mark Farley's place a miss today. Instead, we'll see Pauline at the holiday centre after talking to Richard Turner. See what she has to say about his treatment of the girls working for him."

"But haven't we been told to leave him alone completely?" asked Fiona.

"We need to ask Pauline about the stranger seen outside Frank's house. It could be their guest, Richard Turner. If the conversation moves to Mark Farley, we'll have to go with the flow."

"That's fine, I guess," Fiona said, hesitantly.

"I need to buy a new shirt on the way," Peter added, pulling at his soaked shirt.

In the car, Fiona asked, "How are we going to approach Richard? I mean about him being seen outside Frank's house. I assume that's why we're heading over to Rooksbridge. It's not just to upset the Farley family."

"Quite straightforward," replied Peter. "A quick chat about the offence of stalking and then we ask to see the rear of his car. What we do next will depend on his reaction and the state of the car."

They fell silent throughout the rest of the journey. Peter's new shirt felt uncomfortable around the arms, and he was aware of the deep crease marks from how it had been folded in the packet. The sun was blazing down on them, but he had to concentrate on the road to avoid the flooding from the earlier heavy downpour. He enjoyed the silence. It gave him time to think.

He'd had a long, late-night telephone conversation with Sally. They'd talked through some of their problems, but the barrier between them remained. Sally said she was staying with her parents for a couple more days and he hadn't mentioned Amelia had returned. Both women were important to him. Something had to give so bridges could be rebuilt, but he figured he had a couple of days to work out what that something was.

THIRTY-TWO

Peter drove past the main farm entrance and pulled into the private driveway to the holiday centre. "I'm going nowhere near the family, does that make you happier?"

Fiona had thought she'd kept her growing concern about upsetting the Farley family hidden. "It's fine. I haven't been able to contact Richard by telephone. We'll just have to hope he is in."

Fiona hurried out of the car and up to the cottage. She rechecked the number on the cottage and knocked loudly on the door as Peter joined her. They waited a short time before wandering round to the side of the building. No amount of peering through the windows could alter the fact that Richard was not there. There was also an empty space in his allocated spot in the car park.

"It looks like it was a wasted journey out here," Fiona said.

"I don't think so," Peter replied, spotting Pauline outside the reception chalet sitting on the steps having a cigarette.

As they approached, she said, "Awful habit, I know. I thought I'd given them up for good. I don't believe I'm smoking again."

Peter said, "I don't suppose you noticed what time the young man from cottage number four left this morning, did you?"

"Sorry. No idea." Pauline put out her cigarette and brightened a little. "Why don't you come inside for a cup of tea?"

They followed her into the wooden cabin and sat around the same low table as before.

"How come you started smoking again?" Fiona asked.

"Just the way things have been around here the last couple of days. I shouldn't really let it get to me. I'll give up again once things settle back down. How is Frank, by the way?"

"We haven't heard anything, so I'm guessing no change from yesterday," Fiona replied.

"How bad have things been here?" Peter asked.

"I'm probably overreacting, but everybody just seems so stressed. Without Frank, Graham is taking all his frustrations out on other people. Leaving me to field complaints and smooth things over. It's got to me a bit...And this heat doesn't help."

"Yes. I never thought I'd say it about a British summer, but this good weather has become quite monotonous," Peter replied.

Pauline looked out at the open view of the cottages and courtyard. "I love it here, you know, I always have. But recently I've seriously been thinking about quitting. I've had enough. Maybe I'm getting too old."

"Maybe you just need a break," Fiona suggested.

"That would go down really well. How could I take a break in the middle of the summer season with all this going on? I feel under so much pressure, trying to hold everything together for them."

"Well, by the sounds of it, you've been loyal to them for years. They owe you something in return. Have you told them how you feel?"

"No," Pauline replied. "That's not how it works here. The Farleys are so self-absorbed. They only see their problems. And heaven knows how I've listened and tried to help over the years. Now I feel too drained to be any use to anyone."

Pauline broke off to watch a young woman struggling outside one of the cottages with two small boys. She was trying unsuccessfully to elicit their help in loading the car with a picnic large enough to feed an army. She was left to struggle as the children scampered about the courtyard full of mischief. Pauline smiled sadly. "I do understand the longing to have a family and how disappointed Gillian is. But the stress they put themselves under running this place the way they do is ridiculous. They don't see the damage it's done to their health and relationship, but there's only so much understanding I can give, especially when they appear so oblivious to the upset it causes me...Oh dear! That's done it!"

They all looked towards the car park. One of the young boys had tipped over the massive picnic hamper. The mother had placed it on the bonnet of the car while she tried to round up her other son who was walking across the top of the courtyard stone walls. She was desperately trying to salvage the assortment of treats scattered over the grass. She called out, "Thomas, for goodness sake, come down off that wall and get in the car."

The three of them were going to help when they heard Graham approach. "What the hell is going on here?" he shouted angrily. "Get that awful child off my wall and get that mess cleaned up."

The woman became flustered and was trying to apologise while manhandling the other child into the rear of the car. "I'm so sorry."

"I've had enough of the way you think you can treat my property. When you've got both your brats in the car and that mess cleared up, I want you to go and pick up all the rubbish in the main car park."

"Sorry?" the woman said, looking astonished.

"You heard me. It's full of your rubbish scattered everywhere. I'm going to wait here until you've done it."

Fiona turned her shocked face to Peter. "Should we go out and say something?"

"No, don't do that," Pauline pleaded. "It would only make things worse. The poor woman, I've really had enough of his insanity now."

"I'm sorry, but I'm not standing by watching him behave like that," Peter said.

Fiona led Pauline back to the table as Peter disappeared to confront Graham. Fiona asked, "Does he always treat people like that? I mean, aren't they paying guests?"

"If the mood takes him...but just recently it's been like this all the time. I don't think I can cope any more. And then Gillian hears about it and cries for hours and hours."

"Do you think his behaviour is related to the body found on the farm?" Fiona asked.

"I really don't know anymore."

"You were their housekeeper before, weren't you? What was Graham like as a child? Did he have such a temper then?"

"Oh yes. He's always had that. Although he only showed it when his father wasn't around."

"Did he ever take his temper out on the girls? Physically, I mean."

Pauline thought for a long while. "No, I don't think so. He would verbally attack them. He seemed to enjoy making them cry. But physically harm them? He takes things out on the animals, same as his father. He kicked one of their dogs so hard he broke its ribs once. And I have known him lay into the horses for no good reason, many times."

"Was he into girls around the time of his early teens?"

"I think he probably was. He was a good-looking lad as I remember. Most of the young girls had a thing for him, and as he was big for his age, people often thought he was older. Being the boss's son always has its advantages."

They were interrupted by the woman coming into the reception followed by Peter. She had clearly been crying. "I'm sorry, Pauline. Just to let you know, we're going home later today. If you're not here, should I put the keys through the letterbox?"

"Yes. That'll be fine. I'm so sorry..."

"What sort of man is he? I can't believe he thought I should do that!"

"I'm so sorry," Pauline repeated. "I don't know what to say."

"Don't worry. It's not your fault," the woman replied, as she walked back out to her car.

Pauline rested her chin in her hands. "I'll give them one more day. If it doesn't get any better, that's it. I'm out of here."

"I'm not surprised," Peter said. "Tell me. You've known the family for a long time and seen them at close quarters. Has he always had such a bad temper?"

"We've just discussed it, and the answer is yes, I'm afraid."

"And Mark, his father, does he have the same temper?"

After a long pause, Pauline replied. "I'm sorry to say they both have bad tempers, but they are quite different."

"In what way are they different?"

"Mark tends to be more calculated and vindictive. Graham is more immediate."

"What about all the stories about Mark having an eye for younger girls?" Peter prompted.

Pauline sighed. "In the early days, there was some truth to that. Let's just say he has not been faithful throughout his marriage."

"And how about Graham, has he been faithful?"

"I wouldn't like to say for sure, probably not."

"Do you think either Mark or Graham were capable of murdering that young girl and burying her body on their farm?" Peter asked.

"Do you have any evidence it was them?" Pauline asked.

"I'm doing the asking. Do you think either of them capable?"

"In all honesty, I'm not sure. But I can tell you I have never known either of them to physically harm anyone. It tends to be more mental or emotional abuse," Pauline said.

"Thanks for that and the drink. We must be off. Could you call us when Richard Turner returns?"

"Yes, of course."

"And I don't suppose you know the type of car he has?"

"It's a little sporty thing. I can check the make and model for you now," Pauline said. She collected the empty cups and took them over to the reception desk where she started to look through the bookings diary.

"Have you noticed whether it's been damaged in any way. Been knocked from behind?" Peter asked.

"I haven't noticed any damage," Pauline said, as she passed over the car details on a slip of paper.

As they walked back to their own car, Peter said, "So do you still think we should be leaving the Farleys alone and investigating the grieving cousin?"

"We still need to see him and the rear of his car."

Peter glanced across at Fiona. "I thought you knew about cars. If Frank's Terrano had shunted Richard's MG, it would have gone into the river with him." Reversing out of the car space, Peter received a telephone call. "We're not far away. We'll get over there now."

Peter turned to Fiona. "Well, that's another one from the day out in Cheltenham gone missing."

"What do you mean?"

"David Conley has just disappeared," Peter replied.

THIRTY-THREE

Pulling into the small yard in front of Grange Farm, they were surprised to see a woman in the yard. Despite the deep frown she gave them, she was stunningly attractive, tall and elegant with the figure of a model. She looked immaculate in her riding gear pushing a wheelbarrow full of horse muck.

When Peter introduced them and asked who she was, her eyes acted like flamethrowers. Peter withered under the haughty glare of her annoyance at his very existence and instantly felt self-conscious about his creased shirt.

"I'm Hannah Conley. Lady of this pile of shit house."

Having demoralised them with her black look, Hannah took out her frustration on the horses' beds with her pitchfork. The horses rolled their eyes and pressed themselves against the back wall of their stables as far out of her way as possible.

"We understand, your husband, David has been reported missing?" Peter said.

Hannah replied gruffly, each statement punctuated by a stab of her pitchfork, "Why should I care where he is? I found his will. It said he was leaving everything to some guy called George Ball. I have no idea who he is before you waste my time asking."

Hannah hurled the wheelbarrow to one side and collected a saddle from another shed. It was thrown on to a stable door, causing the horse which had ventured forwards, to shoot to the back wall. From inside the stable, she continued, "In his absence, the farm is to be run by a management team. Where does that leave me?"

Peter risked approaching the stable door. "Do you have any idea at all of where he's gone?"

"How the hell should I know where he is? And before you ask, I have no idea when he'll be back. Go and ask lover boy George."

Peter gave Fiona a shrug. Fiona raised her eyebrows in mock amusement and tried. "Could we have a look around inside the house ourselves?"

Hannah threw a set of keys at her from her pocket. Fiona jumped back to avoid being hit by them. "Help yourself. Leave the keys under the mat when you're finished."

Leading the horse from the stable, Hannah said, "How come you got here so quick anyway? I didn't report the bastard missing." She didn't wait for any reply as she mounted her horse and spurred it straight into a trot, the metal shoes slipping on the concrete as it moved off. Turning the corner from the yard, she almost ran over an elderly man in work clothes. "Get out of my way, Fred," she shouted.

Fred was slight and fit looking with bandy legs. Only his white hair suggested his true age. For an old man, he moved very quickly to let Hannah pass. He watched her disappear along the lane before saying, "It was me who noticed David was missing. I've been working with him on the stone walls. I didn't worry at first when he didn't turn up this morning. But after a while, I thought I'd better come up and find where he'd got to. Hannah told me he'd gone. I don't trust her, so I rang you."

"And you are?" Peter asked.

"Fred. I work here on and off for David. Have done for years."

"How did he seem to you the last time you saw him?"

"David?" Fred scratched his head and made himself comfortable sitting on the stone mounting block. Peter couldn't help noticing the tufts of white hair protruding from his ears. "He seemed right pleased with himself of late. He's always played with his cards close to his chest. But I've had a feeling for a while the old goat has been up to something. He can't fool me. Been around these parts far too long, I have."

"And how long's that?" Peter asked.

"Too long to be bothered anymore by the queer goings-on round here...And don't you go worrying about that old witch on horseback," he said, jabbing his thumb in the direction of Hannah. "She can look after herself, that one."

"So, I've been hearing," Fiona said.

Peter looked at her quizzically before turning his attention back to Fred. "You thought David was up to something? Any idea what that was? Or where he might have gone?"

"None at all, I'm sorry to say. But I bet I know what you're thinking. You're thinking it's something to do with that dead girl at Rooksbridge."

Peter shrugged.

"Doubt it myself. He's been planning something for months. I think it's something else."

"What makes you say that?" asked Peter.

"Like I said, there was just something about him recently. Secretive like...I just had a feeling... He's not a bad bloke. Bit lonely at times. He likes to wind up the locals. Play up to their silly ideas about him." Fred pulled a packet of crushed cigarettes from his pocket. Lighting one, he inhaled deeply and continued, "He was treated pretty rough after the trouble his father caused. But he's nowhere near as crazy as he likes people to think. People think it was his idea to split the house in two. It wasn't, you know. It was the old witch."

"Really, it was Hannah who did it all with the tape?" Peter said.

"Yeah, and of course everyone immediately assumed it was him. He just chose not to correct them. As I said, he knew everyone thought he was crazy whatever he did anyway."

"Have you noticed anything else unusual recently other than he seemed a bit secretive?"

"Not really," Fred replied. "Nothing that would make him up and leave without warning."

"When you were working together, did he say anything about the body being found?"

"Normal gossip, nothing special. But here's a funny thing. A young man stopped by the other day. Not a local lad. They went off together, chatting like. Thing is, he looked the spit of the girl that was buried up at Rooksbridge. Except he was a lad."

"Can you give a clearer description?"

"Like I said, he looked like the girl on TV."

Peter and Fiona had a quick look inside the house. It was silent and still save the odd creaky floorboard. There was nothing noticeably out of place. The kitchen seemed a little darker and sadder without the presence of David and his three dogs. They took the solicitor's details from the will, thrown carelessly on the table.

"Do you think Richard Turner looked that much like his cousin?" Peter asked.

"Quite a bit, yes. You saw him as well. With Rose? Should we check upstairs?"

"We probably should have a quick look."

Walking back to the car, Fiona said, "So what do you think?"

"I think this village is driving me nuts. Remind me when I'm older to retire to the seaside. In a town."

"Maybe there's something in the water?"

They drove to the solicitor who'd handled the will. The family solicitor confirmed he was asked to draw up the new will in favour of a George Ball, but he had no idea what David was up to. George Ball was a surveyor living a few miles south of Birstall. As far as the firm was aware, he'd had no previous involvement in the farm or with David.

Still unable to get hold of Richard Turner by phone, Peter made the decision to visit George Ball and deal with Richard after.

In the car, Peter asked, "What was that all about Hannah Conley, by the way? What was it you had heard?"

"That's what I was on the phone about first thing this morning. When we did the initial cross reference, Hannah Conley's name came up. It didn't seem that relevant to the case at the time. But as I recognised one of the officers on the vice squad, I decided to give him a ring."

"The vice squad, who exactly is she?"

"I'm not sure how involved she was, but her second husband is under surveillance by them."

"Second? Maybe you should have told me earlier."

"Sorry. It didn't seem important at the time."

"So, David is her third husband?"

Fiona blushed and said as apologetically as possible, "Fourth."

Peter thumped the steering wheel and said, "Tell me now what you know."

"The first husband, a wealthy farmer, died in a car accident very shortly after they married, leaving her pretty much set up for life."

"I'm getting a little concerned about all these car accidents." Peter glanced across at her. "What happened to the other two?"

"The second husband is the one under surveillance. He supports a lavish lifestyle from organised crime. The third husband owned an accountancy business in Southampton. Let's just say Hannah has done pretty well financially from her failed marriages."

"So not exactly the innocent, mistreated wife."

"I guess not. But I was surprised she set up the strange living arrangement and not David. Dividing everything up with tape is just plain weird, in my book."

"Could be he refused her divorce terms," Peter said.

"It's equally odd he put up with it."

He was falling, falling, forever falling, falling downwards through branches of trees that didn't hold him. They gave way, letting him slip through. He tried to grab onto something solid, but each time his hand came away full of leaves. The dried-out leaves mocked him. In his head he was screaming, "please catch me." But no sound would come out.

He couldn't call out because his lips had been sewn together roughly, with large stitches of thick, coarse black cotton, by the bogeyman. The bogeyman who had stolen Jenny had come back for him and sewn his lips together forever. Only inside his head could he scream, but no one could hear him. While he was screaming in his head, people smiled and waved and pass on by.

All his irrational fears returned. The dark was closing in on him. He didn't think his medication would get him through this one. Once the thoughts started to come and swirl about in his head, he couldn't stop them.

Once she was laid to rest properly, he would have no further purpose. Maybe he could accidentally take a few too many pills and let himself slip away to join her. No one would miss him. He had never allowed himself to get close enough to anyone in case they got snatched away in the night.

Everyone was interchangeable. Easy to replace. Who would ever grieve for him? He had made sure. He never needed anyone. He could provide everything he needed or would ever need for himself. All he had to do was dig deeper.

He certainly didn't need her.

THIRTY-FOUR

Fiona checked again whether David had been found as they pulled up in front of the house belonging to George Ball. The house was a large, modern, detached property. Peter tripped over the scattered children's toys abandoned in the garden as they walked up the path. They were met at the door by Helen Ball, a pretty girl with open features not wearing any make-up. She looked harassed and anxious with a baby in her arms and a toddler fiercely holding onto her legs.

They were invited into the conservatory with fantastic views over the river. It was decorated with wicker furniture and an abundance of large potted plants. A combination of the tiled floor, a blind blocking out direct sunlight, and a huge overhead fan kept the temperature bearable. "George will be down in a minute. He's just getting changed," Helen said, as she jiggled the contented baby on her hip while pushing various toys on the floor out of the way with her foot. "Can I get you a coffee or anything?"

"If it's not too much trouble, a cold drink would be good," Peter replied.

"The same for me, please," Fiona added.

"Orange squash?"

Helen took the children out with her to make the drinks. Peter smiled as he heard her bribing the toddler to stay in the living room with the promise of their favourite films and chocolate biscuits followed by a bedtime story later.

Peter and Fiona stood admiring the view. A good-looking, athletic guy dressed neatly in a blue short-sleeved shirt, open at the collar joined them. Peter guessed him to be about his mid-thirties.

George held out his hand and said, "We are as bemused by this as anyone. We really weren't expecting anything like this...but do sit down."

Helen came back in with the drinks and said she was just going to put the baby down to sleep, but would they mind if she returned and listened.

George quickly explained he was from a very close family who lived nearby but his parents had always been honest about his adoption. He had been given the option several times previously but had no interest himself in contacting his birth parents. "We were very apprehensive when we were told that an uncle was trying to contact me. We talked about it and took our time before agreeing to meet. We met him at the adoption offices. Over time, we got to like David. He was almost childlike in his wish for us to like him. We were on the verge of inviting him to meet the children. The solicitor's letter was totally out of the blue, and we don't know what to make of it."

Peter was surprised at the connection, but doubted it was relevant to finding who murdered Jenny Turner. "Do you have the letter here?"

"No, it's with our solicitor."

Fiona put down her empty glass and asked, "Could you tell us roughly what the letter said?"

Helen, who had just joined them, laughed. "He's read it so many times he probably knows it word for word," she said, sitting down on the floor.

George gave a look of mock crossness at his wife and admitted, "Yes, I probably can. It said he had no other family and so he had amended his will to make me the main beneficiary. Everything would pass to me, but with the condition, all the financial needs of a Mrs Christina Conley would be met by the estate. I believe that is my mother. The estimated estate value was £3.5 million.

We are still in shock."

Peter wished that was the sort of shock he could receive.

Fiona asked, "Did you get back in contact?" She regretted it straightaway as she could tell George did not like the under-lying implication that the sum of money involved may have changed his point of view.

George replied curtly, "No, I've already told you. We passed the letter on to our solicitors. We really don't know what to do or say about it."

Peter was struggling to see any connection to Jenny Turner. This all predated the discovery of the body by months. Possibly it was something David had been planning for years.

George seemed to read his mind. "You haven't really explained why you are here. Is it some type of fraud? We haven't actually received anything from him."

"No, no. Sorry. I thought I had explained on the phone. We are investigating the matter at Birkbury. You may have seen the press coverage."

"God yes, the missing girl. You don't think...?"

"Your uncle lived in the village and has disappeared. We got your details from his solicitor. We were hoping for some sort of a connection. Did he say anything to you about going away?"

"Sorry, as I said we haven't seen him recently."

"Thanks for your time," Peter said, rising from the chair and handing George a card. "Could you contact us if you do hear any-thing from him?"

Escorting them to the door, George said, "For my own peace of mind...could you tell me whether David is a serious suspect in your investigations? That he's capable of killing?"

Peter slowly turned back towards him, thinking of how best to reply. "Off the record, I quite like your uncle. And no, he is not our main suspect. Does that help?"

"Yes, thank you," George replied, as he closed the door.

It was threatening to rain again when they left. The gathering storm clouds gave a brief respite by blocking out the glare of the hot sun, but the closeness of the heat remained draining.

"What do you think?" Fiona asked.

"I think David is very probably hiding from his wife. And from what you've discovered about her previous husbands, it's not a bad idea."

"I can see why he might want to avoid her for a while."

"It's getting late. How about we head over to The Trout Inn for something to eat?" Peter suggested. "We should be able to get there before they stop serving food."

"Fine by me, I'm feeling a little hungry."

"We can check the alibi Mark Farley gave us and then we'll go and see if Richard Turner has returned. Find out why he's been seen hanging around Frank's home and talking to David. I'd be very interested to know what he chatted to David about."

"It could be totally unrelated. As a private investigator, he may have come across Hannah before. He could have been asked by a potential husband to take a closer look at her."

"You have a very active imagination," Peter said, smiling. "There's nothing to suggest David's disappearance had anything to do with Richard Turner or our investigation, but we need to keep an open mind until we know he is safe and well. As he was with the group in the photograph, he is still a potential witness."

The Trout Inn was located at the end of a narrow winding lane. It was a long building, originally being a row three of terraced cottages overlooking the river.

The porch was blocked by the rapid stacking of oversized umbrellas from the garden following another heavy downpour of rain. A young man started to hastily remove them as they arrived. He apologised profusely for them blocking the entrance.

The interior was full of the sound of chatter and clinking of cutlery, and the low ceiling bar was cosy and welcoming. The food being carried out looked mouth-wateringly tasty. Peter felt his stomach somersault as a tantalising smell wafted in the trail of the plates being carried past them.

The bar manager recognised the picture of Mark and Kim Farley straightaway. "They'd be hard to forget. The man made a terrible scene about his meal being cold. Made sure everyone in the building heard his complaint."

Peter smiled wryly.

The bar manager continued, "It was particularly annoying because there was nothing wrong with it. Everyone agreed it was piping hot. It was reheated briefly and sent back out. As far as I'm aware, it was eaten without complaint."

"How sure are you this was the night before yesterday?"

"Positive. It was my girlfriend's birthday, and she was not happy about me working."

"And are you able to confirm the time?"

"Not sure exactly when it was. We're always busy with food on an evening. Most tables do three covers a night. A lot of people are in and out quite quickly. It wasn't that late, though, as far as I can remember."

A customer wearing a suit sat at the bar nursing a pint. He asked, "Can I have a look?" After a brief study of the picture he said, "Yes, I remember him and all the fuss he made. The wife, if that's who she was, looked mortified by the whole thing. And he made some racist comment to me about the music playing."

"Did you notice what time they left?" Peter asked.

"Yep. Is he in some sort of trouble?"

"I can't say."

"Well, I can tell you the exact time they left. They pulled out of the car park at nine-twenty. They left in separate cars. That's why I assumed they weren't married. They argued briefly in the car park about the incident just before getting into their cars. He seemed quite keen to get away. I assumed he had a wife at home waiting."

"How come you were outside?" Peter asked.

"I was outside having a smoke."

"And you're sure of the time?"

"I'm definite on the time. I didn't want to make it look like I was eavesdropping, so I pretended to be studying my phone. It's got the time on the screen."

Peter was pleased to have some good news at last. It would be tight, but Mark would have had plenty of time to get back and stage Frank's accident. "Well, thank you very much for that."

As they took their seats in a small alcove, Peter said, "Mark Farley had nearly an hour and a half between leaving the pub and Frank's accident. That would give him plenty of time to meet up with Frank."

"But nobody saw him in The Star," Fiona pointed out.

"He could have met him outside, or he could have waited somewhere along the lane for him to show up."

"Are we going to head over there after we've eaten?" Fiona said, with a worried look on her face.

"No. Don't worry. I'm not going out of my way to cause trouble. I'd like to look a little closer into his alibi for the day the girl disappeared first. This horse passport thing? Can the recorded date be a hundred per cent relied upon? It's possible, of course, Kim could be lying for him, and they weren't present when the foal was born or at any celebratory meal."

"You're thinking he meets the girl on the day of their anniversary. He brings her back here and then what? Something goes wrong. He panics and buries her on his own land?"

"That's about it."

"And you think his wife would be prepared to lie for him about that? I'd be furious," Fiona said.

"That's what I'm suggesting. The question is, how do we prove it?"

"Do you really think it was him?"

Peter leaned back in his chair, running things through in his mind. "Everything seems to fit."

"Kim must have been damned angry about missing her anniversary meal."

"But she has a history of protecting him over the grooms they employed," Peter reminded Fiona.

"You're suggesting Kim knew what happened?"

Peter shrugged. "Maybe."

"But would he really try to kill Frank? Whatever low opinion you have of him, Frank was a loyal employee of over twenty years. As far as we know, Mark has shown no outward sign of stress or odd behaviour since the body was found," Fiona said.

"I take your point. On the face of it, he would have to be very cold blooded to attempt to kill someone he had known for years. But I get the impression he would do anything to protect his reputation. The girl may have been an accident. But he still chose to bury her up on his farm rather than face up to the consequences."

"Are you so certain it was him that we shouldn't be looking at anyone else?" Fiona queried.

"My gut feeling is yes."

The bar manager brought over their plates of steaming hot food. "This looks fantastic." Leaning forwards, Peter added, "Smells good as well. Let's enjoy our meal and not talk work until we're back in the car."

As they cleared their plates, Peter said, "I've been meaning to ask you. How did you get along with DCI Harris when I was away?"

"Good...We got along just fine."

Once they finished their meal, Fiona pulled out her phone and tried to contact Richard Turner and then David Conley without success. She had just closed her phone and was about to put it away when it rang again. Peter listened in, wondering whether it was David or Richard returning her call. He looked across when he heard Fiona say, "Oh, my God."

He watched her face pale before she started to ask for the exact location. He watched her close the phone and noticed she took a deep breath before turning to him and saying, "David Conley has been found dead in his car. No other vehicles involved. It appears he collided with a tree at speed. They're moving the vehicle now for tests. Do you want to go straight to the accident site?"

Peter's thoughts were colliding in his head like a kaleidoscope, the shape and form constantly changing. He struggled to think through recent events logically. Which was the correct connection? Could it really be a revenge thing and not Mark covering his tracks? Did David say anything relevant in the gully field? Could the wrong decision lead to a further death? Is it possible I've got things so wrong? Fiona's voice knocked him from his thoughts.

"Sorry, yes?" Peter turned to her, feeling tired and weary.

"Should we go to the accident site?" Fiona asked, again.

"Richard Turner? Has he returned your calls yet?"

Fiona checked her phone screen before shaking her head.

Peter thought, at least George could be assured his uncle was not capable of killing. "You got the location?"

Fiona nodded and passed over the details to Peter.

"I'll get the bill," Peter said. "Keep trying to get hold of Richard Turner. And I want to know every exact movement of Mark Farley, today."

A few miles north of Birkbury, Peter drove up a steep winding lane. Nearing the top of the hill, the navigation system told him to turn right along what seemed more of a private drive than part of the highway. As they climbed still higher, the potholed road seemed to be suspended in the air with steep unfenced drops either side. A short distance along, they saw flashing lights up ahead. Peter pulled over next to the marked cars and produced his warrant card.

The uniformed officer said, "It's down there," pointing to the left-hand side of the road. Peter and Fiona peered over the side. The ground fell away steeply from the track, and in the distance, some way down could be seen the rear of a white Land Rover embedded in the base of a large oak tree.

"Are we going down?" Fiona asked, looking doubtfully at the severe drop.

Peter turned back to the uniformed officer. "Are you in radio contact with the guy in charge down there?"

Nodding his head, the officer pulled the radio from his top pocket. "I understand it's a bit of a mess down there."

Peter spoke into the radio, giving his details and asking for an initial opinion on what had happened.

After the static, a gruff voice replied, "At this stage other than the vehicle left the road for some reason and travelled down the embankment at speed, we've no idea."

Peter spoke into the radio again. "Could you get a report of your preliminary findings to me as soon as possible?"

"Yes, will do."

Returning to their car, Peter said, "Once we get that report, I want to see Mark Farley again. But meanwhile, we've got to find Richard Turner." As an afterthought, he added, "It would help if we had a picture of the guy."

"I could call the Oxford Station on the way back see if they have anything."

When her call ended, she said, "We're in luck. The officer on the desk said Turner often leaves flyers around the place advertising his PI firm. He's sure there's a photograph of him on the front. If he can find one, he'll send a copy through to me."

Pulling into the station car park, Peter noticed Fiona staring intently at the screen of her phone. As he pulled up the handbrake, she grabbed his arm.

"We've a big problem. The guy I saw isn't the cousin. It's James Turner, the brother."

Peter felt like he'd just received a heavy blow to the stomach. "The rest of the evening we spend getting that picture out to everyone. We need everyone available looking for him."

He lay on the bed worrying about the age gap. It concerned him. She'd made it clear she was interested in him, but she was young, lively and attractive. Other younger men would be interested in her. She would become bored with him. In a few days, he would be leaving the area.

What was he thinking? There's no chance of a relationship with her. The state I'm in? I'm not capable of dealing with one anyway. I'm confusing my feelings about Jenny with how I felt last night. I won't be able to stay more than a few days anyway. My medication has nearly run out.

He pulled his stomach muscles in. Love handles. Who am I trying to kid? A few weeks ago, I found a stray grey hair. Why should a vibrant young girl be interested in me? What really could I offer? She might find me entertaining for a while, I would fall madly and deeply in love and then someone her own age would come along. She would move on without a second thought.

He could hear and feel his blood racing through his veins, around his body, pumping his heartbeat. His skin tingled with irritations and his hands clenched and unclenched involuntarily. Thoughts rushed in and out of his brain too quickly for him to hold on to. He was incapable of staying still. He sat down, stood up, laid down, sat up, stood up and finally walked around. Every sense was on fire.

THIRTY-FIVE

Peter was unable to sleep when he eventually got home long after Amelia had retired to bed. Fed up with tossing and turning, he got up early and, despite feeling exhausted, he headed into the station. Grabbing a coffee, he pulled out the psychological reports on James Turner he'd skimmed read the night before. They didn't make comfortable reading.

James suffered from delusional episodes brought on by depression. The report confirmed he had received months of cognitive behaviour therapy, was on serious medication and until recently been quite closely monitored. Peter wasn't reassured by the fact that nothing serious had been reported in the last five years. That was before his sister's body had been found and no one knew whether he was taking his medication.

Peter looked up when Fiona walked in and asked, "Did you read these reports on James?"

"I'm so sorry. When I saw him, I just accepted who he said he was..."

Peter noticed the dark rings under her eyes. She looked exhausted. "You can stop right there. We all assumed the same. As your senior officer, this is my fault, not yours."

"But it was me who interviewed him," Fiona said.

"Yes. And I should have picked up earlier on what you said about him seeming very upset, how he had access to the jewellery..."

He was stopped mid-flow by the arrival of Superintendent

Rogers. "I hear that the deranged brother has been around all this time and no one thought to mention it or bring him in?"

"Yes, sir. Sorry. It was an oversight by me," Peter said.

"Instead of keeping tabs on a known lunatic, you've been harassing innocent businessmen," Rogers shouted.

Peter said, "I accept there has been an oversight about the brother. But we've been looking into the murder of his sister..."

"I don't want to hear it. I want to know you've found this man and he is in police custody. Do you understand?"

"Yes, sir," Peter replied, to bring an end to the conversation as quickly as possible.

As soon as Rogers left the room, Peter said, "Let's get out of here. See if we can find this guy."

"I'm so sorry..."

"Fiona, it is okay, just forget about it. What's done is done. We can't turn back the clock. We concentrate on finding him. We'll start back at Rooksbridge."

"But you took the blame instead of saying it was me who interviewed him."

"As your senior officer, I am responsible. Let's get going," Peter said.

James Turner wasn't at the holiday cottages. They found Pauline who handed over the key to the cottage. Inside was spotlessly clean and tidy and gave no hint of where James might have gone.

Peter pulled open the hand-carved wardrobe door in the bedroom. It contained a handful of tee-shirts and a pair of jeans. "I'm guessing he was planning on returning at some stage," he shouted out to Fiona who was looking around the kitchen. In the adjoining bathroom, Peter found personal toiletries in the cabinet, but there were no prescribed medicine bottles.

Peter returned to the living room as Fiona came out of the kitchen. "I found a few things in the cupboards. It looks like he was intending to return."

"We last saw him with the barmaid from The Bull Inn. She might be able to give us some idea as to his state of mind and where he might be," Peter said. Closing the cottage door, he telephoned to arrange a full search.

It was before opening time, but they felt the heat from the sun as they climbed the steep stone steps to pub entrance. The heavy door was locked. Peter peered through the window behind the terrace and saw the landlord carrying crates of bottles to the bar area. Peter knocked loudly on the window pane.

After a multitude of locks were turned and bolts were drawn, the landlord finally appeared, looking tired and hung over with beads of perspiration running down the side of his face.

"We're sorry to bother you at this time, but is your barmaid Rose around today?" Peter asked.

The watery eyes that stared back at Peter were glazed and bloodshot. The landlord led them inside and used a towel from the bar to dry his face. "I haven't seen her since yesterday lunchtime. She swapped her shifts with one of the other girls." He turned away and walked back to the bar where he started to fill the fridge space with the bottles from the crate. "I feel like climbing in these fridges myself. Still, this weather is good for trade."

Peter leaned over the bar. "Have you any idea where she might be?"

The landlord picked up an empty crate and walked out from behind the bar. "You could try Hillend Farm. She keeps her horse up there," he said, as he walked over and pulled back the heavy doors and attached the chains to hold them open. "I may as well open them up. Might be I can get some fresh air through the place."

"Thanks for your time," Peter said.

"When you do find her, ask her to give me a ring, so I know which of her shifts she intends turning up for this week."

"Yes, will do. What sort of an employee is she?"

"A very good one when she remembers to turn up,"

"She's a sensible, reliable sort of girl?" Peter asked.

"I wouldn't go that far. She's a good barmaid as she's lively and likeable. But like a lot of girls these days, she has quite a casual attitude to things."

"Thanks again and we will ask her to ring you when we find her."

They drove straight on up to Hillend Farm and did a double take as they walked across the yard. Tim was holding a grey horse, which towered above his six-foot frame, in one hand and a bucket of soapy water in the other. Cathy was sitting on the horse's back, wearing nothing but a skimpy bikini, scrubbing the horse's neck and mane with a wet soapy brush. "Hi," she called. "How are the investigations going?" Registering their surprised looks, she added, "Charlie's so big it's the only way I can clean his mane. It's so annoying when you're riding to look down at a dirty mane, don't you think?"

"Umm, I'm sure it is," replied Peter. "We were just wondering if Rose was here."

"Not sure. Is her car parked over there?" Cathy said, as she slipped down from the horse with the agility of a young girl and threw the brush carelessly into the bucket Tim was holding.

Peter, mindful of the bucket of soapy water being slopped about by Tim, took a step back.

"Last time I saw her, she was riding her horse, Jaeica, out towards David Conley's farm," Cathy said. "She had that handsome young man who is staying at Rooksbridge with her."

Peter's stomach lurched at the thought of the danger Rose might be in. They followed Cathy towards where Rose normally parked her car. Tim loped off to join his son at the bottom end of the yard where he was tinkering with a tractor.

"I put those photos in the post the other day, by the way. Here we are. This is her car." Cathy reached for the door handle. "It's unlocked, and I can see the keys are in the ignition. I've told her before about doing that." Cathy turned around to face them. "You don't think something has happened to her, do you?"

"We really don't know," replied Fiona. "Can I take a look?"

Cathy stood back to allow Fiona to peer into the car interior. There was nothing to give any clue as to where Rose may have gone. Peter opened the boot, but it was empty.

"Does she usually leave her keys in the ignition?" Peter said.

"Yes. I've told her loads of times to be more careful. Especially as she sometimes leaves her handbag on the passenger seat, although I see it's not there now," Cathy replied. "You don't think there's been an accident, do you?"

Peter ignored her question and asked, "When was the last time you actually saw her?"

Cathy thought for a while. "Yesterday morning, I think, when she was riding out with her boyfriend. I'm not sure if I've seen her since. But I don't usually take that much notice of her comings and goings."

"Did you see her come back from her ride?"

"Well no, but she must have. First thing this morning when I walked the dogs, she was in the field...the horse, I mean."

"And the car has not been moved?" Peter asked.

"Now you mention it, no, I don't think so. Not since yesterday."

"And you didn't see them leave after her ride?"

"I've told you no. But we can ask Tim." She started to walk down the yard calling, "Tim! Did you see Rose leave yesterday?"

Tim appeared from behind the tractor. "Yes. She left with that boy."

"Any idea what time?" Peter asked.

"Not sure...afternoon-ish."

Cathy gave them the home address she had for Rose, which was on the edge of the village. When they pulled up outside Rose's home, they were met outside by a petite, attractive woman flapping her arms and looking anxious. She was opening their car door before Peter had a chance to pull the key from the ignition.

"Are you the police? That was very quick. I've only just telephoned to report her possibly missing." She suddenly stopped. The colour drained from her face. "Oh God, there's been an accident. That's why you got here so quickly."

"We are not aware of an accident. Can we go inside, please?" Fiona asked, steering Mrs Gwinnet inside. She was trembling and starting to go into shock. "Is there anyone I can call for you?"

Fiona asked.

"My husband, I'll call my husband."

Once she'd made the call, Fiona concentrated on getting her to sit. They needed her calm enough to be able to answer their questions. Despite the occasional attacks of near hysteria, Fiona managed to get some information from the distraught woman. The last time her mother had seen Rose was early yesterday morning. Rose told her she was going riding and then into town to do some clothes shopping.

As Mrs Gwinnet was in no condition to be left alone, they stayed with her until her husband arrived. They took with them a photograph of Rose and contact details for her friend, Sue, who lived near Frank.

They found Sue at home, but she couldn't tell them much. Rose had asked her to cover her shifts because she had met someone and wanted to spend a few days with him. Rose had mentioned he was older, but she really liked him.

"I've rung round all our friends. No one has seen her for days," Sue said. "Do you think something bad has happened to her?"

"We don't know. Would Rose have gone off with someone she'd just met without telling anyone?" Peter asked.

Sue looked at the floor and shifted uneasily.

"Please, just be truthful, this is important. We really do need to know."

"She can be a little unreliable at times... You could say a bit unpredictable. I suppose yes, she might."

Peter's head started to throb as he inwardly berated himself. He'd missed something important. The resultant tension rapidly spread to his neck. First Frank, then David Conley, and now Rose. All victims because he'd missed something. At the time he'd regretted not seeing Richard Turner himself. With his experience, he might have sensed something not quite right about him. But would he have acted any differently?

Before Frank's accident, there was no sense of urgency. They were dealing with an old case in a village full of rural eccentrics, and it hadn't crossed his mind people could be at risk. He hadn't taken things seriously enough from day one, so had inadvertently missed things. And just maybe he'd been far too wrapped up with his own domestic situation.

That had to change. He had to establish if the two car accidents were set up and find James Turner and Rose Gwinnet without delay. He remembered the other man in the photo, Taffy Mark called him. Killed in a farm accident. Was that also connected?

Peter's stomach churned, and his jaw clenched as the overwhelming sense of time running out washed over him. The fear was paralysing his brain, making it difficult for him to decide the best course of action. The intrusive thought of Sally's imminent return filled far too much space in his mind, making it more difficult to think straight.

"We need to set up a separate team to deal with the disappearance of Rose. But we liaise closely with them," Peter said, far more decisively than he felt. "We get back to the station now to chase up the reports on the two car accidents and pull the report on the fatal accident involving Taffy. We need to double-check the alibi Mark Farley gave us with a vet and what he was doing yesterday. We've already got the psychological reports on James Turner. And we need to speak to Frank."

Fiona started to jot the list down. She scribbled the last two as she saw Peter already heading off in the direction of his car.

Pulling away, Peter added, "And chase up whether they've traced the girl who went to Cheltenham with Jenny that day. Stress just how important it is we find her."

THIRTY-SIX

All that could be done to find Rose and James Turner was being done. Officers were seconded from neighbouring stations, and the media were going nationwide. The preliminary thoughts on David's car were the brakes, and the steering had been tampered . with.

Peter looked up at the clock. Amelia had told him their meal would be ready at 7:30. He still hadn't told her Sally was due home soon or Sally that Amelia was back. He'd used the excuse he wanted to talk it through properly with Amelia before ringing Sally. He had wanted to talk about things over their meal, but it looked like he'd cut things too fine.

He picked up the envelopes Cathy had sent but was interrupted by Fiona.

"I think I've got something. We only looked at Mark Farley's record, but I've found something looking at his father."

Peter could see Fiona's face was flushed with excitement. The earlier weariness he'd noticed was gone. His eyes felt gritty and sore from scanning reports searching in vain for a breakthrough, something other than gut feeling and speculation. "Go on."

"Mark's father was done for benefit fraud. He was on incapacity benefit following a factory accident. But on the quiet, he built up his own business sourcing and renovating vintage cars, in Birmingham."

"Cathy told us Tim had a contact in Birmingham. You think..."

"Mark has no record. But his brother does. He was charged with aiding and abetting the rape of a young girl locally. The other boy was never named."

"I get the connection with the vintage cars, but what's the relevance of the brother?"

"The girl wasn't able to confirm the identity of the boy, so the case was dropped. The one who carried out the rape they never traced. She described him as tall, blond and painfully thin." Fiona desperately skimmed back through the report. "Here it is... She described him as a toff, very well to do and not from around here."

"You think the brother was set up to take the blame? It was Mark Farley and Tim Potter?" Peter asked, running through the possibility in his head. He walked to Fiona's desk to read the file still carrying the envelope from Cathy.

Fiona pulled at the envelope from Peter's hand, saying, "May I?"

Without taking his eyes from the screen, Peter spilt the contents of the envelope onto her desk. As he read the report on the screen, he sensed Fiona's attention was focussed on one of the photographs. In black and white it depicted two young boys in greasy overalls standing next to an old car partially in pieces. The photograph was small and grainy, but Tim Potter had changed very little over the years. The second boy was not so recognisable but above the vehicle could be seen the first three letters of a sign. "FAR."

Their eyes locked, both clearly making the same connections. The moment was interrupted by the shrill ring of the desk telephone. Peter grabbed the receiver, his eyes still on Fiona. "Hello. Detective Chief Inspector Peter Hatherall."

"Hi," drawled the voice. "I understand you want to speak to me. How is old Birkbury?"

"Sorry...You are?" Peter asked.

"Gerry Bowden."

Peter stalled for time, trying to gather his thoughts. This was one call he didn't want to get wrong. "What have you been told?"

"Not a lot. A girl has been found on Mark's land, and Frank's in hospital. How is he, by the way?"

"He's fine as far as we're aware. Anything else about why we want to speak to you?" Peter asked.

"Nah. Just you wanted to know something about the girls we chatted up on race days."

"Go on."

"Well...yeah. It's going back a bit. But yeah, I used to know Mark Farley. I did a bit of business with him," Gerry said.

"How about Tim Potter, did you know him as well?"

"Yeah, I socialised with both of them. Good times as I remember."

"And do you remember a trip to Cheltenham Race Festival with them in 2001?"

"The Cheltenham Festival, you mean. Yeah, I remember that trip. Mark arranged it. A group of us went."

"You remember going to the Cheltenham Races. How many times did you go with them?" Peter asked.

"Only the once. I did a couple of other outings with Mark. Racetracks or agricultural shows, but due to one thing and another, Cheltenham only the once."

"You only went to Cheltenham Race Festival the one time with them?" Peter was holding his breath waiting for the reply. Fiona had wheeled her chair over to his desk and was oblivious to the fact their knees were touching.

"Just the once as I remember. It was a good day marred by an argument," Gerry said.

"About?"

"We all had a lot to drink. We were all being incredibly stupid as I remember. We split up and went off in our own huffy groups, vowing not to speak to each other ever again. All very childish."

"And who did you spend the rest of the day with?"

"Taffy mainly and then later we went to find David Conley as he was the only other person with a car."

"Do you remember what Tim and Mark did for the rest of the day?"

"I saw them once later that day from the other side of the bar."

"Were they with anyone else?"

"They were with a couple of young girls. They were joking about with them, by the look of it. But how long they were together, I have no idea. Once I bought my drinks, I left the bar," Gerry said.

"Can you remember what the girls looked like?"

After a brief pause, Gerry replied, "One was dark and the other blond. They were quite young, but they seemed happy enough."

"Did you see any of them again that day?" Peter asked.

"No. I left shortly after with David and Taffy."

"Do you think you would recognise the girls they were with that day?" Peter asked.

"It was only a brief glimpse, but I'd be happy to try."

"How well did you know Mark?"

"Not that well. I did some business with him. Is he in some sort of trouble?"

"We're not sure. How about Tim Potter, did you know him well?"

"I only knew Tim vaguely through Mark. They'd been friends for a long time."

"Do you remember what you all argued that day?"

"It was over some women we'd met earlier in the day. I can't really remember any details, but I do recall we'd all had far too much to drink."

"Did you regularly pick up women on these days out with Mark?" Peter asked.

"I didn't. Mark and Tim would chat up the girls. Free of their wives for the day they threw a bit of money about and had some fun. Sometimes they went too far. I don't really know. It wasn't my sort of thing."

"What happened? With the girls, when it went too far?"

"I don't know. Like I said, it was not my thing. And I admit I didn't like Tim Potter anyway... Thinks way too much of himself."

Peter was distracted by the ringing of a phone. The prickle of

THE SKELETONS OF BIRKBURY

irritation was relieved when Fiona lifted the receiver. "If I send over a photograph of one of the girls we believe Mark and Tim met that day at Cheltenham, do you think you would recognise her?"

"It was a long time ago, but I'll have a look."

After ending the call, Peter said, "Let's go and see Frank, now."

Arriving at the peak of hospital visiting hours, they struggled to find somewhere to park. Peter took the steps two at a time as he hurried up to the ward. Joyce got up from his bedside when they entered. Frank looked pale and drawn and a little ill at ease in his paisley pyjamas. Peter thought how some people always looked odd if you took them away from their everyday environment. In Frank's case, it was as if the work clothes and the farm were a natural part of him. He felt a pang of guilt that hit hard into the pit of his stomach, reminding him it was empty.

Once the pleasantries were out of the way, Frank was keen to tell them all he could. Peter guessed he should thank Joyce for this. She sat by his side almost willing the words from his mouth, supporting and cajoling whenever he faltered.

"Yes. I was in Cheltenham at about the time the girl went missing," Frank confirmed.

"Did you see Jenny Turner that day?" Peter asked, leaning forward in his chair.

Frank shook his head and fell silent a short while, looking to Joyce for guidance. "I didn't see the girl. Or go to the race track. But earlier that day, I did see Mark Farley, David Conley, Taffy Jenkins and Tim Potter walking along the street."

"You saw all four of them in Cheltenham that day?"

"Yes, I saw them in Cheltenham."

"Did they see you?" Peter asked.

Frank shook his head. "When I saw them, I turned the other way. I don't think any of them saw me."

"Are you quite sure it was them?" Peter said. He looked across at Fiona, who was biting her lip anxiously.

Frank thought for a bit and then nodded his head.

"What happened next?"

"Well, nothing happened really. I'm not even sure how I spent the rest of the day. Probably inside betting shops and pubs and then asleep most of the late afternoon and early evening. I do remember later that evening I couldn't sleep. The dreariness of the bedsit became too much, so I decided to drive home."

"You didn't see them again that day or know where they went or who with?" asked Peter. Trying to hide his disappointment, he asked, "So is there anything else you can tell me about that day?"

Frank paused for a long while. Joyce touched him gently on the shoulder. "You need to tell the rest, Frank."

Frank continued hesitantly, his eyes focused on Joyce. "I got back to Birkbury about two am, I guess. As I was driving past Rooksbridge, I noticed David Conley's car. It was abandoned haphazardly a little ways down the lane. I knew Mark and his friends after a particularly good day out would continue the party into the night. They often played cards in the caravans used by the winter, stable staff. Mark kept a stash of booze in there when they were empty. It could get quite rowdy at times. Kim would have never allowed it inside the house. So anyway, feeling wide awake I thought I would go and see if they were playing and if I could join them for a hand."

"You headed towards where the caravans were parked?" Peter prompted, when Frank fell silent again.

"Yes. I drove around to the back of the stables where the caravans were. They were in pitch blackness. I was about to leave when I saw something by one of the caravans. When I looked closer, I saw it was Graham Farley. He was a young lad back then, of course. He was in a trance-like state; sat cross-legged, rocking forwards and backwards. He was renowned for sleepwalking when he was younger."

"You didn't see or hear anyone else by the caravans? It was just Graham you saw?"

"Well, as I pulled Graham to his feet, I thought I may have heard a vehicle engine somewhere in the direction of the homefield. But when I looked, there were no lights. I guessed maybe I imagined it or the sound had come from somewhere farther away. It could have come from the motorway even."

"The homefield, that's what you call the first field heading out from the main yard? It's the field you'd go through first if you're heading in the direction of where Jenny was discovered?"

Frank again nodded. He motioned to Joyce to pass him a glass of water.

Peter's mind was racing. He needed something to link Mark to Jenny.

Frank continued, "I led Graham to the back door of the house and, knowing the key was kept on top of the door frame, I bundled him inside. I didn't want to disturb them, so I relocked the door, put the key back and headed back to my car. As I drove back up the drive, I stopped by David's car. It looked like it had been abandoned in a hurry, but there was no sign of him anywhere. I went home then and have never thought much about the night again. Until the body was discovered, that is. Now I seem to be thinking about it constantly."

"Go back to the caravans. You say you found Graham by the caravans? And these were used mainly in the winter?" Peter asked.

"Yes, the ponies were only stabled winter time. The girls weren't all needed when the ponies lived out in the fields in the summer. They were often used for storage until they were needed again. But I remember around that time they were completely cleaned out and refitted."

"And that's what is shown in the photograph," said Peter, more to himself while he was trying to recollect Graham's reaction to the picture.

"Yes, when I found them, I put them all together, as a way to jog my own memory."

"Why didn't you tell us this earlier?"

Frank looked sheepishly down at the sheets on his bed. He pulled the corner into his hand and made a fist. Looking down, avoiding eye contact, he quietly continued. "I did meet them in the bar on one Gold Cup day, and I'm pretty sure the date on the back of the photograph is correct. But I wasn't with them when they went back in May. After the body was found, I was worried you'd think I killed her." He steeled himself to look Peter directly in the face. "And you did. Didn't you?"

"We weren't sure. Joyce has always thought not," Fiona said, smiling at Joyce. "We thought you were hiding something."

"Did you see them with a group of girls, Jenny Turner in particular?" Peter asked.

"I'm not sure, possibly. There were some girls hanging about I think. One of them looked like her. But it was such a long time ago, and I wasn't with them long. Mark and Tim were always picking up girls."

"Tim Potter?"

Frank brightened. "Yeah, you should have seen the au pair he used to have staying with them. Grant was away at boarding school most of the time. Never quite sure what her duties were." Frank started to chuckle but was stopped short by the pain it caused.

They waited for him to recover and Fiona asked, "What about Mrs Potter? Didn't she have something to say?"

"She was just as bad. When they were younger, she always had a bloke on the go. She was quite a stunner back then."

"And James Turner, have you had any contact with him?" Peter asked.

"Sorry, who's that?"

"The brother of the murdered girl. Were you aware at any time of somebody hanging around outside your house?"

Frank shook his head in surprise.

Joyce said, "He's not the brother. He's a cousin. I saw him the other day with Rose. I had a little chat with him, in fact."

"What did he say? Did he say anything about leaving the area for a while?" Peter asked, turning his full attention to her.

"If I remember rightly, he said he was going to travel around the area sightseeing for a few days and then check back to see if there was any further news about his cousin's disappearance before deciding whether to go home. He definitely said cousin, not sister."

"Did he mention Rose going with him or where he was going?"

"No. I thought they made a nice couple. He asked something about David Conley and Mark Farley, if I remember rightly," Joyce said.

"What did he ask?"

"Nothing really, just wondered if I knew them, asked what they were like and where he could find them."

Peter asked Frank about the accident.

"All I can remember is being blinded by headlights just before the bridge. The other vehicle seemed to be in the middle of the road." Frank drank some more water. "It appeared from nowhere right in front of me. I tried to steer hard to the right to avoid a head-on collision. It was instinctive. I can't remember anything else after that."

This confused Peter as the debris found had been from a rear light, not a headlight. "Frank, are you absolutely sure you were blinded by headlights?"

Frank replied with certainty. "Yes, headlights on full beam suddenly appeared right in front of me. I had little time to brake. I can't think where the vehicle came from. One minute it wasn't and then it was just there."

The nurse came in at that point and asked them all to step outside for a short while.

In the corridor, Peter said, "Why do you think Frank didn't mention any of this before, Joyce?"

"I don't think he was really sure what he saw at the time. And like he said, he was scared you would think he was involved. He probably didn't want to implicate the others, especially when he didn't really see anything. I believe him when he says he didn't see the relevance to start with. I think he wanted to sort it all out in his own mind first. And God only knows why, but Frank does genuinely like Mark, for some reason."

Peter asked, "What do you think of the Farleys generally?"

He smiled at her curt reply "Self-centred wankers, the whole lot of them. And what was that about the brother earlier?"

It occurred to Peter that if Joyce had been maintaining a round-the-clock vigil at Frank's bedside, she would know nothing about Rose disappearing or David Conley's accident.

"It's just something we're looking into, Joyce." He could tell from her face he was not going to get away with saying so little. He was tired and wanted to go home. Also, he was wondering who would sit beside his bed if he were ill.

"What are you looking into?" Joyce asked.

Peter felt the intensity of her stare. "It's probably nothing."

"But?"

"As you know, he was seen outside Frank's house before the accident, and he and Rose seem to have disappeared somewhere together."

"You're saying he was responsible for the accident. If you thought he was dangerous, why was he allowed to roam the village freely?"

Peter replied, "Nobody is saying that. But we can't find either of them at the moment."

Joyce walked away a few steps and then turned. "Rose is a flighty girl. She is the sort who would dash off without telling anyone. But what are you really saying? That Frank's accident wasn't an accident? I thought it didn't really make total sense, how he says it happened. What are you going to do about that? That's what I want to know."

"We are looking into it."

"Looking into?" Joyce repeated with disdain in her voice.

Peter thought how fierce she could look at times. He was rescued by the nurse reappearing.

THIRTY-SEVEN

Peter felt tired and irritable confined in the hot, cramped office. Fiona was coping better with the heat, the frantic phone calls, the re-reading reports and the strong sense of failure. She was calmly chasing Cheltenham to track down Jenny's friend, Ellen Frost.

Peter took a deep breath and dialled Mark Farley's home number. Despite all the unspoken criticism, he felt sure of his convictions about Mark.

Kim answered the phone. After a long silence, she said, "I will call him." Peter felt the sweat run down his sides as he was forced to wait on the empty line a full five minutes. He'd almost given up waiting when Mark picked up the receiver.

"This had better be good. Do I need to call my solicitor?"

Peter replied, "Some new information has come to light. We'd like to talk to you again."

"I repeat. Do I need to call my solicitor?"

"That is entirely up to you, but can we agree on a time?"

"Well, how on earth am I supposed to know when he's available?"

Peter said, "Shall we say three o'clock here at the station? If your solicitor is unavailable, I am sure we can provide one."

Mark replied, "Three o'clock," and hung up, leaving Peter unsure whether that was an agreement to the time or not.

Checking his watch, Peter tried the landline for Rooksbridge and Graham's mobile leaving messages on both for a call back.

He leaned back in his chair and closed his eyes momentarily. This proved to be a mistake as it allowed space for a critical stream of thoughts, highlighting his failures on the case.

Peter's domestic life was on an equal downwards spiral. When he'd arrived home the previous night, Amelia had gone to bed and had not resurfaced when he'd left this morning. He'd tried to call Sally, but that had gone straight to answer machine. Sally was going to be driving home shortly, and he'd not told her Amelia was back.

Sally was probably already on the road. Hopefully, Amelia would still be at work when Sally arrived home, but she would soon realise Amelia had moved back in during her absence. Sally would be angry and then defensive, and if he was late getting home again, Amelia would arrive before him. He felt as powerless to avert the disaster at home any more than the one unfolding at work.

His mind flew back to when Amelia was born as if it were only yesterday. At first, people said it was all quite normal. Jordan was suffering nothing more than the baby blues. It would pass in weeks if not days. But the weeks had turned to months of dark despair. He'd been sympathetic and supportive to start, as were family and friends. Gradually, one by one their friends began to lose interest and patience with the situation. He became angry and irritated by Jordan. Where had the happy, lively girl he'd married gone? He had no understanding of the devastating effects of depression at the time.

His frustration turned to resentment. He couldn't become a recluse because she felt unable to socialise. The long periods of time she never left the house became unbearable. Then there followed equally long periods when she did not even leave her room. He tried and tried to understand.

He felt he had every excuse. He was lonely. He was tired. He was stressed. He was hurt. And the girl was pretty and interested in him as a man. She offered a light at the end of the long, dark tunnel Jordan was dragging him into.

If only Jordan had not gone to the station that day to find him.

She should have been home in a darkened room with the curtains closed, as usual.

He would never erase the look on Jordan's face when she caught them together in the car park. It was imprinted on his brain forever. The big scene where Jordan walked across the car park played over and over in a never-ending loop.

Peter was knocked from his melancholy mood by the arrival of Superintendent Rogers. Red in the face, Rogers boomed, "I've just received a call from Mark Farley. Can you explain that?"

Peter stood up to face him. "Yes, sir. New information has come to light that we need to discuss with him."

"And yet the only new information I've heard is that the bereaved brother with a history of assault has been seen hanging around two villagers. One is in hospital and the other in the morgue. And he has disappeared with a young girl from the village." Rogers stopped to draw breath, before shouting, "And you want to go bothering Mark Farley again."

"I am very concerned about the whereabouts of James Turner and Rose, but everything is being done to find them. I am also concerned about finding who murdered his sister," Peter replied.

"And what is this new evidence you have?"

"We have eyewitness evidence Mark Farley and Tim Potter were in..."

"Stop right there. You're talking about Tim Potter, the local magistrate?"

"Yes," Peter said, carefully. "We understand they may have been friends since their teens and they were both in Cheltenham on the day Jenny disappeared. They were well known for chatting up women on their days out and the alibi..."

"And that's it? Show me a married man who doesn't like the attention of attractive women. If anything, you should be offering them police protection until James is found, not harassing them," Rogers shouted.

Peter felt his temper slipping away from him. "Has it ever occurred to you that James may have disappeared after seeing

Mark. That..."

"I've heard enough of this. When you've calmed down and have something more concrete, bring it up to me. And I'll decide whether you have sufficient evidence to bring in Mark Farley. And the same goes for Tim Potter as well." Rogers turned on his heel to leave the room but spun back round before he reached the door. "I've been very patient with you, and you are a good officer. But I have to say, I am very close to asking you to step down from this investigation. Concentrate on finding James Turner before anybody else goes missing." Rogers said, before slamming the door shut behind him.

Fiona tried to hide behind her computer screen while PC Bains and Mann looked intently interested in a file they were holding. Peter unclenched his jaw, which he'd been grinding. DCI Jenkins chose that moment to poke his head around the door. "Thought I heard things get a bit heated in here."

Peter said, "I've had enough right now. What really gets me is when you see the cop shows on TV, they get to crash cars, leave buildings burnt to the ground and beat confessions out of their suspects. And get medals for bravery. Can you imagine us doing that? We'd be hauled up and threatened with demotion, and we'd have to file reports in triplicate. And that would be before wasting time with complaints committees, victim liaison and the insurance company."

"Tell me about it," Jenkins replied. "Do you want to come somewhere quiet and talk about it?"

"No! And stop patronising me. Just give me a bit of space to wind down," Peter said, storming out of the office through a row of downturned eyes.

THIRTY-EIGHT

Joyce had been spending all her time in the hospital with Frank. She was finding it exhausting, as although Frank was slowly recovering from the physical injuries, he was slipping into depression. She was doing all she could to remain cheery and encourage his other friends to visit.

She feared he was disappearing too far down into the black pit. She knew the deeper he fell, the harder it would be for him to drag himself back up. She was losing the battle against a ticking clock and had run out of ideas of how to distract Frank, and to give him something to look forward to.

She was furious that Mark hadn't visited Frank and felt this failure increased Frank's sense of worthlessness. Frank had been so badly used and discarded by him and the whole family that she wanted to spit. All his hard work and loyalty over the years had meant nothing to them. She hadn't dared tell Frank that according to Pauline, he'd already been replaced at the farm.

What did they think he was going to do when he came out of hospital? He'd worked for them all his life. He knew nothing else.

In desperation, she had lowered herself to telephone Mark and Graham to ask them to visit. But still neither had come. Mark hadn't even bothered to return her call.

Joyce hated Frank's reliance on them at the best of times. They just weren't worth it. Frank said it was only his employment worries that were upsetting him, but Joyce knew it was more than that. It was the realisation that the friendship he had put himself out for was all one-sided.

His entire working life had been helping that one selfish family. In her view, he had held back about seeing them in Cheltenham solely to protect Mark. In return, they couldn't even find the time to visit. While Mark had done all the big talk about helping Frank at the beginning when he was first arrested, it had all come to nothing.

She could not believe she had been taken in by his earlier concern and she also felt used and angry. That was the thing about Mark. When you were in his company, he could make you believe black was white and you'd want to believe every word he said. Only afterwards, when it was all too late, you'd realise you'd been duped and taken for a fool. The skills of a good con man never go away, she supposed.

The newspapers were hinting at failures by the investigating officers. They should have at least warned Frank of the danger they had put him in.

The nurses had been fantastic. But this morning, when one of them told Joyce she should give herself a break and go home for a bit, she'd felt quite resentful. She thought they just wanted her out of the way, but now she was beginning to realise just how tired of the hospital she was.

She decided to visit Mark to give him a piece of her mind. She'd been to Mark and Kim's home a couple of times with Frank and thought she could remember the way. She was very sure she would recognise the pretensions gates and driveway once she got there.

She told Frank she was heading home for a few hours and set off. The heat was stifling as she clambered into her small car. The steering wheel was burning her hands and the air, cooked by the sun, was suffocating.

She crunched through the gears of her old Ford Fiesta as she exited the hospital car park. Not used to driving in town, she angered her fellow motorists. She was overly cautious at roundabouts and junctions and constantly found herself in the wrong lane. The blare of horns and shouts of abuse she received, flustered her even more. She felt so lost and overwrought with emotion she started to stall the engine at every junction. Her vision was blurred by furious tears, making it difficult to read the signposts. Still, she propelled herself forwards towards the cause of all her outrage.

Once out of town and on more familiar country lanes she relaxed. Sensing she was nearing Mark's home, doubts crept into her mind. She felt the tears beginning to form again. What exactly am I going to accuse Mark of? Being a lousy friend and bad employer? Beg him to visit Frank? It would only inflate his ego, and possibly upset Frank. What if Mark merely laughs? Is it my own feelings of hurt and pride compelling me to confront him?

She pulled into a lay-by to consider her options. I've already travelled all this way. All I need is a plan, a reason for appearing at Mark's doorstep unannounced. I can't just launch into an attack on him for not visiting, can I? Something less confrontational and emotional would be best. Does he know Frank has told the police he'd seen him in Cheltenham? But they were all there. That was why Frank was taken in for questioning in the first place. It didn't make them all killers.

While thinking of what to say, a red pickup truck pulled into the lay-by in front of her. Joyce instantly remembered the driver from when he did some work on Frank's cottage. It was Chris, a local builder Mark used to maintain his various properties. He was a large, friendly man with curly red hair and freckled arms. He had the typical build of a middle-aged man who liked a drink. Long skinny legs but a beer belly that hung precariously over the belt of his jeans, defying gravity. He greeted Joyce jovially. "I thought I recognised the car. Is everything okay?"

"Everything is fine," Joyce said. "I pulled over to get my bearings. I'm on my way home now. But thanks for stopping."

Unfortunately, her car felt it had been abused enough for one day by her driving across town. When she turned the key, the engine refused to turn over.

Chris came back from his pickup, hoisting his jeans up as he walked. "Flip the bonnet open. Let's have a look."

Joyce struggled to remember how to release the bonnet. She knew there was a catch somewhere. She was relieved she found it, more by luck than judgement.

She got out and stood to the side under the shade of a tree. After a short while, Chris swaggered back to her with a knowing smile on his face. "You're out of water and oil. It's probably just overheated. Were any of the warning lights on before you stopped?"

"I'm not sure," replied Joyce, creasing her forehead.

"Mark Farley has a workshop just up the road he lets me use. I'll tow you over there. Get you back on the road in no time," Chris said.

Chris quickly reversed his truck and attached chains to his tow hitch. Joyce had no time to decide whether this coincidence was very good or very bad.

Sat in the cab next to Chris, Joyce's heart was beating so hard she wondered if she was going to have a heart attack. It felt like it could break out of her chest at any moment. Now that she had an excuse for her visit, she was thinking it probably best not to say anything. Maybe Mark might say something about Frank, and she could take it from there. She glanced out the window but didn't recognise the lane they were travelling along. They pulled up in a small yard. Chris said, "I know where he keeps the keys to this workshop."

Joyce felt the release of pressure from her body. She hadn't realised how tense she'd become until that moment. How tightly she'd been holding herself, thinking she was going to be confronting Mark. She took deep breaths and started to think clearly.

Chris mistook the look on Joyce's face for concern. "Don't worry, he knows I borrow stuff from here all the time. He rarely uses this workshop himself. Not since he built that new one up by the house anyway. That one is full of all his new gadgets."

Joyce watched Chris feel along a ledge by the side of the workshop door. After a while, he turned back to Joyce with a look of confusion on his face and said, "That's odd. The key isn't in its usual place. Bob across the way has a set of spare keys. I'll pop over and borrow his. Up to you, you can wait here or come along. I'll be about fifteen minutes."

Joyce thought she'd use the time for a quick snoop around, now she knew Mark was not nearby, so she waved Chris off.

As soon as he was out of sight, she wandered round to the back of the workshop. She noticed amongst the long grass the same imitation stone key-hide, as Gillian had. It wouldn't fool any burglar with an IQ above twenty. As she anticipated when she retrieved it from amongst the weeds, the bottom could be slid across to reveal a key-hiding box. She vaguely remembered Gillian saying hers was a gift from a child of a family friend. Maybe this one came from the same donor.

It took only a second to consider whether she should wait until Chris returned. She pulled out the bunch of keys and started to try the lock. Knowing she may only have another ten minutes for her private snoop, she worked as quickly as possible. On the third key, she was in.

Parked in the middle of the workshop was a large black van, the back of which was damaged. The left-hand rear door seemed to be the most severely buckled. It looked like it had been hastily hammered back into place, so it could be shut. The rear lights were smashed and covered with black tape. She tried to pull the doors open but they were locked. Joyce walked round to the cab and saw the keys were in the ignition.

Apart from the van, the workshop was nearly empty. The shelving along the sides had been cleared of the previous contents. Only a few odd screws and bolts were dotted around in the dust. In the corner were some empty paint tins and dried out brushes. There were no tools except a broken spade and a crowbar abandoned on the floor.

She tried the front door of the van and, finding that unlocked, took the keys from the ignition to the back doors. The keys didn't help. The rear doors weren't locked either. They were jammed shut due to the damage. She remembered Peter querying Frank's description of the collision. Something about, are you sure you saw headlights, not rear lights? She picked up the crowbar from the floor and used it to force open the rear doors. The van was empty except for a large piece of plywood propped up along one side. Joyce clambered in to have a closer look.

She pulled the sheet of wood towards her. Attached to the other side was a large sheet of material that mimicked a mirror. She remembered Frank saying something about it. He had fixed it to several stable walls. Owners believed it fooled a horse into thinking it had company. Frank had found it hysterically funny, and they'd had a good laugh about the gullibility of some people. "Most horses got more sense than their owners," Frank had joked.

Joyce wasn't laughing now. She noticed the metal clips attached to the board coincided with some makeshift catches on the van's ceiling just behind the doors. Her brain was making connections she couldn't keep up with. This was crazy. She couldn't believe what she was thinking.

On a dark, unlit country road, a black vehicle would be hard to see. If the mirror was in place and the back doors were suddenly thrown open, a driver would see the reflection of his own lights on main beam. He would be partially blinded and swerve to avoid a head-on collision.

Joyce was stunned. All the thoughts in her head collided. They came to one awful conclusion. Initial disbelief gave way to panic. She had always disliked Mark and Kim, knew them to be callous, deceitful and manipulative. But this was something else. Mark had tried to kill Frank. And here she was being a silly old woman going to confront him about treating Frank unfairly, for not being a good friend! The colour drained from her face, and she felt suddenly faint. What if he had been here? What a bloody fool she was. The bastard, how could he?

Joyce knew she was running out of time. Chris would return shortly. What was she? Man or mouse? She ran to pull the chain that fully opened the main workshop door. Running back to the van, slamming the rear doors shut as she passed, she tripped and nearly fell.

Once in the van, she struggled to release the catch under the seat to move it forward. It was no good. She couldn't pull the van seat forward, and she was running out of time. She had to act quickly. She decided she could drive it where the seat was if she stood to reach the pedals.

She turned the key, adrenaline pumping. The engine started straightaway. Deep breaths, I can do this. She forced the gear into reverse, making a loud crunching sound. The van shot backwards, hitting the side of the door as she reversed out. She then clipped her own car turning the van around. Once she had the van pointing in the right direction, she was sure it would be easier.

She drove as fast as she could for the police station. If she had irritated other motorists on her journey from the hospital, she terrified them on her way to the police station.

THIRTY-NINE

The march around the block had not cooled Peter's temper one bit. He felt angry and frustrated. Not feeling ready to return, he sat in his car brooding. Mostly he felt incredibly tired. Whether he was just tired from lack of sleep over the last few days or tired of everything, he was not entirely sure.

Everybody talked about stress and stress management, but this felt like something else. He felt overwhelmed with the belief that he just couldn't handle it any more. All aspects of his life, both personal and professional, seemed to be spiralling out of control. Spinning ever faster like a huge twister in a storm picking up more and more baggage as it went. A feeling somewhere low in the pit of his stomach telling him he'd screwed up and he didn't know how best to regain control and turn things around.

He started to question himself over his handling of Mark Farley. Tried to break down the facts and view them dispassionately. But the more he went through things in his mind, the surer he was that his judgement was correct. Was that his problem? When had he become so oversensitive to his credibility being questioned? Could it be that it was his own ego and conviction that he was right that was preventing him from reviewing the evidence objectively? If that were the case, his conscience told him he should withdraw from the case. But there was still a small voice inside, telling him he was correct and had to stick with it.

Normally he would trust his inner voice and go straight back out there and prove he was right. What was stopping him this time? Why was he sitting alone in his car considering giving up?

He remembered a conversation with his granddad, amazed how quickly his mind could send him back in time. He saw himself as a twelve-year-old sitting on the porch steps trying to ignore the effort the old man was making to lower himself down to sit next to him. It was about six months after his friend had been knocked from his bicycle and he still felt the pain of loss and loneliness. Granddad had been staying with them a few weeks but was all packed and waiting patiently for his lift back home.

"You know, son, I can remember when I used to call you the 'adventure kid.' Always up to mischief somewhere or other and giving your mother grey hairs."

Peter remembered how he had felt hurt by the comment which made him defensive. "Yeah, well. Now I'm the wimpy, scared kid." He wished his parents would hurry up and take his grandfather away. He turned his back to look across the back-yard and pretended the old man was gone already.

"Well, you know, young man, you don't have to stay that way. It's entirely up to you."

His grandfather struggled back to his feet and left in search of his lift home. Peter refused to acknowledge him or turn to say goodbye. He remained on the step thinking about those words. That comment had kickstarted his life back then.

Peter returned to the station, apologised for his absence and threw himself back into the case. It wasn't an easy day. Frustrations at the delay in reports and returned calls were still there, but he felt more able to cope. Calls from locals wanting to arrange search parties for Rose didn't help. As she was seen leaving the area, he didn't think they would find anything, but he told them it would do no harm to search their outbuildings if they so wished.

The extensive press coverage hadn't given them any useful leads about where James and Rose could be. A shop assistant thought she may have served her that day, but that was about it. Peter closed his eyes and cringed whenever he remembered earlier comments about the young man seen hanging around, looking just like the girl in the photograph. He tried to block them from his memory.

He had two experienced officers dedicated to leading the search for James and Rose. He was briefing them when they were interrupted by a flushed PC Mann rushing into the room. "Sorry, sir…" She paused, gasping for air. "The phone lines were all busy, so I ran up. A Joyce James is in the car park causing total chaos. She says she'll only speak to either you or Fiona."

"The car park?" Peter said, as he and Fiona moved simultaneously to the window.

"Yes, sir… in a black van."

They looked down on the roof of a white van surrounded by a group of officers. Peter pointed dumbfound at the police patrol vehicles that had been tossed to one side like toy cars making a path from the car park entrance. "I thought you said a black van? It's white."

PC Mann looked out the window. She was still catching her breath from the exertion of running three flights of stairs. "Downstairs it was black."

At the corner of the car park, Peter and Fiona were confronted by an angry crowd of officers surrounding the van. When they got closer, they could see Joyce had locked herself in the cab. They elbowed their way through the other officers trying to persuade Joyce to get out of the cab. Joyce spotted them, gave a cheery wave as if meeting on a social occasion, and unlocked the door. Peter pulled it open and said in exasperation, "What on earth are you doing? You've damaged half the station's patrol cars!"

As the throng of officers moved back, Joyce awkwardly stepped down from the cab. She took Peter and Fiona by the hand and led them to the back of the vehicle. She didn't say a word, just pointed to the damage to the rear doors and the tape covering the rear lights. She then started to struggle to open the doors which had re-jammed. Only when Peter helped her did the door finally spring open, sending them tumbling backwards. Had it not been for other officers behind, they would have both ended up flat on their backs when the doors opened with a jerk.

Peter didn't know what he was expecting to see inside. Certainly, more than an empty space with a length of plywood propped against one side.

Fiona and the other officers who had crowded forwards looking over Peter's shoulder were also confounded by the empty van. Joyce was not deterred. She held up a finger indicating, 'wait one moment,' as part of her silent film actress moment. She clambered clumsily into the van with Peter giving her a helpful push up. With a struggle, she managed to swivel the plank of plywood around. As she did so, she spoke for the first time. "Would this explain why Frank saw headlights suddenly appear from out of nowhere, but you found traces of damage to rear lights?"

Peter looked up in wonder at the attachments for the mirror on the ceiling of the van and turned to one of the officers crowded round. "Can someone arrange for this vehicle to be moved? We have to get this to the forensic team as quickly as possible."

Now that her moment of theatrical glory was complete, the enormity of what she had just done hit Joyce. The colour drained from her face, and she looked like her legs were about to buckle. Peter jumped into the back of the van and was immediately at her side with his arm around her. He carefully helped her down from the van, which he now noticed had been hurriedly sprayed black and said, "Fiona, take Joyce upstairs Have the station medic check her over, and I'll join you in a bit."

Fiona gently led Joyce away, supporting her as they walked into the station. Joyce was insisting she was fine and wanted to go back to the hospital. "I need to explain all of this to Frank. I don't want him hearing about it from somebody else first."

Fiona admired her strength and courage. "First we want to

make sure you're okay. Then we need to talk about what you've been up to. Where this van came from? Then I will personally drive you back to the hospital. Do we have a deal?"

Joyce nodded her agreement. "Frank is going to be so upset. I don't know how I'm going to explain it all to him. I don't know how he's going to take it. He's going to be devastated."

Fiona repeated, "You need to explain everything to us first, Joyce, when Peter gets here. You're probably in shock. We'd like someone to check you over."

"Don't talk such nonsense, there's no time for that. You need to get someone to arrest Mark Farley for attempted murder."

"Slow down, Joyce. Let's wait until Peter gets back," Fiona said. "You must think a lot of Frank."

Joyce paused briefly before she replied, "Yes, I do. We've been friends a long time, proper friends." Joyce smiled and added, "At school, I used to have a terrible crush on him. The friendship we've had over the years has proved to be far better, though." She thought a bit more before adding shyly, "Don't you go telling that old fool I said that, mind?"

"Your secret is safe with me," Fiona said.

"I didn't get a look in, once Maggie arrived on the scene. Frank worshipped her. I wanted to hate her, but she was such a lovely person, we ended up being friends. It was terrible what happened to her," Joyce said. "They were so worried when they thought she was pregnant. That's why they married, super quick. Maggie endured the sickness thinking the child growing inside her would make it all worthwhile. What do you think it did to them, when they discovered it was not a bouncy baby growing? It was a monster draining and destroying her. It was cancer."

"I can't even start to imagine how devastating that must have been for them," Fiona said.

Peter supervised the removal of the van and joined in with the initial speculation of whether the mirror would cause a driver to swerve thinking another vehicle had just appeared in front of him. "Even on a dark rural lane, wouldn't the outline of the van be seen?" Peter asked. "Possibly not, if the driver was blinded without warning. They wouldn't have time to notice anything else."

"But I mean before. Before the mirror could be seen?"

"Was there a hedge or gateway the van could have been hidden behind until the moment it was reversed out?"

"In that case, wouldn't a second person be needed to time the reversal out from behind the hedge at exactly the right moment?"

The officer shrugged.

Peter had not previously considered two people working together. But that was before the recent revelations about Tim Potter.

Once satisfied the van was receiving all the attention it deserved, he made his way upstairs. He found Joyce at his desk with a blanket around her shoulders, drinking a cup of tea. He made eye contact with Fiona to check she was okay and up to questioning. He gave Joyce a weary but genuine smile. "Now young lady, would you like to tell us what you have been up to today?" Peter said, as he drew a chair up next to her.

Joyce quickly gave her story from the time she broke down in the lay-by. She did not admit she had intended going to the house to confront Mark. When she completed her story, she reminded Fiona of her promise to take her back out to the hospital.

"Slow down a minute, Joyce. There are a couple of things I need to check with you before you leave," Peter said.

Joyce looked at Peter, her feisty nature returning. "I don't know what more you need to know. I've solved the case for you. All you've got to do now is get out there and arrest Mark Farley."

Peter ran his hand through his hair and sighed. If only things were that simple. Joyce showed every sign she disliked him, but he had grown to feel quite fond of her. Under her sensible matronly appearance, she was quite a spirited lady. He wondered what she was like as a young woman. He said patiently, "We know this workshop was on Mark Farley's property, but you said it was some distance from the house? We need to know exactly where it is. Also, you said yourself it wasn't used by Mark, and at least two other people were using it."

Joyce looked crestfallen. "You mean I did the wrong thing driving it here? I should have left it where it was and called you? Oh no. And now it'll be covered in my fingerprints. I'm so sorry. Have I ruined your crime scene?"

"Don't be silly, Joyce. You did a very brave thing. You found it for us," Fiona said.

Peter could see Joyce was shattered by her experience and wanted to leave, but he had a few more questions before he could let her go.

"If...and I say if, this was Mark. Do you think Kim would have assisted her husband in setting up an accident?"

Joyce thought very carefully before replying. "Well, Kim only cares about Kim and her image and status. She probably would do anything to protect herself if she knew she could get away with it. But, she is not a stupid woman and wouldn't do anything that might incriminate herself. If it was a question of her or Mark, she would save herself. Does that help?"

"Yes, it helps a little. Can you tell us anything about Tim Potter?"

"Tim?" Joyce said in surprise. "He is friendly with Mark. Not someone I really know. He thinks himself above the likes of me. Why do you ask?"

"No reason," Peter said, as dismissively as he could. "You said Fiona was taking you to the hospital."

"If you're still happy to take me?" Joyce said, turning to Fiona who nodded agreement.

"Can you promise me you won't breathe a word about the van until we've had the chance to investigate it further?" Peter said.

"Not even to Frank?"

"Not even to Frank."

Joyce nodded her agreement.

Peter stood up and held out his hand to Joyce. "Say hi to Frank for me." He turned to Fiona and said, "Keep in contact. I'm planning on having a quick look at this workshop and then going out to see Mark Farley."

"Are you going to arrest him?" Joyce asked.

"We'll see," Peter said, wearily. "But please just leave things to us now."

Peter felt Fiona gently pull him to one side. "You are going to see Rogers before pulling in Mark, aren't you?"

Peter was surprised to see a genuine concern for him in her eyes. He gave her a wide grin in. "It'll be my pleasure."

Peter shot back to his desk, pulled out the notes he'd already prepared on both Mark and Tim and headed upstairs. The meeting with Rogers wasn't quite the victory he would have liked, but he had the go-ahead to question Mark about the van and workshop. Peter quickly re-read the file on Frank's accident. From a quick look at the photographs of the bridge, there did appear to be an area where the van could have been partially obscured by trees before reversing out. He would drive by tomorrow and have another look at the scene.

He tried to ring Mark several times without success. He then tried Tim Potter's number.

His son Grant claimed he was the only person at home. "They went off first thing this morning in one of the cars."

"Have you any idea where they were heading?" Peter asked.

"Sorry. No idea," Grant replied. "But they are due back later this evening. Shall I get them to give you a call?"

"That would be most helpful," Peter said. He ended the call thinking how jolly for them to be having a lovely little jaunt in one of their fancy cars.

From the directions he had, the workshop was not as close to Mark's house as Peter had hoped. He was concerned and a little disappointed that not only was it some distance away but more importantly, it was not within the area secured by his security gates and wall. It could be reached by anyone with local knowledge via the narrow country lane. He needed something else to prove Mark guilty.

Peter arrived at the workshop at the same time as the forensic team. He introduced himself and walked through the bent door into the workshop. He smiled to himself when he saw the damage Joyce had caused to the workshop door and to her own car. Looking at the door, he noticed that the padlock which had been locking it appeared to be brand new. He spotted the key-hide, mentioned by Joyce, in the long grass.

After a brief look around, he telephoned Mark Farley again. Although he received no reply, he decided to drive out to the house. The gates barred his entrance, and a quick look at the panel on the wall confirmed he could not operate the gates from outside. He parked his car and telephoned again. Receiving no reply, he checked the lane before pulling himself over the wall and jogging up the driveway. The house, as he expected, was deserted. The warrant they had only covered the workshop, but he was debating forcing the door. He took out his phone to ring Mark again with no success. He then tried Graham.

"It's DCI Peter Hatherall here."

"Graham isn't here," Gillian said.

"Can you tell me where he is?"

After a long pause, Gillian replied, "Is it important?"

"Yes, it is. Where is he?"

"He's driving his parents to the airport. They're going to Kenya for a break. It was a spur of the moment thing. They left first this morning, so he should be back sometime soon."

"Which airport is he taking them to? And what time was the flight?"

"I think he said Gatwick. I've no idea what time they were due to take off."

Peter had already closed his phone and started redialling.

FORTY

Peter considered breaking into the house while he frantically called the station. They had to stop Mark and Kim from getting on their aeroplane. He thumped the front door with frustration, bruising his knuckles. The physical pain gave some distraction from his feelings of anger and helplessness. There was nothing more he could do where he was. He just had to hope they were not too late and jogged back to his car.

He rammed the car in reverse sending up a spray of gravel and dust. He drove at speed trying to force his phone to ring. Only when he felt his fingers start to ache did he release his tight grip on the steering wheel. By the time he arrived back at the station, his neck and shoulders were in spasm.

He raced into the incident room, shouting, "Have they been stopped?"

DS Steve Jackson replied, "Not yet. The flight they're booked on hasn't boarded yet."

Relief flooded through Peter. It felt like opening the windows of a long boarded up house and allowing a breeze through. He slid down into his chair. "Well. That's something at least. And thanks, Steve."

"No problem. Happy to help."

Peter thought he saw the young man blush as Fiona walked in. "Did they say whether they'd actually spotted them?"

"They're trying to keep a low profile at the airport, so they don't startle them. But ..." Steve faltered. "They haven't as yet been able to spot them in the terminal."

Fiona crossed the room, slipping her handbag from her shoulder. "Maybe they're leaving it to the last minute. Have they booked in?"

"Yes. According to the airline, they booked in as soon as the desk opened. But they haven't been seen in the terminal since," Steve replied. "As soon as they try to board..."

"When do they start boarding?" Peter asked, feeling his tension start to rise.

"Any minute now," Steve said.

"Has anything come in about James and Rose?" Peter asked.

"No sightings despite the media coverage," Fiona replied.

"Where the hell are they? Has Rose been in contact with her friends or family?"

"I can check again," Fiona said.

"Have we heard anything further from Gerry Bowden?"

"Not yet," Fiona said.

"I can chase up on that," Steve offered.

"Thank you. And has Tim Potter returned yet from his jolly jaunt around the countryside?" Peter asked.

They jumped when the phone in front of Steve rang. He was slow to react. Peter shouted, "Answer it, for God's sake."

Everyone in the room stared at Steve, listening intently to his comments, hoping for some reaction that would release the taut atmosphere. Steve gave the universal 'thumbs up' sign.

Peter shouted, "Yes!" thumping the air in a victory salute. "At last the self-absorbed snob is going to be held accountable."

Steve paused briefly after replacing the receiver before swinging his chair round to address his captive audience.

"Apparently they made quite an amazing scene at the airport. Claimed to be absolutely astounded at the suggestion they should be suspected of anything."

"I bet they were," Peter replied, his voice laden with sarcasm.

"They couldn't believe we expected them to forgo their trip, as it was a terrible error. They thought we could just wait for them to come back!"

"Yeah, of course, we could do that. Anything else?"

"Not really. They're expecting a full refund of the holiday. Heads would roll, that sort of thing," Steve said.

"But they are both now safely in custody?"

"Yes. Once Mark had at least in part accepted the situation, he called his solicitor who he claims will sort out this little misunderstanding in the morning."

"And how did Mrs Farley take it?" Peter asked. "Floods of tears, by any chance?"

Steve replied, "No. She remained as cool as ice. She insists she should be allowed to continue her journey alone if need be, as it has nothing to do with her."

Peter smiled. "Not exactly the loyal, supportive wife then. That could be very useful to us. Any idea when they are likely to be transferred here?"

"They're ready and waiting for us as soon as we can get someone over there to pick them up."

"Steve, I don't suppose you'd like to do the honours?" Peter asked, as a wave of exhaustion washed over him.

"Could do...Do you fancy a trip?" Steve said, looking at Fiona.

It was no contest for her. It was that or another evening trying to conquer the yoga training programme she'd purchased. "Yes, sure, if you'd like the company."

Before they left, Peter said, "Thanks again... And Fiona, try and not worry about James and Rose. I promise I'll ring you if anything is heard from them."

"Thank you."

"I'll see you first thing in the morning. We will need to head over to Birkbury at some point tomorrow. I want to see what Graham has to say about the night Frank found him by the caravans before we interview his father." Peter added, "We'll also go and see Tim Potter."

"Will we be arresting him as well?" Fiona asked.

"We haven't got enough evidence to bring him in at the moment. But get off now, and we'll start afresh tomorrow."

Fiona hesitated by her desk. "I'm worried about Rose."

Peter sighed. "Half the country is looking for them."

He knew his answer was insufficient. He was increasingly concerned they had not heard anything from Rose. His hope her disappearance was unconnected was fading as the media coverage failed to get any response.

An hour later, with no developments and nodding off at his desk, Peter decided it was time to leave for home. He dreaded the conversation Sally would want once he arrived. The break had supposedly been for him to come to some conclusions. But it seemed every time he questioned his feelings, the more questions appeared. He had to be fair to Sally. He had to let her know one way or the other. He had missed her and been irritable all the time she was away.

For once, he was happy to be held up in traffic due to an earlier accident. It gave him more time to delay the inevitable conversation. He fought the urge to stop for a drink on the way.

His stomach lurched when he saw Sally's and Amelia's cars, parked side by side on the driveway. He sat in his car, reluctant to go inside. Whatever he was expecting, it was not what he found inside.

He pushed the front door open as quietly as possible, listening out for sounds of shouting and smashing glasses. He walked into the silent kitchen feeling on edge. Through the open French window, he could see the twins playing in the garden on their trikes. Sitting at the table sharing a bottle of wine, were Sally and Amelia. They turned and smiled simultaneously, a picture of domestic bliss and happiness. Sally called to the boys who leapt from their trikes, tumbling and fighting to be the first to reach him with outstretched arms calling, "Daddy!" Peter's stomach turned somersaults, a lump rose in his throat as they wrapped themselves around his legs.

Disentangling himself, Peter mumbled, "I'll go upstairs to change out of my work clothes," and fled. He pulled on a pair of jeans and t-shirt. He sat on the bed trying to understand what had just happened. Why had he felt so overwhelmed with feelings of suffocation, and an urgent desire to escape? His mind flew back to the first time he'd been overwhelmed with emotion. Then he had a reason.

The expression on Jordan's face pierced straight through him. Despite the unbelievable hurt he thought he could fix it. If he said sorry often enough and for long enough, eventually he would be forgiven. One day Jordan would look at him again with love and trust in her eyes. Well, maybe not trust but love certainly. Not hurt and anguish.

Why did you have to do it? I would have made you so happy. I would have shown you every day how sorry I was. You could have hurt and hurt me again in return, and I would have forgiven you. I could have forgiven you anything except what you did. I did wrong, but your punishment was too cruel. Did you kill yourself to punish me? I deserved it, but it wasn't fair on our beautiful daughter. How could you have done it? Left us all like that. What if it had been Amelia who found you, not me?

Peter was startled by a knock on the bedroom door.

"Can I come in?" Sally asked.

"I'll be down in a minute," Peter replied, not moving from the bed. I can never make amends for Jordan. How can I? She killed herself before I got the chance. But I can make amends with Sally. I have to pull myself together and go downstairs to face them.

Listening to Sally walking down the staircase Peter realised why he'd been so angry with Sally and Amelia. He'd thought it was his responsibility to bring them back together. After all the sleep he'd lost, they'd done it without him. They hadn't needed him at all. His reaction had been ludicrous and childish. His only excuse was he was tired, angry and scared by the strength of his feelings. He loved them all but was too damn scared to admit it or how vulnerable that made him feel.

Peter walked into the kitchen where Sally was waiting for him. He could hear Amelia entertaining the twins in the living room. He shoved his hands as far down into his pockets as he could. Took a deep breath and looking directly at her, he said, "Sorry."

He saw the tears in her eyes as she replied, "We're all sorry. But you have to stop hiding from us."

Peter nodded as he held her tight.

"Will you be here in the morning?" Sally asked.

Peter gently pushed her away. "I need to get away early to see two people before interviewing..."

Sally interrupted him. "Peter. It's all right for tomorrow. But I need to know about other days. The days when you choose to stay away."

Peter took her hands in his. "I will try."

"Peter, we love you. We all do. And that doesn't change."

Peter had to look away. "I know. And I love you all back...but it terrifies me."

Sally pulled him towards her and held him tight. "I know, but I promise I won't let go," she said softly in his ear, as she led him upstairs.

FORTY-ONE

Peter left a note in the morning next to the kettle telling them all how much he missed them. The note felt inadequate to convey all he felt or wanted to say. But it was a start.

The temperature was already rising as he headed to the car. It seemed such a long time since he'd felt the sharp coolness of more typical British weather against his skin, or even a gust of wind against his face. Despite the continued heaviness of the weather, he could not ignore a slight lifting of his spirits. His mind felt less cluttered by random thoughts darting in all directions.

He saw Fiona pulling into the car park as he was locking his own vehicle. He waited for her to catch him up. "Thanks for coming in early. I want to get over to Birkbury as soon as possible this morning."

"No problem, sir. To be honest, this weather makes it hard to lie in."

"How did it go last night with the Farleys?"

"Surprisingly quiet."

"I hope you weren't too late."

Fiona shook her head in reply.

"I'm guessing they'll be meeting with their solicitor this morning before they agree to speak to us, which gives us a little more time." Peter wanted to ask about Steve but didn't want to risk embarrassing her by overstepping the boundaries of their relationship. "We'll just check on that and whether anything new has come in overnight, grab a coffee and get going."

"That sounds good to me," Fiona said.

Nothing new of note had happened over-night. Fiona found a note on her desk advising the vets had returned her call. "I need to make a quick call before we leave."

"I'll go get some coffee for us," Peter said.

He returned to find Fiona looking very pleased. "Won the lottery?"

"No, but Mark Farley's alibi for the day Jenny disappeared isn't as strong as we thought."

"Go on."

"That horse's passport he showed us? They're not strictly regulated like a register of human births and deaths. Nobody would hold the vet who signed it to an exact date unless it was a thoroughbred destined for the race track. Chances are the vet would have written down any date Mark gave him as long as it was roughly correct."

"Good work. That creates doubt. Considering the time they left The Trout Inn, in separate cars, that alibi is weak as well. I wonder what he got up to around the time of David Conley's accident? Have we got a copy report on the work accident involving Taffy, the other man in the photograph?"

"Yes. Nothing suspicious noted."

Peter gulped the last of his coffee, and said, "We'll see Graham first and then Tim."

Peter was worried about talking to Tim Potter without anything more substantial than a photograph and a hunch about an unsolved rape case. He didn't need Rogers to tell him that arresting a rich landowner and a local magistrate would cause quite a stir. "Let me see that photograph of the two boys again."

"Here you are," Fiona said, efficiently.

He looked at it closely and thought about his own childhood. He remembered waiting for the bus to take him to his comprehensive school. On the opposite side, the posh kids waited for their coach painted in the colours of their private school. They used to shout abuse across the road. Mostly it was good-natured, but it showed the clear social divide.

Mark Farley grew up in a council flat and attended the local comprehensive school. Would a shared hobby break down the class barrier? How would Tim's wealth and privilege have affected the relationship? Mark's father was a genius at finding and restoring old vehicles. As wealthy, multiple collectors, the Potters would have been viewed as important customers by him. Where did the balance of power lie?

He looked up at Fiona. "I'm playing devil's advocate a moment. Could it be we've been looking at this the wrong way around?"

"How do you mean?"

"I've assumed Mark to be the leader, and Tim covering for him. Wouldn't it make more sense the other way around?"

"You mean it was a repeat of what might have happened when they were younger? When the girl couldn't identify her rapist, other than saying he was blond and posh."

"That's exactly what I mean. Just unfortunate for Mark, this time it happened on his farm."

"Possibly makes more sense. Or it could be a case of I-covered-for-you once. Now it's your turn?" Fiona suggested. "But, we've no evidence Tim Potter was the toff in Birmingham."

When they arrived at Rooksbridge, Peter was surprised to see Gillian out on the yard kitted out in jodhpurs and gloves despite the summer heat. Her shoulders still slouched in their downturned way, yet she appeared head and shoulders above everyone else. The erratic waving of her arms suggested she was trying to direct proceedings. The women who kept their horses on the yard seemed as bemused as he was.

Her voice was shrill, and as they approached, she gave a high-pitched false laugh. Peter decided he preferred her sullen silence and mournful eyes. He flinched at the sound and hunched his shoulders as if they could somehow block out the dreadful sound.

Fiona whispered, "That screeching just went straight through me. Like chalk on a board."

Gillian greeted them briskly, abruptly holding out her hand.

Peter shook it as he asked her where Graham was.

"He's sulking in the kitchen," Gillian replied.

"We need to see him. Will you be coming back to the house with us?"

"I have farm work to do. I will be finished in half an hour." Before turning away, Gillian added, "I hear you've arrested that horrible little man."

Peter whispered to Fiona with a raised eyebrow, "A little harsh." He wondered at her attitude. Was it the arrest that had cheered the woman and lifted her from her easy chair? He was also mystified by what her 'farm work' could possibly consist of. Previously the place seemed to have managed quite fine without her.

Walking towards the house, they heard Gillian shout, "That's not the proper way to push a wheelbarrow. Here, let me show you."

Peter said to Fiona, "There's more than one way to push a wheelbarrow?" He felt a slight pang of sorrow for Graham.

They saw Graham through the open door to the farmhouse. He sat at the kitchen table looking ashen-faced. When they knocked, he raised a hand indicating they should come in.

Graham was unshaven, and his eyes were bloodshot. Peter noticed the unsteadiness of his hands when he insisted on making them coffee despite them declining the offer. As he carried the mugs to the table, they slipped out of his hand, crashing to the floor. Fiona jumped up and tried to help as he frantically wiped the floor. Long after Fiona had picked up the broken crockery, Graham continued scrubbing hard at an invisible stain. If they had more time, Peter would suggest he seek medical attention before questioning him.

Gently, Peter said, "I am sure you know we have your parents in custody. We have to ask you some questions."

Graham turned his dull eyes towards Peter, his face expressionless.

"We need to ask you about the evening Frank found you by the caravans when you were a boy."

There remained no response from Graham, sat heavily in his usual position at the head of the table. On their earlier visits, Graham had filled the space, the position reinforcing his control over the room. Now he appeared a broken man uncomfortable with the amount of space he took up.

"We understand you told Frank you could remember the incident vaguely. Could you tell us what you remember about that night?" Peter prompted.

Graham gazed at him with unseeing eyes.

"It really would help if you could tell us what you saw that night, Graham," Peter coaxed.

Graham continued to stare at his coffee mug, and an uncomfortable silence filled the room. Peter felt at a loss at how best to proceed. How hard he could push a man in this state?

Gillian marched in with a look Peter couldn't quite read. "I need some keys." She rummaged in a drawer, not giving her husband a second glance. "Well. I'll leave you to it," she said, oblivious to her husband's suffering.

Peter could not fathom the callousness of her behaviour. For all his faults, Graham had seemed genuine in his attempts to shield and protect his wife. Her cold indifference seemed shocking in comparison.

Graham looked up at them with dull eyes and said, "Green and yellow. What do you think of the colours green and yellow?"

"Sorry?"

"I'm thinking of getting a new tractor, a John Deere maybe, but they're green and yellow," Graham said.

"I'm sorry I don't know anything about tractors," Peter said. "Can you tell us about the night you were found wandering about near the staff caravans when you were a boy?"

"I have tried, but I can't remember a time when I was wandering about outside in the early hours," Graham stated.

Peter sighed and patiently said, "That's not what you told Frank."

"I have no idea what you are talking about," Graham said slowly as if explaining something to an idiot.

Peter felt frustrated. He really wanted to push the matter, but felt he had no choice other than to leave it there. Finding Graham tomorrow morning with a shotgun between his knees wasn't something he wanted on his conscience. "Thank you for your time. We will need to talk to you again," Peter said, trying to keep his voice as neutral as possible.

Graham waved them away wearily.

Outside Fiona asked, "Should we have left him alone? The state he's in?"

Peter tensed. "His welfare is not our responsibility. His wife is around, and he is protecting his father by withholding information from us. There's nothing we can do for him. He's a grown man."

"Realising what his father has done and dealing with that vile woman would drive anyone over the edge," Fiona retorted. "Did you see the way she blanked him? It was almost as though she was pleased he was suffering."

Peter agreed with her, and he really didn't want to be responsible for him doing something stupid, but he knew they were powerless to help. "He has to work it out for himself. You can't save everyone," Peter said, sternly. He felt cold and callous saying it, but he didn't want Fiona carrying around such a burden of guilt. "We'll see if Gillian has finished doing whatever she was doing. See what, if anything, she has to say about her in-laws. Maybe we could encourage her to check on her husband, afterwards."

They found Gillian in a stable, feeding an endless supply of mints to a horse, saying, "Your owner doesn't deserve you. None of them does."

Peter called, "Mrs Farley. Could we have a word please?"

Continuing to address the horse, Gillian said, "About Father, I assume."

"Yes," Peter replied.

Gillian stepped out of the stable, and said, "Can we take a walk?"

They followed her across the yard, towards the wooded walkway to the holiday cottages. Small talk was not invited or given. A short way along the path, she turned left through the trees. As they emerged on the other side, they were confronted with a breath-taking view over the farm and the fields beyond. The fishing lake could be seen below, its surface glistening in the sun.

"What a fantastic view!" Fiona said, as Gillian led them to a worn wooden bench shaded by the trees behind them.

"You don't seem very upset about the arrest of your in-laws, Mrs Farley?" Peter said, as they seated themselves.

Gillian stared straight ahead. "You know. When I first came here, I thought this was the most beautiful place in the world."

"It still is very beautiful," Fiona replied.

"It's all ugly and horrid. All ruined."

When Fiona asked what she meant by that, she merely shrugged.

"You were quite young when you came here first. Sixteen, I think. What was your father-in-law like then?" Peter asked.

After a long pause, Gillian replied, "A bully, same as now."

"Why do you call him a bully?"

"He has to control everything. He's not happy until he has everything and everybody exactly where he wants them. And if he can't, he becomes cruel and vindictive."

"What do you think about him being arrested?"

"Pleased. He deserves it," Gillian said.

"Do you think he murdered that girl?" Peter said, watching Gillian as she continued to stare morosely out to space. "Gillian?"

"I couldn't say. I was just thinking of how uncomfortable it must be for him waiting in a police cell."

"How did he treat you and the other girls when you first came to work here?"

"Badly, he liked to intimidate us. He was mean and shouted at us a lot. If he was in a bad mood, he'd switch off the gas supply to the caravans."

"Was he physically violent?

"Yes, sometimes. He liked to thump the horses in their faces as he walked along the yard. But it was mostly more calculated and cold. We were all terrified of him."

"Were you aware of any time he was violent towards any of you girls?"

Gillian fidgeted, before replying, "No."

"Your husband seems in a pretty bad way, Mrs Farley."

Gillian stood abruptly. "He's spent his entire life trying to win his father's approval and now this," she said, waving her arms to the side. "Are we finished now? I've work to do."

"For now," Peter, replied. "But we may want to see you again."

They walked back the way they had come in silence. Entering the yard, Gillian said, "Mr Turner, I understand, is the brother and not the cousin of the murdered girl?"

"That's right, what about him?" Peter asked.

"He lied to me about being the cousin."

"Have you any idea where he is? If you do, it is important you tell us. Rose could be in danger," Peter said.

"He seemed a nice guy, not the type to harm anyone. Quiet. It was me who booked him in. He said he wanted to be near where his cousin was buried. Graham was furious. Rose is a feisty girl, quite capable of looking after herself."

"Did Mr Turner say anything about what he hoped to achieve or where he might be going?"

"Not really. He told me, everyone is searching for something. Find it, and everything else falls into place."

"Do you have any idea where he might be, now?" Peter repeated.

Gillian shook her head in reply.

As Gillian walked away, Peter rang Tim Potter's home. Grant answered, saying his parents had popped into town to do some shopping.

FORTY-TWO

Arriving back at the station, Peter was disappointed to find there was nothing to suggest Mark had been near the workshop recently. "We'll keep the initial interviews brief," he said. "Just cover what we already know. See how he reacts. Then we'll chase up the outstanding enquiries and any further alibis he gives."

"Is there anything you'd like me to do?" Fiona asked.

"Just watch him really closely. Make a note of any slight reactions you might see. Anything at all that might give him away."

Steve finished his phone call and raised a hand in greeting to Peter.

"Is there any news of Rose?" Peter asked.

Steve shook his head. "We've received nothing at all yet."

"Please keep me updated on any developments. We're going to interview Mark Farley now, but you can interrupt me with any news."

As anticipated, Mark had secured a top London solicitor, who directed his every move and response. His expensive suit and shiny shoes shouted his exclusive hourly rates. Tall and athletic, he had all the arrogance and self-assurance of a public-school education.

The solicitor immediately tried to take control. He was pretentious in his anticipation all their evidence would be circumstantial and demanded the immediate release of his client.

"My client is a successful businessman of good character. He has no previous convictions or involvement with the police but is keen to help with your enquiries. He is prepared to surrender his passport and forgo his paid-for trip. But when he is finally cleared of all this nonsense, we will be seeking a full refund of the cost of his holiday. We will take action for his wrongful arrest and detention. The damage to his reputation is immense, and it must be compensated for."

Peter chose to ignore the solicitor and direct his questions to Mark. "We have eyewitness evidence you were in Cheltenham on the day Jenny Turner disappeared. This contradicts your earlier insistence you were on the farm."

"You are talking about one day nearly twenty years ago."

"Yes, the day you said you were watching a foal being born. We have the passport showing the time of birth. Can you explain that?"

"I was present the day that foal was born. You can ask my wife. Maybe your eyewitness is incorrect about the day. That's more likely than the vet not knowing the date," Mark replied smugly.

"Our witness is sure it was the day of the show. And you said it was also your wedding anniversary? Surely you remember whether it was the same day? You told us earlier how special that particular horse was to you."

"I have been married for over thirty years, have owned more than one hundred horses and probably watched at least twenty foals being born. It all merges into one after a while. As I said, it was a long time ago, and as far as I was previously aware, there was nothing special about that day. I had no reason to query the date of birth written on the passport. It was correct. It was the day of my anniversary."

"You are adamant that, on the twenty-fifth of May 2001, you were in Birkbury all day witnessing the birth of a foal after a celebratory meal with your wife?" Peter asked.

After consulting with his solicitor, Mark calmly replied, "Could anybody confirm exactly what they did on a particular day nearly twenty years ago from memory alone? I have provided evidence that says I was in Birkbury on that date. I can't add anything more."

"Did you attend the Cheltenham Gold Cup that same year?"

"Yes. I have never missed a year, along with thousands of other people. But I can't confirm exactly what I did, which horses I bet on or where we had lunch from so long ago."

"Did you meet Jenny Turner at this event?"

"No, I did not."

"Did you meet any girls?"

"For goodness sake, how do you expect me to answer that question? It was a long time ago. I probably spoke to a lot of people. If the young lady was at the same event, it is very possible we may have been in the same area together. But I have no recollection of ever meeting the girl."

"Did you and Tim Potter make a habit of meeting young girls on your days out?"

Mark's jaw twitched as he clenched his teeth. "This is absolutely outrageous. We were young men. I'm quite sure we did flirt on occasion with women when we got the chance."

"Young married men," Peter said, feeling like a prude and hypocrite for saying something so crass. He added, "Can you explain why she was buried on your property?"

"No. I can't. It's a large farm a few miles from a motorway junction. I was not running around burying bodies on my wedding anniversary."

Peter ignored the withering look the solicitor gave him. "On the night Jenny disappeared, a vehicle was heard driving across your land around two o'clock in the morning. Could you give any explanation for that?"

"I can't give an explanation for something I know nothing about," Mark said.

Peter consulted the file he carried and said, "Is there anything more you would like to say about the renovation of the staff caravans that summer?"

"No."

"What can you tell us about the van we found in your workshop?"

"What van? I don't own a van," Mark replied.

"So, what was it doing in your workshop?"

"I have no idea."

"Who else has access to your workshop?"

"The workshop by the house? Well, I would, of course and Graham. I think Kim would know where I keep the spare key."

"The other workshop," Peter said. "Who has access to the old workshop to the rear of your property?"

"Several local people have access to that one. Since I built the new one up at the house, I don't think I've used it myself for ages. Why should I?"

"When was the last time you were in that workshop?"

"God, I don't know, six to twelve months ago. If you found a van in there, it could belong to any number of people. I let lots of other people use it. Graham, Chris, Bob, they all have keys to it. As far as I'm aware, nothing of any great value is kept there. It's too open. That's why I built the one up at the house."

After a brief discussion with his solicitor, Mark added. "My solicitor can arrange signed statements from several people who use that workshop and confirm they know where the key is kept."

"Where were you on the evenings of Frank's and David's accidents?"

"I haven't a diary with me," Mark replied sarcastically. "What was the first date?"

"Surely you don't need a diary to tell you the evening of Frank Codrington's accident?"

"Ah yes. I remember now...I thought I told you already. I was in The Trout Inn in Lower Sudbury with my wife having a meal."

"But we understand you left early in separate cars."

A flicker of annoyance crossed Mark's face. "We're both very busy people. We met there. And then we followed each other home."

"And do you remember where you were on the day of David Conley's accident? That was three days ago. Surely you can remember that far back?"

"Let me think." After a brief pause, Mark said, "Yes. I know what I was doing that day. I had an appointment with my bank. And then I went on to the travel agent next door. To book the very break, we should now be on. I didn't book with them in the end. I went online and got a better deal. I'll write down their details."

"That would be helpful," Peter said, handing Mark a pen. While Mark was writing, Peter asked, "Can you tell me about your friendship with Tim Potter?"

Mark completed his note and handed it over. "Tim? Not much to say. He was our neighbour when we lived at Rooksbridge. We got along very well with him and his wife. We have gradually seen less of them since we moved out of the village."

"And when you were younger? I'm talking about much younger, when you lived in Birmingham with your parents."

Mark hid his reaction by turning his head to speak to his solicitor. "Our fathers knew each other vaguely through a shared hobby."

"Did you become friendly with Tim at that time?"

Mark shook his head and said, "No. Not particularly. He was the son of a customer."

"And how well did you know David Conley?"

"Again, he was a neighbour. We mixed with him when we lived locally. A little odd but we got along all right."

"When was the last time you saw David?"

"I passed him in the lane about a week ago when visiting my son."

The solicitor interrupted, "My client has helped you all he can. Can I ask why a greater effort isn't being made to find Mr Turner? I believe he is the brother of the deceased girl and has a history of mental health problems and assault. The newspapers suggest he has abducted a young girl from the village."

Peter tensed. "Thank you, yes, I would like to talk about Mr Turner." He turned his attention back to Mark. "Could you tell me whether Mr Turner has contacted you in the last few days?"

"No, of course not. I only know what I've read in the news-papers," Mark replied.

"Are you quite sure he didn't contact you?"

"Yes, I am quite sure. I don't understand why you think he would."

"We understand Mr Turner has spoken to people who would have been in the area around the time of his sister's disappear-ance. As you were the owner at the time of the farm where her body was found, we consider it likely he would have tried to make some sort of contact."

Mark looked genuinely surprised as he turned to his solicitor. After a brief discussion, the solicitor said, "My client has had no contact with Mr Turner. He is, of course, a very busy man and it is possible an attempt to make contact was made but failed. Could you tell us which people Mr Turner has spoken to since arriving in the village?"

"I'm afraid I can't give that information at this stage."

"We would like to formally request that information."

"Gentlemen, that will be all for now, and we will bear your re-quest in mind," Peter said, standing up.

Peter came out of the interview convinced Mark was guilty of killing Jenny and David and attempting to kill Frank. He was also unnerved by the reaction to James Turner and needed to think that through. In the corridor, he said, "We'll take a break before seeing Mrs Farley. And I mean a proper break."

Peter had no pity for Mark Farley. His actions were motivated by nothing more than his cowardice, greed and pride. He could concentrate fully on proving this was the case if only he knew James and Rose were safe and well.

FORTY-THREE

The sun beat down on them as they walked along to his favourite coffee shop. "At least they have proper air conditioning and an edible selection of snacks in here," Peter said, holding open the door for Fiona.

They sat in the window watching people hurrying by. The relaxed atmosphere, smell of real coffee and the coolness of the room contrasted sharply with the red-faced passers-by struggling with the heat outside.

"Do you think Mrs Farley had any part in all of this?" Peter asked. "I don't like the woman, and I'll be disappointed if all we can charge her with is perverting justice by giving false alibis."

"But if that's all she's done, what's wrong with that?"

"Because she must have known what her husband was capable of when it came to young girls. She didn't do anything to protect the girls they employed, or her son for that matter. Whether she played an active role or chose to turn a blind eye to her husband's behaviour she was motivated by the same greed as her husband," Peter said.

"Do you think she had any part in the murder or the burial?" Fiona asked.

Peter stretched out the knots forming in his back. "My gut feeling is no, but at the very least she must have doubted her husband's innocence when things came to light. Her lies are just a different way to bury the truth."

"I guess. Do you think she will be willing to tell the truth now?"

"I think she'll do whatever is best for her. Are you sure you're okay with just water?" Peter asked, watching Fiona start to peel the corner of the label from the bottle with her thumb.

"Yes. What's the plan after we've seen her?"

"Checking that alibi Mark gave us at the bank and travel agent and digging up anything we can about his friendship with Tim Potter back in Birmingham. Did you see his reaction when I mentioned it?"

Fiona nodded. "It was the only time he looked rattled."

"Yes, it's definitely worth digging a little bit more into their time in Birmingham. See if there's anything else we can dredge up to unsettle him. And re-double efforts to find the girl with Jenny at the Race Festival. What was her name?"

"Ellen Frost." Fiona carefully peeled the wrapper from the bottle in one piece before adding, "Are you totally satisfied none of the accidents has anything to do with James Turner? I mean with his disappearance with Rose as well."

Peter asked, "Is that what you think? Or what Steve Jenkins thinks?"

Fiona raised her eyes from the bottle. "I just think it's something that should be considered."

"And you think I haven't? If he was going after possible suspects, why has he been nowhere near Mark Farley? Or maybe he did. And that's why he's disappeared."

Peter broke the uncomfortable silence. "I am concerned about their whereabouts. I just don't think...We haven't a clue where they are. But there's also been nothing to suggest Rose has been harmed. I'm worried there have been no sightings of them, but all that can be done to find them is being done. Meanwhile, I want to concentrate my efforts on Mark Farley who I'm convinced is as guilty as hell."

The same solicitor represented Kim, and her interview went much as Peter had anticipated. She gave the same explanation for the date of the foal being born and confirmed she was with Mark on the evening of Frank's accident. She couldn't say what time they left The Trout Inn, but she insisted Mark followed her home and arrived shortly after she did. She had no interest in the workshops, and of course, they socialised with their neighbours.

"Several people have now suggested your husband's relationship with some of your grooms was improper in the past. Is there anything further you would like to tell us about this?"

"I've told you before. It's just malicious gossip from people who have nothing better to worry about. The girls we employed over the years were of different ages and abilities. If some were given added responsibilities, the others would become jealous. They were silly young things trying to cause trouble and people jealous of our success were happy to encourage them."

"And you confirm you have spent every wedding anniversary together?"

"Of course, we have," Kim insisted.

"And was it always planned for the farm to be given to Graham on his wedding day? To give up your home and the business you'd set up together?" Peter asked.

"He was our only son, marrying a groom. It seemed the natural thing to do."

"And the evening you went for a meal at The Trout, you are quite sure Mark followed you home, and you spent the rest of the evening together?"

"Yes."

Peter was convinced Kim was lying and would continue to do so until they had solid evidence to prove otherwise. "You do understand lying under oath is an offence, Mrs Farley?"

"Of course, I do."

Not wanting to waste any more time, Peter stood up abruptly and terminated the interview.

When they got back, the preliminary report from the workshop was on his desk. Despite reading it twice, it was not much help. There were no fingerprint matches on the mirror or the van, which had been recently reported stolen.

"Nothing else come in?"

"Sorry," Steve replied.

Peter picked up the report again and said, "You've rung Cheltenham and Birmingham?"

Steve nodded in reply.

"Come on," he said to Fiona. "We'll head to the bank. And I'd like us to pay a visit to this Chris character, the one who took Joyce over to the workshop. He might be able to tell us something more about the van and when it appeared."

At the bank, they were shown up the stairs into a standard interview room. The advisor joined them later. He was tall, and his suit jacket hung off his skeleton-thin body. When he greeted them, Peter recoiled at the limp dampness of the handshake while wondering how recently he'd left school.

The advisor took his seat, crossed his legs and checked his trouser creases before saying, "I understand you are here about Mr Farley. I was, you know, quite traumatised by his visit."

"Really?" Peter said, feigning interest in his upset. "Could you tell us what happened?"

"Well," said the advisor, crossing and re-crossing his legs. "I can't tell you the details of what we discussed, but I can tell you he was here that day and was incredibly rude. He called me, 'an insignificant, little pencil pusher.'"

Peter worked hard to suppress a smile as the young man told his story with rolls of his eyes and dramatic hand gestures.

"Well," he continued, holding his hand to his chest, "You can imagine how I felt being personally attacked in this way. And then he ranted on about the government destroying jobs and small business. And this apparently was my fault. I asked him to stop upsetting me, but he continued to attack me personally. He even said he was annoyed that his money was being used to buy gold-nibbed pens for me! I mean really! It was at that point I called security, and he stormed out." The advisor leaned forward and said, "The whole experience terrified me. I'm pleased you're taking some action against him."

Peter heard Fiona cover a stifled giggle with an elaborate fit of coughing. Keeping a straight face himself, he asked, "What time was the appointment?"

The advisor moved his chair to a position behind his computer screen. "The appointment was booked for two o'clock. He arrived half an hour early, which flustered me to start with. I'd say his disturbing attack on my personal integrity lasted about fifteen minutes."

"You're sure about the time?"

"I could check what time my call to security for assistance was logged."

"Yes, that would be helpful."

As they left, the advisor asked, "Do you think I would be entitled to compensation for the distress I was caused?"

They both struggled to compose themselves before going into the travel agency next door. Peter tried through his laughter to tell Fiona it was a serious enquiry and they should pull themselves together.

At the travel agency, at first, none of the row of girls with their perfectly manicured nails could recollect Mark Farley or his enquiries about a holiday to Kenya. It was only by chance Peter saw a young girl coming from a side door heading towards the exit.

She glanced quickly at the photograph of Mark before saying, "Yes, I remember him. But I really must be going."

"Can you tell us what time you saw him?"

"Yes, it would be about the same time as it is now. I remember him because he made me late leaving that day as well. I only work a few hours in the mornings."

Alibis annoyingly confirmed, they headed over to the address they had for Chris.

As they walked across the small yard in front of his tumbled-down cottage, they disturbed a group of hens. The birds showed their irritation by running across the yard flapping their wings. The cat curled in the sun on the doormat raised its head, quietly stretched and moved lazily to the low stone wall as they approached the front door. Chris looked nervous and uncomfortable as he met them at the door and led them through to his kitchen. The furnishings were heavily worn, carpets threadbare in parts, but the easy chairs of the living room were comfortable, and the room was neat and tidy.

As soon as they were seated, Chris blurted out, "Look, about that van. It is nothing to do with me. I hadn't been over there in weeks."

"Calm down. No one is suggesting it was. We just need to ask you a few questions," Peter said. "Firstly, how do you know about the van at all?"

"I only know what Joyce told me. I mean, when I got back with the key. Well, I didn't know what to think. I rang her to…"

"What has Joyce told you?"

"Nothing other than there was a van," Chris replied nervously, pulling at a thread on the armchair.

"We want to know more about your agreement to use the workshop, what you used it for and how regularly you used it."

"It would kind of depend on what I was doing. I used it more in the winter when there was less to do outside."

"Did Mark still use the workshop? Or visit from time to time?"

"I'm not sure. Once Mark built his new high-tech workshop up at the house, he moved all his tools up there. He said he didn't mind me using the old one. In return, I'd do odd favours for him. You know, when he just needed an extra pair of hands for half hour or so. It wasn't just me. I didn't have it to myself or anything. He gave me a key, but a spare was always left up on the ledge."

"Do you know who else used the workshop?"

"Not really. Bob across the way had a key. But he said he'd not used it for over a year."

"That's fine. Can you tell us the last time you were there?"

"Yes. It would have been about two weeks ago. And I can tell you, there was no van in it then."

"And two weeks ago, when you were there, was the spare key on the ledge as normal?"

"Yes, it was."

"Was there anything else different about the workshop?"

"Apart from the damage Joyce did, you mean? I was worried sick when I got back. Thought something had happened to Joyce. The workshop door wide open, the damage to Joyce's car. Tyre marks all across the grass. Well, you can guess the stuff going through my mind. I couldn't find Joyce anywhere. When I couldn't find her, I went to lock the workshop back up. That's when I noticed it was a different padlock. My key wouldn't have opened it anyway."

"You are quite sure? The padlock on the door had been changed within the last two weeks?" Peter asked.

"Yes. It was the same make and everything. But different."

"Thank you, Chris. Unless you can think of anything else, that's all we need to know."

As Chris showed them out, he said, "I understand Frank was hurt pretty bad. Lucky he wasn't killed. Is it right what Joyce said? That it wasn't an accident but deliberate like?"

"That's something we're looking into," Peter replied.

FORTY-FOUR

The atmosphere in the station and around the village of Birkbury had become increasingly tense. They still had nothing substantial to prove Mark had anything to do with the van or anything else, for that matter. Peter was working flat out chasing up leads but getting nowhere. James and Rose had still not resurfaced, and there was a clear sense of resentment from the locals. There was also increasing criticism from the media about the handling of the case and their failure to protect the public.

It didn't help that he'd been warned off bringing in Tim Potter without something more. Even Fiona, who was spending more and more time with Steve Jackson, seemed to be doubting him. The only good news he'd received recently was that Frank had been released from hospital.

When Fiona came in, he suggested they pay a visit to Frank. He hoped he would be one person in the village not to show increasing hostility towards them as the case seemed to drag on.

"He may have remembered something more now he's at home. Sometimes being in familiar surroundings can jog the memory."

The journey back to Birkbury continued mostly in silence. Just like the night before, Peter's mind stayed resolutely awake. It restlessly went over all the possibilities as the various characters of the village circulated around his brain.

When they knocked on Frank's door, Peter was not surprised it was opened by Joyce.

"Come in. Come in," she said. She then added in a whisper, "I don't really think he should be at home. But I don't think he could have stood one more day in that hospital bed. He could do with some distraction, but please don't tire him."

Frank did look very pale and tired, laid out on the sofa. Joyce curled herself up on the end of the sofa. The cottage had received a meticulous cleaning, along with the spray of an air freshener.

"Good to see you're at home, Frank. How are you doing?" Peter asked.

Frank was restrained by Joyce when he tried to sit up. He smiled weakly at Peter and Fiona. "I could be better." His face then fell as he said, "But then I could be a lot worse."

"We're sorry how things have worked out."

Frank averted his gaze to the corner of the room.

"Well. Have you charged him?" Joyce said.

"Not yet. But we're working on it." Peter looked over at Frank with concern. He looked far weaker than when he'd been in hospital. "We wondered if it was possible for you to go through things again. Just to see if there was anything we missed before. But if you'd rather leave it for now, that's fine."

They all looked to Frank, who gave a firm, "No. I'd rather get it over and done with, to tell you the truth."

"Thanks," replied Peter. "This can't be easy for you."

Frank went through his recollection again of the afternoon in Cheltenham and his return in the early hours. There was nothing new he could add, other than insisting he was quite sure Graham had seen something that night by the caravans.

"Isn't it true that when stressful things happen children block it from their minds on purpose?" Joyce said. "I'm no shrink, but I've been hearing all sorts of strange stories about Graham's bizarre behaviour recently. Pauline is not one to gossip, but she reckons it's all got too much for him. Gone totally bonkers, she reckons."

Frank said, "When I mentioned the night I found him by the caravans, he was very vague. He said he couldn't remember much."

"Well, maybe he's had time to think," replied Joyce.

"What sort of things has he been doing?" Peter asked Joyce, thinking back to the broken man he'd seen on their last visit to the farm.

"Constant fits of rage about the most ridiculous, trivial things."

"And what about Gillian, how has she been?"

"Paying regular visits to the yard and the holiday centre as if nothing was wrong. That everything was quite normal. Pauline described her behaviour as manic."

Frank said, "Probably the first time she's set foot over there since they were opened."

"Pauline is at her wit's end," Joyce said.

"Joyce, is there anything you have thought of since your infamous van escapade? Anything at all you might have heard or seen that you didn't tell us at the time?"

Joyce furrowed her forehead." I don't think so. I know there is a weird atmosphere up at the centre. A lot of silly gossip going on, but then there always is."

"No, I meant when you found the van. We know the padlock was new. Can you think of anything else that looked out of place? Something that might suggest Mark had been there recently? We've still got nothing to link him to the van."

Joyce suddenly beamed from ear to ear. "The key-hide!"

"Sorry?"

"The key-hide! That tacky imitation stone. Gillian has an identical one. That's why I knew straight away what it was. Something so cheap is very unusual for Kim to have. But I remember Gillian told me hers was a gift from a child. That's why she kept it. She uses it by the back door where it can't be seen."

"Can you remember which child?" Peter leant forwards from his chair. "Would the parents be someone who knew Gillian and her in-laws?"

"I'm thinking," Joyce said crossly.

Frank was racking his brain before having his eureka moment.

"Gordon's grandchild! Don't you remember? They all spent last Christmas together. I bet that's where they came from."

Fiona was already on the phone checking that the officers had picked up the key-hide from behind the workshop.

Peter was on his feet. "Let's go over to Rooksbridge now."

When they pulled into the yard, they saw Gillian writing a long note on the main notice board. Peter quickly skimmed the set of amended rules over her shoulder.

Gillian turned and said, "It's very rude to come up behind someone like that. What do you want, anyway?" she demanded in a shrill voice, causing a small flock of birds perched on a nearby fence to fly away.

"I am sorry," Peter said, feeling anything but. "Can you tell me if you have an imitation stone key-hide about so big?" He made the shape with his hands.

"What a strange question," Gillian said, making a point of looking down at him along her long, thin nose. "But as a matter of fact, yes we do. It's by the back door."

"Where did it come from?"

"It was a gift." Gillian started to walk away.

"Can you tell me who from?"

She spun round to face Peter. "Oh, for goodness sake is this important? I really am quite busy. Gordon's grandchild, Jack. Is that all? Can I get on now?"

"Could you show us where it is, please? We would like to have a look," Fiona asked.

Gillian turned abruptly and began to march towards the farmhouse. Pushing the front door open with some force, she carried on through the kitchen and hallway to the rear garden without looking back. Peter and Fiona followed as far as the hallway, both trying not to look towards the locked door that hid the macabre nursery. Gillian returned with the key-hide. Handing it to Fiona, she said, "Ugly thing, but as you are so interested in it, you can have it."

Fiona thanked her and slipped the stone into her pocket, giving Peter a quick smile.

"You said it came from a friend's grandchild. Do you know if he gave the same gift to anyone else?" Peter asked.

"Yes. Jack is Kim's godchild, so she had one as well. The child bought it out of his own money. It seemed mean to throw it away, even though it was so ugly. He is just a child, after all."

FORTY-FIVE

Driving back to the station, the message came through. James Turner and Rose Gwinnet had just turned up in the village safe and well. James was waiting at the station to speak to them. Peter was immediately flooded with a sense of total relief. Muscles he never knew he had, relaxed. This was followed by anger towards the young man and the additional burden of stress he'd caused. By the time they arrived back at the station, Peter's blood pressure was on the way back up.

He marched towards the front entrance. "Do you think he has any idea the trouble he has caused? The time we have wasted on him? I'm going to charge him with something. I just don't know what yet."

Fiona was struggling to keep up. They were almost taking the corridor at a run.

As they entered the interview room, Peter said, "Ah, Richard, or should I say James. We meet at last."

James jumped from his seat, his face full of apprehension.

Peter barked, "Sit down."

Fiona took a seat, watching the two men. James looked worn out with dark circles under his eyes. Peter was also tired, but his anger seemed to have given him renewed energy.

"What exactly do you think you have been playing at? Did you see all the press coverage? Half the nation has been out looking for you," Peter said.

James mumbled something inaudible, digging his thumbnail

into his hand. His right leg was rhythmically knocking the table leg.

"Have you any idea what you put Rose's family through? They thought…" Peter regretted the words as soon as they left his mouth. The raw nerve he'd touched showed clearly in James' face. An awkward moment of silence hung over the room. Realising his gaffe, Peter tried to soften his tone and move things on. "You've wasted a lot of valuable time. But I am more interested in finding out what happened to your sister. I assume you are as well?"

James nodded and mumbled, "But Rose left a note for her parents. She left it on the table. She told me she did."

Peter heard the pleading in his voice and said, "We'll be talking with Rose later. Can we go through the original statement you gave the Oxfordshire police? You said at the time your sister had met an older man at the Cheltenham Gold Cup that year?"

James glanced up at Peter for the first time. "Can't you just read those statements? Do I have to go through everything again?"

Peter spoke as softly as he could. "We are looking at the matter afresh. So, it would help if you could."

"That's fine. I do understand."

"Thank you. Can you tell us all you know about the man your sister met in Cheltenham?"

James started hesitantly at first. "I told the police several times, but they didn't seem interested. Because she hadn't mentioned it to her friends, they didn't think what I had to say was important. But then nobody did at the time. Her friends said she had men hitting on her all the time. That it was nothing unusual. They dismissed the whole thing and told me I was reading too much into things. But she did mention him twice to me."

"Twice, there's no mention of a second time in the reports."

James' leg continued to knock the table in time to an irregular inner beat. "Yes, the first time she mentioned it directly. She told me this wealthy looking man had bought her drinks and said he could give her a career with horses. A few days later, she mentioned it again but indirectly. She wondered if Mum and

Dad would freak if she chose to work with horses rather than go on to university. I had the feeling at the time there had been a follow-up conversation. I don't know why... I just did." James had stopped knocking the table leg. Instead, he was incessantly rubbing his temples with both hands.

Peter noticed his fingernails were bitten until they bled. "But she didn't mention anything about him to her friends?"

James started rocking in his seat, rubbing his hands up and down his legs. "I don't know... Maybe her main concern was our parents' disappointment if she gave up her studies. Maybe that's why she asked me. I don't know."

Annoyed by the constant jiggling around, Peter wanted to scream, "Any chance you could sit still for a minute?" Instead, he sat back, trying to feel some compassion and not push the bundle of stressed nerves sitting in front of him too hard.

Fiona said, "James. Can you think of anybody else Jenny may have confided in? Somebody she trusted enough to talk about your parents' expectations with? Somebody the police didn't question at the time?"

James momentarily stopped fidgeting. "Yes, her best friend, Ellen. But she had left for the states for a year on some sort of exchange thing. It was something to do with the Rotary Club. She was at the races that day with Jenny. Her mother still lives in the same house." He pulled his mobile from his jeans and started tapping his legs. "Ellen still lives in the states. But I see her mother around occasionally. Here. I can give you her number."

Peter took the number and handed him the group photograph taken at Cheltenham in return. He made a mental note to call Ellen's mother as soon as they were finished. "Do you recognise anyone in this picture?"

James squinted at the photograph. "Is that the guy whose father did weird things with sheep heads? When he was younger?" He was pointing at David.

"Yes. Yes, it was but have you seen any of the others?"

James stared again at the picture. "No. Sorry."

Peter's nerves were on edge due to James' constant jigging

about in his seat. "Thank you for coming in. We will try and contact Ellen and her mother. Why don't you go and get some rest? We will need to speak to you again later."

Fiona added, "And James, can you make sure your mobile is switched on so we can keep in contact?"

Peter kept hold of Mrs Frost's telephone number, knowing he was probably clutching at straws. He was sure the local police would have called Ellen's mother, but he still wanted to speak to her himself. They still had no real evidence Mark and Tim had ever met Jenny.

Jim Harris and Steve Jackson were waiting for them when they returned to their office. "How did the interview go?"

"Not too bad."

"I was wondering if either of you fancied a pint?" said Jim.

Peter noticed again the way Steve Jackson looked at Fiona and the slight blush on her face. "Not for me, thanks. I want to get off home."

Steve said, "Fiona?"

She turned to Peter. "Is there anything else you'd like me to do here, sir?"

"No. You get off."

Peter watched them leave together before dialling the number James had given him. Mrs Frost answered on the second ring. He explained who he was and apologised if she had already been contacted by the local police.

He felt like weeping when she replied, "No. But then I've only just got back from a three-month trip visiting my daughter in America. She lives there now. She's travelled back with me for a short visit. We've literally just walked through the door."

"Ellen is there now with you? Can I have a quick word with her?"

"Is it important? We're both exhausted."

Peter was unable to keep the urgency from his voice as he replied, "Yes, it is. It's about Jenny Turner."

He could hardly believe his luck as he listened to Mrs Frost calling her daughter to the phone. He spoke briefly with Ellen.

She vaguely remembered meeting a group of men. She wasn't sure if she could recognise them now, but she would certainly try. She was tired from her journey but of course if the local police showed her the photograph she'd do her best.

He immediately rang the local station asking them to interview Ellen and to ring as soon as they'd finished. He knew there was no point going home, so he settled himself down to re-read all the reports on the case. There was always the possibility something had been missed or not considered relevant at the time. He was asleep with his head on the desk when the call came.

He rang Fiona after ending the call. He could hear the background chatter and music in the background from the pub and had to shout to be heard. "I've spoken to Ellen Frost! Yes! Ellen Frost. She couldn't definitely pick out Mark or Tim, but she's absolutely sure she remembers David Conley. She remembers the round glasses and the fact she felt sorry for him because of the way the others treated him. We should be able to seriously rattle Mark tomorrow morning."

Fiona's voice sounded slightly slurred when she replied, "That's fantastic news."

"It gets better. Ellen couldn't say for sure from the photograph that Mark and Tim were the men she met with Jenny. However, she gave a brilliant character description of the men they met. She remembered one as a stereotypical Hooray Henry right down to the striped jumper tied casually around his neck and how he was stick thin. The other she thought was a bit of a chancer with a sharp and cruel wit. She has never forgotten a comment he made on infidelity. Something along the lines of, 'Young men promise to be faithful but can't, older men want to be unfaithful but can't.'" Peter paused before adding, "Who do we know who would say something like that?"

"It certainly sounds like them," Fiona replied.

"Enjoy the rest of your evening. But I expect you bright and breezy tomorrow morning," Peter said.

FORTY-SIX

Fiona arrived looking hung over the following morning. Nothing could dampen Peter's spirits after receiving confirmation the two key hides were a match. He felt on top of the world and miles away from the man he had been just a few days ago, struggling with self-doubt. He waited for Fiona to finish her second coffee before ushering her towards the interview room.

They were intercepted on the way by PC Bains. "Graham and Gillian Farley are downstairs. They want to talk to you urgently."

Peter felt torn. He was desperate to get in the room with Mark. He was itching to blow his arrogant manner apart by telling him they had two eyewitnesses and something to link him to the workshop. "Is there nobody else who could deal with them?"

"Yes, there probably is. But Mrs Farley wanted to talk to you about Mark Farley. And I thought you'd want to see her personally."

"We'll come down and see them. But if she starts talking a load of garbage, I'm walking out," Peter warned. "Can you let Mark Farley and his solicitors know we've been delayed a few minutes?"

Downstairs, Graham and Gillian sat apart in silence. Gillian was dressed simply in cords and a smartly pressed shirt. Peter noticed she wore a hint of make-up and perfume for the first time since he'd met her. Graham was wearing smart chinos and a shirt. He had combed his hair and shaved, but he still appeared haggard and tired.

Gillian spoke in a strong but calm voice, surprising all of them. "I would like to give a statement about Mark Farley. About the relationships, he had with the grooms when I lived in the caravans." Her whole character seemed altered. She sounded self-assured, the recent shrillness in her tone gone. Peter wondered if that was merely a stage to bridge the gap between sullen silence and finding her true voice, as he led them to an interview room.

Once seated, Gillian continued with growing confidence in her newfound voice. "You have to remember we were all young and terribly homesick but too proud to admit it. We thought we were grown up when in reality we were naïve and vulnerable. For most of us, it was our first job, and we were all in awe of Mark and Kim. We all wanted to do well, and he used this against us to his full advantage."

"Go on," Peter urged.

"Well, I was unusual. I'm not sure whether I was more naive or more terrified than the others. I stayed in those caravans for years while other girls came and went. Some only managed a few months, some a little longer. Every time a new batch of girls would start, the atmosphere of mistrust and paranoia would develop. There would be a massive argument, and someone would leave. It was a cycle that constantly repeated itself in a loop."

"What part did Mark play in this?" Peter asked, keen for Gillian to get to the point of her visit.

"Mark was masterminding it all. Playing us off against each other. He was cruel and controlling. Horrid to work for, but we didn't know any different. He would shout and scream at us, do vindictive things like disconnect the gas to the caravans."

"Yes. You already told us that, Mrs Farley. Is there something more you want to tell us?" Peter asked.

Gillian gave him one of her cold, hard stares. "Yes. There is. At the same time, he would systematically pick a certain girl and use his charm on her. Give her special duties and treat her differently. This would make the rest of us jealous and not trust her. We'd isolate her, partly due to jealousy, partly due to our fear she would report something back to Mark that would cause trouble. After a while, the favoured girl would leave suddenly without warning. We were too young and immature to understand the principles of divide and rule. I began to think it was wrong, but I chose to ignore it."

Peter interrupted. "We get the point. Mark was not a good employer. Quite callous from what you say, but we are considering something far more serious."

Gillian calmly raised a hand. "Would you let me continue, please?"

Peter nodded agreement to her carrying on.

"I admit I had my suspicions, but I kept them to myself. It was easier to keep my head down and not become involved." Gillian pulled out a slip of paper from her bag and handed it to Fiona.

"Here is the telephone number of a girl who was a friend back then. I spoke to her earlier today. She will explain to you about the special favours."

Fiona gently asked, "Could you tell us what you mean?"

Gillian covered her face with her hands. "I am so sorry. I should have done more, but I was too weak to speak up."

Peter leaned back in his chair and waited for Gillian to compose herself. "We understand you were very young at the time. Could you explain what exactly was going on?"

"She will tell you," Gillian replied, pointing to the sheet of paper in Fiona's hand.

Peter said, "It really would help if you could tell us."

Gillian straightened up in the chair. She raised her head to look straight ahead, past Peter and Fiona. She focussed her attention on the wall behind them. "Okay. I will. My friend was sixteen. Mark charmed her, promised her the world, made her feel special, slept with her and then spat her out."

"And this girl will confirm that?" asked Fiona.

"Yes. I spoke to her today."

"And you're saying this was something he repeated over and over again?" Peter asked.

Gillian nodded.

"Gillian, I have to ask you. Did you have a relationship with Mark?"

Gillian shook her head without changing her focus on the wall behind. "No."

Fiona folded the sheet of paper and slipped it into the case file. "Was Kim aware any of this was going on?"

Peter concentrated on Graham's reaction. His face showed none of this was news to him.

"I honestly don't know. We were all just as scared of her as him. She was so cold," Gillian replied. "Graham has something to say, now."

Graham was the reverse image of his wife. He was hardly recognisable from the self-assured man they had first met. He appeared to have shrunk. He mumbled into his chest, "It's about that night."

"Sorry. Can you speak up?" Peter said.

"That night I did see something. I should have said ... I don't know... I didn't know..."

"Okay," soothed Peter. "You saw something that night. Could you start at the beginning? Why were you outside?"

"I..." Graham started but then faltered.

After allowing a brief pause, Peter asked again, "Why were you outside?"

Graham slumped in the chair. "It was hot. I couldn't sleep. I had hidden some cigarettes earlier in the day behind the main barn. I thought I'd go out for a smoke."

Graham looked towards Gillian before continuing. If he was looking for some support, none was forthcoming.

"I heard noises coming from the caravans. They should have been empty because I knew the girls had already left that year. I crept up to the window. It was dimly lit, but I could see." Graham made a fist. "It was lit by a night light I had as a child, for Christ sake." Graham closed his eyes, closing out the unwanted vision that had returned from his childhood to haunt him. He couldn't face his wife anymore. He had to turn away from her.

"What did you see, Graham?" Peter asked, leaning forwards.

"They were... I couldn't see the girl's face. Father had his hand over her mouth. She had dark hair. I saw her legs kicking. She was struggling and trying to push him off."

"Was there anybody else in the caravan?"

"Yes. Tim Potter. He was pinning her arms back. He sat by her head."

"Then what happened?"

"I backed away to the side of the barn where I could hide in the shadows. Then I heard a scream, Father shouting, a thud and then silence. I wanted to run away, but my legs wouldn't work. I curled myself up into a tight ball at the foot of the barn. Then Father was swearing. Tim was laughing. Laughing! Then I heard the caravan door click open. I was terrified. Then nothing. The next thing I remember is Frank shaking me awake."

"And you're sure you don't remember anything else? No sound of voices or vehicles being started up?"

Graham shook his head in reply.

"Well. Thank you very much for coming in today. It can't have been easy for either of you," Peter said, as he rose from his seat.

"There's one more thing I should let you know," Gillian said. "I'm leaving the area shortly. But I will leave you contact details when I know where I'm going to be."

After seeing them out, Peter said, "Shall we go and tell Mark the good news?"

FORTY-SEVEN

Peter felt Sally reach for his hand under the table when their plates were taken away. Fiona and Steve sat opposite them in the garden of The Trout Inn. A slight chill was starting to creep into the beautiful late summer evening, and he could feel the soft breeze on his arms. He acknowledged Sally's hand with a squeeze but couldn't pull his eyes away from Amelia playing at the bottom of the garden with Liam and Thomas. He felt a dull ache in the pit of his stomach. It was perfect moments such as this the guilt about Jordan tore at his heart, a torture he felt at times he could hardly endure. He was jolted from his musings when he heard Sally said to Fiona, "You're looking a bit distant."

Attention was turned to Fiona, who smiled. "I was just thinking about what Tim Potter said when we brought him in. 'All this fuss over one silly girl who probably wouldn't have amounted to much anyway.' I just don't get it."

Peter replied, "I hope you never do."

The End

I hope you enjoyed reading my debut novel as much as I enjoyed writing it. Although my writing style has since improved, as my first, this book has a special place in my heart.

Peter Hatherall Series

The Skeletons of Birkbury
Bells on Her Toes
Point of No Return
Who Killed Vivien Morse?
Twisted Truth
The Paperboy

The Trouble Series

Trouble at Clenchers Mill
Trouble at Fatting House

Stand-alone novels

Fool Me Once
Debts & Druids

BOOKS IN THIS SERIES

Peter Hatherall Mystery

The Skeletons Of Birkbury

Bells On Her Toes

Point Of No Return

Who Killed Vivien Morse?

Twisted Truth

The Paperboy

BOOKS BY THIS AUTHOR

A Fiery End

Trouble At Clenchers Mill

Trouble At Fatting House

Fool Me Once

Debts & Druids

Made in United States
Orlando, FL
20 February 2023

30202035R00168